Cursed

Elise Noble

Published by Undercover Publishing Limited

Copyright © 2018 Elise Noble

v7

ISBN: 978-1-910954-88-1

Edited by Nikki Mentges, NAM Editorial

Cover design by Abigail Sins

www.undercover-publishing.com

www.elise-noble.com

To me, death is not a fearful thing.
It's living that's cursed.
- *Jim Jones*

.

CHAPTER 1 - RANIA

I KNEW SOMETHING was wrong the instant I reached the ornate iron gates of Daylesford Hall. Not because I could see the crowd next to the front doors or the police officers traipsing in and out, but because the spirit perched on the moss-covered boulder at the top of the winding driveway told me so.

Lucy had been sitting in the same spot since a carelessly driven carriage clipped her in 1883, causing her to lose her balance and hit her head on that very rock.

"Rania! You'll never guess what's happened."

I checked around for watchful eyes, then smiled. Lucy was one of the few spirits I'd come across who didn't make me want to run screaming. Not that I ran out of fear—more from frustration.

"What?" I whispered, careful not to move my lips.

"Something big's happened. Six cars with flashing lights have driven past this morning, and a big yellow van, but that left a while ago."

"Flashing lights... Do you mean police cars?"

"The lights were blue, and the cars had words on them."

As a servant girl, Lucy had never learned to read, and with Daylesford Hall hidden away at the end of a winding lane in the sleepy English village of Enderby, she wouldn't have come across the police too often. So why were they here?

"How long ago did they arrive?"

"This morning, a little after first light."

At this time of year, late November with patches of snow still left on the ground, that meant around eight a.m. The cold snap started in October and hadn't let up since, and while I'd been fascinated by its icy beauty at first, the novelty soon wore off. Crisp white sheets turned to grey sludge, and the walk from the bus stop down the road took twice as long and left me with a bruised ass on one occasion. Back home in Syria, the flurries lasted a day or two at most, and the snow rarely settled.

"I'll take a look and see what's going on," I said.

"Please, tell me. I do wish I could see for myself."

If the situation was serious enough to warrant six police cars and, I presumed, an ambulance, it probably wasn't something either of us wanted to see, but Lucy loved to gossip and I was the only person she had to talk to now. I closed my eyes for a second, imagining her back in Victorian times, very much alive and chatting with the other household staff in the huge old kitchen at Daylesford Hall. I hadn't met any of them myself, but in the summer months when the evenings were warmer, Lucy had told me about her life in bite-sized chunks, a minute or two each day.

"I'll give you an update on my way out," I promised.

She smiled, and when I glanced back, I saw her settle onto the boulder again—an illusion, because she could have passed right through it if she'd chosen to. At least ghosts didn't feel the cold.

Not like me as I tucked my gloved hands into my

pockets and trudged up the gentle hill to the hall. Once home to a wealthy family, it had been converted to the headquarters of my current employer, The Weston Corporation, a firm of engineering consultants headed up by Lloyd Weston and his two children—Anthony and Helene. Rumour had it the older man would be retiring soon, but every time I'd seen him, he still seemed sprightly.

As I rounded the kink in the drive, my worst fears came to life. Or rather, death. Two men wheeled a black body bag out of the front doors on a gurney, slowing to lift their cargo carefully down the steps. A groan escaped my lips, but I forced myself to keep walking towards the cluster of people gathered in front of the blue-and-white tape that fluttered in the breeze.

A woman turned in my direction, and I recognised Martha, the receptionist who spent more of her time reading gossip websites than answering the phone.

Her eyes widened as she saw me. "Rania, I'm so sorry. I thought I'd called everybody, but I forgot about you."

Of course she did. I was just the cleaner, invisible to everyone unless they had a spill that needed clearing up or an overflowing wastebasket. Well, almost everyone. A handful of the building's occupants noticed me, and today it looked as if that count might increase by one.

"What happened?" I asked.

She dropped her voice to a whisper. "Helene Weston died."

One of the others shuffled closer—a brunette who had no idea how to place a cup into the dishwasher. I cleared at least four from her desk every day. "Stabbed, apparently. Mr. Weston found her this morning."

The whole group, mostly women, leaned forward as the men loaded Helene's body into a black van and closed the door. Ghouls, the lot of them. Someone had even brought out a flask of coffee and a packet of biscuits, and the blonde at the end snapped a few photos when she thought nobody was looking. A father had lost his daughter today, and the waiting crowd was treating it as an opportunity to update their Facebook statuses with something really juicy. Only one person looked appropriately solemn—a guy at the end in a suit and tie. What was his name? Adrian? Something like that. He offered me a small smile that I struggled to return.

"Do they know who did it?" I asked.

"I don't think so," Martha said. "The forensics people have been going in and out all day."

The brunette shuddered. "Tell you what, I'm never working late on my own again, not when some madman's on the loose."

Martha nudged her and jerked her head in my direction, and the brunette grimaced as she patted me on the arm. "But don't worry, Rania. I'm sure you'll be just fine in the evenings. You're used to being alone, right?"

"Perhaps keep your phone handy, eh?" Martha said.

Of course, because my phone would be excellent protection against a knife-wielding maniac. "Sure."

A car drew up next to us, and the receptionist smacked her head. "Oh, crap. I forgot to phone Geri too." She slipped on a patch of ice as she hurried to the vehicle, and the group gasped before she regained her footing. "Geri, you're never gonna believe what's happened."

I was dismissed as the group went to talk to the yoga teacher who taught a class in the basement relaxation room every Monday at five thirty, part of Weston Corp's commitment to work/life balance. Fruit bowls on every floor, yoga on Mondays, Indian head massage on Tuesdays, reflexology on Wednesdays, and reiki on Thursdays. All that healthiness offset Fridays, when everybody headed to the nearest pub straight after work.

I glanced up at the facade of Daylesford Hall. Even in the gloom of winter, the building was grandly imposing, three storeys high plus a basement, with more rooms than I cared to count. Old photos in the lobby showed the walls had once been red brick, but in the last decade, someone had decided they'd be better off painted cream. A curved wrought-iron balcony formed a focal point above the main entrance, pretty as a Romeo-and-Juliet picture with a vine growing up one side. I'd always found the place peaceful. Serene. But it was far from tranquil today. Lights blazed in every window, and I saw people walking back and forth upstairs. The scene of the crime? I'd soon find out.

***

Back at home, my flatmate, Shannon, swore under her breath as she tried and failed to get the cork out of a bottle of red wine.

"I don't believe this. It's gone crumbly. The one night I really, really need a drink."

I didn't touch alcohol, but Shannon used it to treat all of life's ailments. Wine for general stress, Guinness for a cold, and vodka whenever she broke up with a boyfriend, which happened roughly every other month. Each time a new man came along, she swore she wanted a casual relationship, then fell hard and cried her eyes out when they left. Right now, she was trying internet dating.

"Why do *you* need a drink?" I asked.

"After what you've just told me? Come on—how can you even ask that question? If the killer had come today instead of yesterday, it could've been you lying there tomorrow morning."

I closed my eyes and leaned back on the sofa. Dark-blue leather, squashy, and best of all, we'd got it free when the guy in the flat under ours bought a new three-piece suite. He'd been only too happy to help carry it into our lounge instead of driving it to the tip. Normally, I loved curling up against the cushions, but it didn't seem so comfortable tonight.

When I didn't answer, Shannon pushed more. "Surely you must have thought of that?"

"Of course I have. I'm just trying to block it out."

"Maybe you should get a new job. I mean, you've worked there for what, eight months?"

"You know why."

"Oh, yeah. Right. The 'ghosts.'"

She made little quote marks with her fingers around the words, and although I used to find that hurtful, I'd soon realised it was just Shannon's way of dealing with my...curse. I'd confided in her a little over three years ago when we were both twenty-one and sharing a room in a run-down bed and breakfast on the outskirts of London. She'd fled to England from an abusive boyfriend back home in Ireland, while I'd escaped from hell itself.

Back then, we'd needed a more permanent place to live after our previous apartment building got condemned, and have you seen house prices in the south of England? There wasn't much a cleaner and a girl who worked the early shift in a bread factory could afford.

And when I'd rejected what on the surface looked like a very nice flat, Shannon had understandably been a bit upset.

"What's the problem with it?" she'd asked.

"It feels wrong."

"You said that about the last three places. I'll agree the place above the betting shop was kind of icky, but this one?" She waved a hand around the living room. "It's perfect."

"I just can't live here."

"Don't you want to share with us? Is it Aisling?"

"No. I love Aisling."

"Then what?"

Eyes followed me around the room, and they belonged to the teenage boy sitting on the sofa with blood dripping from the stab wounds in his chest. Small eyes, set too close either side of a long, thin nose. Hard eyes. Predatory eyes. He didn't speak, but he didn't need to. Everything about his expression and his posture told me he hadn't been a pleasant person when he was alive.

I took a deep breath. Sharing my secret was hard, but Shannon was my best friend and she deserved to know the truth. "A man died in this room, and it creeps me out."

"How do you know that?"

"Because he's still here, watching us."

Shannon scoffed and rolled her eyes. "No, seriously —did you read it in the paper?"

"He's on the sofa."

She glanced over, but to her, it would have looked like a slightly shabby maroon leather three-seater without so much as a dent under his bottom. Spirits couldn't touch our world.

"Rania, stop messing around."

"I'm not. I wish I was, but I'm not."

Baby Aisling started crying, and Shannon's mouth set in a thin line as she backed out of the door. "Fine. You look for a place for us to live."

I'd upset her, I knew I had, and she didn't even believe me. But while Shannon worked, it was just me and Aisling, and I couldn't bear to spend my mornings with a man like that, even if he wasn't physically able to hurt me. Shannon would come around. She always did. Neither of us had anyone to lean on but each other, and our desperation had turned into a lasting friendship.

We hadn't spoken about my abilities again until one grey Sunday evening, six months later. Sure, she heard me crying out from my nightmares, but those were easy enough to write off as reminders of a time I'd rather forget. After all, the horrors of daily life in Syria had been plastered across every news channel for years.

But that evening, the malevolent sky swirled above us as we walked home from the supermarket with little Aisling in a pushchair, and as the first spots of rain fell, a Ford Focus mounted the pavement and missed us by inches. Aisling let out a wail, but I couldn't take my eyes off the girl jogging in front of us, oblivious to the drama as she listened to her iPod.

The *crunch* as the car hit her would stay with me

forever, but I'd still run forward to check her vital signs as Shannon puked.

Dead. The girl was dead, killed instantly, and as I looked up from her broken body, the pale form of the spirit guide vanished and left the girl staring down at me.

"Please, you have to help," she whispered.

How many times had I heard that request? "I'm sorry—"

"My cat's all alone. There's nobody else to look after him. He's called Taffy, and he'll be expecting his dinner soon."

A cat? She'd just died, and her first thought was for a cat?

Most people wanted a different kind of assistance from me, a kind I couldn't give, not anymore. But feeding a cat was doable.

I sighed. "What's your address?"

Shannon thought I'd gone crazy when I insisted we sit outside the girl's house and wait for Taffy.

"We just watched a girl die, and you're worried about a cat?" She wrinkled her nose and rubbed at the vomit stain on her trousers.

Shannon hadn't taken the sight of the body well. Me? Unfortunately, I'd seen so much death I feared I'd lost some of my humanity.

"I promised."

"You promised a dead girl." She laid a hand on my forehead. "Have you taken something?"

"I told you before—"

"I know, I know, you think you can talk to ghosts. And I never judged you, even when you rejected a perfectly good flat because of it. But do you not reckon it's time you spoke to somebody about this? A professional, I mean. I can help you find—"

Taffy chose that moment to walk around the corner and rub up against my legs, purring. The bell on his collar jingled as he leapt into my lap, and I checked the tag. Yes, this was the one.

Shannon lost a little of her colour, which wasn't easy since she was paler than most of the spirits I encountered.

"How did you know about the cat? Seriously?"

"I told you."

"You told me you talked to a corpse, Rania. That's crazy."

I shrugged. "I didn't ask to be able to see them."

"You're my best friend, and that'll never change, but I always thought the ghost thing was a bit...you know." She whirled two fingers by her head in the universal sign for crazy.

"It is. But that doesn't mean it isn't true."

Shannon being Shannon, she dealt with the situation in the best way she knew how: by pretending it didn't exist. A minute of silence passed, then two, before she finally spoke again.

"So, are we keeping the cat?"

Even now, two years later, Shannon avoided the subject of my strange ability. I didn't have to be psychic to understand it freaked her out, but at least that meant she didn't joke about it. Taffy wandered in and curled up next to me, and I reached out to scritch his head. Thankfully, our current landlord turned a blind eye to him, mainly because he kept the mouse population down.

"Right, I don't want to work somewhere else

because of the ghosts," I said in answer to her question. "Remember how many jobs I went through before I found a place that only had three?"

"But what if Helene's killer comes back? You could end up joining them."

"It doesn't work like that."

As one of the chosen, the Electi, I had to pass my curse on to another. If I died before I produced a child to act as my heir, then according to what little I knew about the process, my soul would get allocated to a random newbie, and the remaining three Electi would have to find the poor sod and educate them on the job we were supposed to do. And that meant I couldn't remain tethered in the spirit world.

Shannon poked at the cork until it fell inside the bottle. "Yeah, I forgot. You have a higher purpose." She stood up. "I need to get a sieve for this wine."

I laughed softly to myself as she disappeared out to the kitchen. A higher purpose. According to my mother, and her mother before her, our gift would one day save the earth and mankind, only she'd been slightly hazy on the details. Just the kind of pressure I needed on my twenty-four-year-old shoulders, and now I had the prospect of Helene waiting for me at Daylesford Hall to deal with as well.

CHAPTER 2 - RANIA

TURNED OUT MARTHA was more efficient than she looked because she phoned me on Tuesday and Wednesday with updates on the happenings at Daylesford Hall. I suspected she hadn't developed an altruistic streak so much as a deep-seated need to spread a particularly juicy piece of gossip as far as humanly possible. She even tried to get me to join the Facebook group she'd set up specially for the purpose, but I didn't have any social media accounts. When I told her that during the second call, she gasped so dramatically anyone would have thought I'd confessed to the murder itself.

"No Facebook? But you've got Twitter, right?"

"I don't even have a computer."

"But how do you keep in contact with people?"

"I don't."

"But what about your family and your friends from...wherever you were born?"

Aleppo. I was born in Aleppo. Thanks to years of civil war, I had no family left, and I'd never been great at making friends. Yes, I'd had acquaintances, but I certainly hadn't wanted to stay in touch with any of them.

So I changed the subject. "Has anyone said if we'll still get paid for this week?"

"No, but I can't imagine we won't. It's hardly our fault there was a murder."

She sounded remarkably casual about Helene's death, but even so, I sure hoped she was right. My job at Weston Corp was the first salaried position I'd held. Until then, I'd worked through agencies, and if I didn't turn up and do my hours, I didn't get paid—simple as that. And if I didn't get paid, I couldn't afford my rent. A reasonable landlord might have granted Shannon and me some leeway, but our current slumlord wasn't that man.

"When do you think we'll be able to get back to work?" I asked.

"The police are talking about Friday."

Two days away. "Will you let me know either way?"

"Definitely. Although I'm not sure I want to go back with a maniac still running around. Aren't you nervous about being there on your own?"

Being the only person at Daylesford Hall hadn't bothered me until that point. Perhaps because I'd never truly been alone. But Martha was right—if the police hadn't managed to find whoever killed Helene, I'd need to stay on my guard in case he decided to make a reappearance. But was I nervous? Not really. More tense. Death came to all of us in the end, and I knew exactly what to expect.

But I could hardly tell Martha that. "Yes, I'm a bit nervous. Do the police have any idea why she was killed?"

"Not that I've heard. But you know, the Westons are really rich. Maybe it was a robbery gone wrong? Or a botched attempt at kidnapping?" Martha gave a nervous laugh. "Forget what I said about being on your own. I'm sure you'll be fine."

***

I tried to block out Martha's words as I walked up the driveway to Daylesford Hall on Friday. England was supposed to have been the start of a new life for me. A safe life. A life where I didn't wake up each morning wondering which side would drop bombs next or how many more tethered souls I'd have to deal with as I tried to find something to eat that day.

And although life as a refugee in a country where many attitudes ranged from suspicious to downright unwelcoming had its difficulties, the tension that hummed constantly through my body had eased a little. Four years, and I'd done my best to fit in. I learned the language, worked on my accent, and bought my clothes on the high street like everybody else.

But in so many ways, I'd always be an outsider.

Lucy waved, and I muttered a quick "hello" under my breath as I passed through the gates, but with cars driving past, I couldn't risk stopping for a chat. She understood that and settled onto her rock to wait again. And wait. And wait.

Daylesford Hall was busier than usual. Extra cars parked outside, more shadows flitting about in the brightly lit windows, and a random group of people deep in discussion in the lobby. A couple of women I vaguely recognised were standing by the reception desk chatting to Martha when I tried the doors and found them locked. She looked up, fiddled with something in front of her, and the light on the security panel flashed green.

"Mr. Weston upgraded the entry system," she said. "He got some company out to install everything yesterday—cameras over each entry and exit, more swipe-card points inside so the building's divided up into sectors, and even panic buttons."

One of the girls talking to her giggled. "They've installed a panic button in the ladies' loo on the first floor. Overkill if you ask me."

Her friend raised an eyebrow. "What? Worried you might hit it accidentally if you get frisky with Stuart from sales again?"

"Shh!" She put a finger to her lips. "Nobody's supposed to know about that."

"Honey, everybody knows about that."

I had no desire to hear the details of a virtual stranger's sex life. I didn't even want to think about my own, or rather the lack of it.

"So, do I need a new pass card?"

Martha opened one drawer after another in the fancy reception desk, all polished wood and shiny granite, before coming up with a slim plastic rectangle already printed with my name and photo. "Here you go. This'll get you in everywhere. And those panic buttons are linked straight to the police." She shrugged one shoulder. "You know, just in case."

She sure knew how to make a girl feel secure.

"And does the burglar alarm have the same code?"

"There's no code anymore. As soon as the last person swipes out of the building, it sets automatically."

Sounded straightforward, but I'd never quite trusted technology. Or people. Or in fact anyone but myself. And most of the time, I doubted my own mind too.

I left Martha and her minions behind and headed for the top floor. Like many companies, Weston Corp didn't want a cupboard marked "cleaning" anywhere visitors might see, so they put it in the most inconvenient place possible—beside the toilets two floors up. Boy, I loved carrying mops and buckets everywhere.

But today, I didn't get that far before I encountered the very thing I'd been dreading since Monday.

Helene.

I'd barely spoken to her while she was alive, just a few words here and there—a quick hello in the corridor plus the occasional request that I empty her rubbish bin or clear the dirty cups off her desk. But she'd been striking to look at. Pale skin, thick honey-blonde hair she'd recently cut shorter, and sparkling green eyes. Everybody always said those eyes were her best feature.

Except now she didn't have any.

It was always hard to predict the exact form a ghost would take. The spirit world captured them close to death, at the precise moment when the soul left the body. As only those taken too soon became trapped, their tethered forms were rarely perfect. I'd seen it all. The damage a gunshot wound could cause to a person's head, blood pouring from stab wounds in a never-ending waterfall, the harsh ligature marks on victims of strangulation. But whoever killed Helene either hadn't wanted her to see them or had borne a grudge against those beautiful eyes. A trickle of scarlet marred each of her freckled cheeks below sightless eye sockets.

Even blind, she still sensed I was there. They always did. I'd talked to several spirits about how they saw me, or rather, felt me. Some said I had a glow around my body, an aura that set me apart from other humans. Others said the air crackled when I was near. And they knew I was coming—one of the few people who could help set them free for reincarnation—because the spirit guides helpfully told them of my existence.

Oh, how I hated those spirit guides. If it weren't for them, I'd have been able to ignore the ghosts and get on with my life.

Like now. I could have walked right past Helene, fetched the vacuum cleaner, ignored Arthur on my way back downstairs, cleaned Daylesford Hall, and spent the rest of the evening watching bad television with Shannon.

Instead, I was greeted with a faint gasp, a pointed finger, and an accusing, "It's you."

There was no point in denying it. "Hello, Helene."

"The...the thing told me you'd come by if I was lucky, but it gave the impression you wouldn't turn up so soon."

"Lucky..." I sighed. "Yeah."

"So, we can get started then?" She adopted a businesslike tone, one that told me she was in charge, or so she thought. But under that confident exterior, I detected a faint tremor.

"Started?" I played dumb. It was worth a try.

"The thing told me I'm stuck here for good unless you exchange my killer's soul for mine."

Helene's breath hitched on the word "killer." No, she might be pretending to be okay, but she was only one step away from breaking down. And I hated that part. Not only was I expected to be the angel of death, I was also supposed to combine that with playing guidance counsellor. Whoever created the Electi all those millennia ago either hadn't realised what a burden they'd be placing on us, or they had and they simply didn't care.

"It's not quite that simple. I can't just go around killing people."

"Well, I have to admit, it sounded a bit strange when the thing—"

"The spirit guide."

"Yes, whatever, when the *spirit guide* told me how this system worked, but it seemed quite certain."

And so did Helene. I needed to set her straight.

"The problem is, the spirit guides have been spouting the same spiel for thousands of years. Back at the beginning, maybe the Electi did perform that role, but now we have a police force and jails to punish criminals."

At least, England did. Syria? Not so much.

"Okay, so if the police catch whoever did this, how does that set me free?"

I shifted uncomfortably from foot to foot, thankful that she couldn't see me. "Well, it doesn't."

Now she lost it. The occasional sniffle turned into great racking sobs, and her shoulders shook as she cried not tears but more blood. And now that she'd turned towards me, I saw the red stain on her chest glistening against her dark-grey jumper. If I had to guess, that was the wound that killed her. A stab to the heart.

I could offer little comfort. No arm around her shoulders, no squeeze of her hand. I might be able to see ghosts, but I still couldn't touch them.

How did a person get over their own death? Some

stayed in denial, talking to themselves and anyone else who happened to go past, even when nobody answered. Others retreated into themselves, ignoring everyone and everything. The ghost on the second floor at Daylesford Hall was like that. A teenage girl suspended naked in mid-air, two feet off the ground, blonde hair floating around her as blood spread from her wrists in puffy red clouds. Although we'd never spoken, I could tell she'd died in a bath that had long since been ripped out to make room for the sales director's fancy glass desk and oversized leather swivel chair.

I classed those ghosts as type one and type two, and they were the easiest to deal with because I didn't have to do anything. Type threes wanted to talk, like Lucy at the gates. Quite friendly, a little lonely, but they took time to deal with and caused embarrassment and awkward questions if anyone happened to see me conversing with them.

Then there were the type fours like Arthur on the ground floor. They wanted justice and they wanted revenge, and they were determined I should get it for them. Sure, some of them were friendly, but at the end of the day, they wanted me to do their bidding and never let me forget it. Finally, there were the type fives. Those needy souls who demanded attention and never let me get a moment's peace.

Which type would Helene turn out to be?

Based on a combination of guesswork and experience, I predicted she'd turn out to be a combination of four and five, which meant I'd need to start using the other staircase more often.

But for the moment, I tried to comfort her with words. "I understand how this must have been a terrible shock for you."

"Do you? Do you really? Because you're still alive, and I'm dead."

"I know that, but I've seen a lot of death, believe me."

"Seen it? Is that all? What about your duty?"

Helene wiped a hand across her cheek, which didn't make a blind bit of difference to the trickles of blood. If I didn't know better, I'd have said her sobs were loud enough to wake the dead.

I'd heard rumours about her being highly strung, and it looked as if they were true. Now what? I couldn't avoid this corridor completely. The executive offices lay at one end, with meeting rooms and a kitchen at the other, and they all needed to be cleaned.

"Like I said, times have changed," I told her. "And even if they hadn't, I have no idea who killed you. Can you shed any light on that?"

Helene tried to lean against the wall next to her, and I caught the look of surprise on her face when she fell right through it. No, I shouldn't have laughed. There really wasn't anything funny about the current state of affairs. But even so... New ghosts had a steep learning curve. The spirit guides whispered just enough information to make them a thorn in my side and give them false hope, but never imparted the basics, like the tethered could no longer sleep, that solid objects presented no obstacle, and if they were hungry when they died, they'd be hungry for all eternity.

Best not to mention those little facts to Helene right now.

She scrambled back to her feet and scowled as if it were my fault she'd lost her balance. I imagined that hands-on-hips pose might have carried some sway in life, but it wouldn't get her far with me now.

"No, Miss High and Mighty, I don't have any idea who murdered me. One minute I was walking towards my office, then somebody grabbed me from behind. I felt a prick in my neck, and the next thing I knew, I was staring down at my own body."

"That's it?"

"I imagine they must have drugged me with something."

"And the prick in your neck was from a needle?"

"Unless you have a better idea?"

I shook my head, then realised she couldn't see me. "No."

In fact, I didn't have any ideas at all, mainly because I'd been trying to forget about the whole situation while I'd been off work.

"Well, it's a start," she said. "Maybe the police found fingerprints or something. You can begin there."

"I already told you, I'm not starting anywhere."

"Don't you realise who I am? My father owns this company. One word to him, and you won't have a job anymore."

"Aren't you forgetting something? You've got no way of talking to your father."

Helene burst into tears again. Understandable, but ultimately it got neither of us anywhere. All it did was add a little more weight to the burden of guilt that had built up inside me over the past twenty-four years. A burden I struggled to carry at the best of times. I backed away, and Helene must have sensed the distance opening up between us, because she held out a hand and gulped back sobs.

"Please, don't go."

"I'm sorry. I'm sorry, but I have to." Hands over my ears, I rushed down the corridor, beyond caring whether the offices of Weston Corp got cleaned today. Most likely, the forensics team had hoovered thoroughly anyway. Rather than taking the back stairs I'd come up and risking another run-in with Helene, I hurried down the main staircase and headed for the kitchen on the ground floor. As long as I cleaned up the dirty cups and plates and emptied the bins, nobody would notice I'd done a half-assed job this evening. They were all too busy gossiping in any case.

It seemed nobody else wanted to work past six. Whether out of fear, laziness, or because Mr. Weston hadn't come in today to keep an eye on them, I didn't know, but I only had to hide out downstairs for an hour before the building fell silent. Well, almost silent. I could still hear Helene weeping upstairs, and as I crossed the waiting area next to reception, Arthur's voice piped up from his position at the bottom of the stairs.

"Heard young Helene Weston got bumped off?"

"Please, Arthur, not today."

"Is it true?"

"Yes, it's true."

"Is that her making all the noise upstairs?"

"She's a bit upset at the moment."

"How's a man supposed to get any sleep around here?"

I cracked a smile, my first that day. We both knew he couldn't sleep no matter what the circumstances.

"Good night, Arthur."

Time to leave. The fancy new alarm panel beeped

behind me as I pulled the front door closed, relieved to have my first meeting with Helene over with but also dreading my second. Why me? For what seemed like the millionth time, I wished I'd been born as anyone but Rania Algafari, with my screwed-up soul and a moral compass that got knocked off course long before I'd ever been born.

CHAPTER 3 - RANIA

"THE POLICE WANT to talk to me," I told Shannon.

After a weekend of sleepless nights and bad coffee, tempered only by putting on a pair of trainers and pounding myself into the pavement, I'd spent Monday morning looking after a grumpy Aisling and counting down the minutes until Shannon got home. The afternoon didn't improve when Martha phoned, asking me to come in a little early tomorrow for an interview. Just routine, she said. The cops wanted to speak to all the staff. And, she confided, the younger officer was kind of cute. Would I mind assessing whether or not I thought he was gay? Because opinion was divided fifty/fifty at the moment, and she didn't want to embarrass herself by asking him out if he batted for the other team.

As if I'd know.

Shannon bounced Aisling on her hip, cooing softly. "I'm sure the police thing is nothing. Do you think I should take Aisling to the doctor? I reckon her sniffles are just a cold, but she seems really miserable."

"She'll probably catch something worse if you do. Think of all the people who'll be coughing and spluttering at the surgery."

Less than a month until Christmas, and I was full of cheer today, wasn't I?

"I guess. Maybe I'll wait and see how she is tomorrow."

"Sorry for being so snappy. Take her if you think you should."

"No, you're right. Rania, is everything okay? You know, with work? After the murder? You don't think the guy'll come back, do you?"

"Mr. Weston's upgraded the security for the whole building."

"But what about when you go home? I mean, the bus stop's a ten-minute walk away."

"What choice do I have? It's not like I can afford to take cabs."

And getting my own car was a distant dream. I couldn't even pay for driving lessons on my salary, let alone the vehicle itself. Yes, I'd driven in Syria, everything from small hatchbacks to military trucks when the need arose, but I'd never exactly got around to getting my licence. And in England, with all its laws and regulations, that piece of paper was everything.

"You should get one of those rape alarms, just in case."

Nobody would hear an alarm out at Daylesford Hall. The estate may have been beautiful, but it was also isolated. But Shannon meant well, and I didn't want to let on how worried I truly was, so I forced a smile.

"I'll look into it."

"Will you wake me when you come back so I know you got home safely?"

It was a strange feeling, having somebody care about me. Shannon was the first person to do so since my mother passed away three days after my sixteenth birthday, the first person not related to me by blood who cared whether I lived or died, and I still found the concept slightly awkward.

"Sure, I'll wake you."

***

I palmed the folding knife in my pocket as I walked from the bus stop to Daylesford Hall, my body humming with dark energy the way it once did every day when I lived in a war zone. Somewhere out there, a black soul could be watching, waiting...

Shadows danced as the wind whispered through the trees, mainly skeletons now that winter had arrived, but the odd evergreen stood out against the full moon. I'd once lived constantly on the alert, waiting for the worst to happen, and now those old feelings had come rushing back, albeit not with the same strength. And the environment was so different here. Woods and fields instead of rubble and abandoned buildings. The backdrop of peace interspersed with the odd car passing versus bombs, gunfire, and screams as more death came.

That peace was broken by Lucy's cheery greeting.

"Hello, Rania. Is it cold today? It looks cold."

Being a ghost did have some advantages. Lucy could watch as the sun's rays heated the earth on a baking August day and marvel as the early-morning frost twinkled from bare branches in December without ever feeling the change in temperature.

I kept my hands jammed into my pockets and my chin tucked into my scarf. "Yes, it's cold. Minus three Celsius according to the television this morning."

"I still don't understand this television thing. You say it's a square with a person inside?"

How strange it must be to live on the edges of the modern world, seeing it change around you but never being able to explore or fully understand. Lucy had watched as the road leading to Daylesford Hall turned from hard-packed mud to asphalt, the traffic changing from horse-drawn carriages and bicycles to metal boxes on wheels that whizzed along at sometimes alarming speeds.

"Television is more like a moving picture."

"Like a drawing? I used to draw when I had time. The lady of the house gave me a sketchbook and pencils for Christmas one year. Is it Christmas soon?"

"Three weeks to go."

"I miss Christmas. The children were always so happy, even when their governess insisted they have lessons before they could play with their toys. And the food... We had roast turkey and goose, and Cook would boil the stockpot for days to make the gravy. What will you have for dinner on Christmas Day?"

Last year, we'd eaten cheap—roast chicken and wonky vegetables, with a Christmas pudding Shannon had found on the discount shelf for dessert. What would this year bring?

"I'm not sure yet."

A car engine sounded in the lane, cutting our conversation short. "Got to go. I'll talk to you later."

***

Daylesford Hall had three staircases. The main set wrapped around the waiting area, wide and ornate with its fancy iron railings, which were now painted in pale grey and white. High on the wall opposite, a mural of the ancient world—either painted long ago or made to look that way—appeared out of place above the navy-blue block letters of Weston Corp's motto: *Innovation, integrity, ingenuity.*

Arthur's spirit dwelled beside the bottom step, sometimes sitting, mostly standing, as corporate clones walked past and often through him. Arthur had died at fifty-two, he'd told me, tipped over the top-floor balcony as he paused to reflect while working late one night. The railing up there was only waist height, curved into an oval so the servants could discreetly check on the owners of the house and their guests without intruding. I never liked to step too close to it. Arthur's neck canted permanently to one side where it broke on impact, and he'd adopted a tilted posture to compensate. It went well with his attitude, which veered from morose to chatty to cantankerous on a regular basis.

The second flight of stairs, the one where Helene now lurked, stood at the rear of the property and led from the basement to the second floor. That was the one I'd habitually used, but now I headed for the third set in the middle of Daylesford Hall, narrow and twisty, and liable to break *my* neck if I tried carrying the vacuum cleaner up and down it.

Even so, Helene noticed my arrival.

"Hey, you! Cleaning lady!"

A guy my age brushed past, and I recognised him from the sales department. The "World's Best Daddy" according to the mug he always left on his desk, half-filled with milky coffee he never drank. Father or not, that didn't stop his eyes from dropping to my chest before briefly meeting my gaze.

"Evening," he said. "Are you staying here on your own?"

What business was it of his? "I always do."

"Be careful."

Why did he say that? Friendly advice? Or a warning? "I always am."

My fingers touched the knife once more, safely tucked into the front pocket of my jeans. According to a TV programme Shannon had watched the other day, anyone carrying a knife was, statistically speaking, more likely to get stabbed with it than successfully ward off an attacker, but I'd never cared much for statistics.

Helene's voice rang out again. "I know you're there."

Honestly, the woman had no sense. I stomped to her corridor and checked both ways.

"Shut up!" I hissed. "There are people here, so I can't talk."

"Oh. I see."

I turned to walk away, but she wasn't finished. "Will you come back later?"

"Maybe."

"You'd better! I hate being on my own."

Yes, definitely a type four-slash-five. Just what I needed to go with the job of my dreams.

I spent half an hour collecting the dirty crockery to put in the dishwashers, which was the task that annoyed me most. Did these people just leave plates and mugs all over the place at home? If not, why did they do it at the office? Then I emptied the wastebaskets, which included picking up the wadded sheets of paper and misshapen piles of discarded Post-it notes that people had thrown in their direction and missed. I dusted, I polished, I vacuumed the sales office and the accounts office, and finally I could put it off no longer. I needed to deal with Helene.

"What do you want?" I asked her. "And my name's Rania, not 'hey you' or 'cleaning lady.'"

"Okay, whatever. I've been thinking."

Well, it wasn't as if she had much else to do. "And?"

"I may totally disagree with your decision, but I guess I understand why you can't hunt down the man who murdered me and do the same to him."

Wonders would never cease. "I'm glad you see it that way."

"But you can't let this go. Like you said, times have changed, which means you have to find the perpetrator and make sure he goes to jail."

"That's the police's job."

"And they're not doing it. I heard my brother speaking to Derek yesterday. The police haven't got the faintest clue who killed me, even though they've been questioning everyone."

"Derek was your boyfriend?"

I'd seen the pair of them in a photo on the staff noticeboard in the kitchen, front and centre at some charity gala last year. I suspected he drove the brand-new BMW that was always parked right outside the front door, shiny white with the "B1 GDK" vanity plate.

"Derek was my fiancé." Helene waved her left hand at me, and even in death, the rock on her ring finger sparkled. "He's devastated."

Who wouldn't be cut up at missing the chance to

spend the rest of their life with such a winning personality? *Rania, stop it...* I sighed. Maybe Helene hadn't been so bad when she was alive, and it wasn't her fault I'd inherited a gift I hated.

"I'm sure he misses you terribly."

"Which is why you have to investigate my death. Your job has evolved, and I imagine that's why I'm here. You know, to help you. Why else would I be stuck in this bloody corridor?"

Annoyingly, she was right. The tethered were left to help us find the black souls who took the lives of others, but that still didn't mean I'd follow her wishes.

"Look, I'd help if I could, but I need to work or I don't eat. Between that and babysitting duties, I don't have time to investigate crimes, and even if I did have the time, I wouldn't know where to start."

A little white lie. In Syria, I'd known exactly where to start, but that was a world away. I could hardly waltz into a police station in the UK and steal their files, nor could I persuade people to help by less-than-palatable means.

Helene waved a hand. "I'm sure you'll figure something out. I mean, if you don't, if you keep ignoring your purpose in life, how will you live with yourself?"

Her words sliced into me, a sharp blade delivered in an upper-class English accent. Because that was the exact same question I'd been asking myself since my mother explained to me who I was. *What* I was. And so far, I hadn't found the answer.

"That's my problem," I muttered, heading for the main staircase.

"You can't keep pretending I don't exist," Helene

yelled after me.

No, but I could try.

As if my discussion with Helene wasn't bad enough, Arthur was standing with his hands on his hips when I reached the ground floor.

"She's not happy, huh?"

"Nope. How much did you hear?"

"Enough. She's right, you know. You're the only hope for us, and until you start doing your duty, we're all stuck here. The police think I killed myself, for goodness' sake. My own *wife* thinks I killed myself, and every night I wonder how much she must resent me for taking the coward's way out. My kids are grown up now, and I've missed their graduations, their first dates, maybe even my grandchildren."

"I'm sorry, okay?" I took a deep breath and softened my tone. "Perhaps I could find out about your children? You know, where they are now."

"I'd like that, but it still wouldn't change the fact that there's a man walking around out there who ended my life, and nobody's even looking for him."

"I wish I could help, but I can't. Now there are two murder victims just in this building. Where would it end? I barely have time to sleep as it is."

Arthur folded his arms and smiled, a cunning grin I hadn't seen before. A trap, and I'd walked right into it.

"I know," he said. "Which is why I've got a deal to offer you."

"A deal? What kind of deal?"

Arthur had been dead for twelve years. What could he possibly have to trade?

"If you find my killer, I'll help you to catch the person who did Helene in."

Realisation dawned. "You saw them?"

He nodded, his cat-that-got-the-cream expression growing ever more smug. "Walked right past me on the way upstairs."

A tiny spark lit inside me at the thought of bringing Helene's killer to justice. Of doing something *good*. But a tsunami of doubts extinguished the flame before it got a chance to take hold. Sure, Arthur could help me solve Helene's murder, but to do that I'd have to find the key to a twelve-year-old case that was colder than the Arctic. And I was no detective. Hell, I couldn't even pick out the culprit in the daily reruns of *Columbo* I watched with Aisling.

"Sorry, Arthur. I can't do it."

His expression blackened. "But I'm offering to help you solve a crime."

"No, you're asking me to do the impossible in return for information that any civic-minded citizen would pass over in a heartbeat. And even if you did hand me Helene's killer on a plate, what would I say to the police? I can hardly explain a ghost saw the crime, can I?"

"Maybe you could say *you* saw it?"

"No way." Because then they'd start digging around in my life and my past, and besides, I had an airtight alibi.

"I can see you need some time to think about this."

"I've already thought about it."

"Sleep on it. I'm sure you'll do the right thing."

Great. Now Arthur was delusional too. All I needed was for the weird floating girl in the bath upstairs to wake up and join in, and I'd have to hang up my dishcloth and start picking cabbages for a living. Apart from cleaning, that was the only job I'd been offered since I arrived in England.

"See you tomorrow," he called, sounding worryingly cheerful as I headed for the door.

I didn't bother answering. Denial was a wonderful thing.

"You look like you need a drink," Shannon said when I got in.

I never touched alcohol, but the temptation had never been so strong. "Just a paracetamol."

"What's wrong? Is it work?"

"Sort of."

Ghosts. I was being blackmailed by ghosts. Quite possibly a unique problem, because although there were supposed to be three other Electi on Earth at any one time, I was quite sure they handled their affairs more appropriately than I did.

Shannon put one arm around my shoulder and squeezed, a comforting gesture for any normal person, but I didn't take or give affection well. In fact, physical contact made my skin crawl. But Shannon meant well, so I kept still and hoped my grimace looked more like a smile.

"You're not still worried about the murderer being out there? I doubt he's hung around what with the police being there all the time."

"It's not that. I'm beginning to think you're right, and I should look for a new job."

"Do you want me to see if there's any evening shifts at the bread factory?"

Knowing my luck, I'd probably come face-to-face with some poor sod who met his maker in a vat of dough or something. But Shannon was trying to help,

and goodness knows, I needed that.
    "I guess it wouldn't hurt to ask."

CHAPTER 4 - RANIA

"SO, MISS ALBAFERRARI, you say you didn't come near Daylesford Hall between Friday evening and Monday afternoon?" the older of the two policemen interviewing me asked.

I didn't bother to correct him on my name. I'd already spelled it out for him twice, so I'd come to the conclusion it was a lost cause.

"That's right. I finished at around ten p.m. on Friday, and when I came in on Monday, your people were just carrying Helene's body out."

"And what were you doing on Sunday evening between the hours of seven and eleven?"

"I was on a date."

He raised an eyebrow. "A date?"

Was it really that hard to believe? "Yes, a double date with my friend Shannon."

Of course, she'd arranged it. The closest I got to chatting up a guy was smiling at the boy behind the supermarket deli counter in the hope he'd be generous with the portions.

At least the younger policeman didn't share his colleague's surprise. No, he fixed me with a hard stare and tapped a blue biro on his notepad. I noticed he'd chewed the cap.

"We'll need the details of your date. A man?"

Martha's question about the cop's sexual orientation popped into my head. Why did she suspect he might be gay? I mentally catalogued the details—light-brown hair, cropped short; matching eyes with flecks of grey; a thin nose with a little bump at the end; a jaw slightly too angular to be attractive. To me, anyway. It obviously hadn't bothered Martha. And from what I could see as his shirt stretched across his chest when he leaned towards me, he probably spent some time in the gym.

"The details of your date, Miss Algafari?"

"What? Oh, yes. It was with a man."

"Can you give us his name?"

His name… His name… Joe? John? Jim? "It began with J. I think. Try Jason?"

"Are you asking me or telling me?"

Okay, now I sounded like a complete ditz, although perhaps that wasn't so bad under the circumstances. Better for them to think I was stupid than figure out the truth.

"Uh, I can't quite remember. My friend arranged it through one of those dating websites."

In truth, after he'd leered down my top before we'd even spoken, I'd mentally filed him in the "nope" pile. Then when his hand landed on my thigh halfway through the starter, I'd peeled his fingers away and moved him from "nope" to "not even if the survival of the human race depended on it." And when he'd tried it a second time, I'd been forced to sit on my hands so I didn't pin his fingers to the table with my fork.

Shannon's companion hadn't been much better. They rarely were. Aisling's father had been a rat of the first order, a wealthy businessman named Richard

Albernarle III who'd abandoned her when she discovered she was expecting Aisling and hid behind his lawyers to avoid paying child support, mainly in case the wife he'd conveniently forgotten to mention to Shannon found out. I'd christened him Slick Dick. Worse, Shannon had confided in him that she'd run from her ex in Ireland, and gentleman that he was, Dick had threatened to tell the ex where Shannon was if she breathed a word about Aisling's parentage.

And his parting shot? Shannon would never be worth more than a quick roll in the sack.

I'd have thought that would have been enough to put Shannon off men for life, but instead, she'd gone in the other direction, determined to prove Dick wrong by meeting her perfect man. Mr. Average, she said. Somebody more in her league.

But so far, she'd only managed to attract players and fruitcakes. She did get as far as the fourth date with one guy, but the second she mentioned her daughter, he ran for the hills.

And Sunday had been more of the same. Her date and Joe-John-Jason had obviously been interested in only one thing, which neither Shannon nor I were willing to give. Well, Shannon had a brief wobble after the idiots poured her three glasses of wine, but I'd excused us to go to the bathroom and shoved her out the front door and into a taxi instead. That was the reason I went on those double dates with her—to save her from herself.

But I wasn't about to explain our history to the cop sitting opposite me.

"I'll need your friend's details so we can get his information," he said.

"It didn't go very well, so she deleted all the messages. Can't you check with the restaurant? We went to Pizza Express on the high street. They might have a CCTV camera or something." No "might" about it—the camera to the right of the front door would have caught us arriving and leaving, and even though I'd ducked my head out of habit, they should still have enough evidence to provide me with an alibi. "I was wearing black jeans and a red jumper," I added, just in case.

He huffed, no doubt at the thought of having to do some extra work, but jotted the details down in his notepad.

"How well did you know Ms. Weston?" he asked.

"Not at all, not really. I said hello to her in the hallway once or twice, and occasionally she asked me to skip cleaning her office if she was still working. I doubt she even knew my name. I'm only the cleaner."

"Have you seen any strangers hanging around?"

"Nobody."

"Delivery men? Visitors who looked out of place?"

"Sometimes the postman comes to pick up the mail when I'm here, but it's always the same man. White hair, in his fifties, wears shorts whatever the weather. And there are often visitors, but nobody that gave me the creeps. I think Martha makes everyone sign the visitors' book when they arrive."

"We're aware of that."

Silence. They were trying to make me feel uncomfortable. Amateurs. I'd once spent a week being tortured with water and knives and electricity back in Syria—a little peace and quiet barely blipped my radar.

Finally, the older cop spoke. "Well, Miss Aldehari, I

think that's all for now. Keep your wits about you when you're here late at night, and if anything makes you uncomfortable, I'd suggest you ring 999 straight away."

I nodded, perhaps a bit too enthusiastically. "I'll make sure of that."

The other cop slid a business card across the table towards me. Chris Turner, Detective Constable. "And if you think of anything else, here's my number. Thank you for your time."

I stuffed the card into my pocket and rose from my seat. *Stay calm, Rania.* My feet wanted to run, but I forced them to take slow, measured steps until I got into the corridor. The police had borrowed one of the second-floor meeting rooms to do the interviews in, so I slunk away until I reached the cleaning supplies cupboard. Once inside, I retrieved my knife from behind a bottle of bleach and tucked it back in my pocket.

The most difficult part of the day was over. Now I just had to finish the cleaning and deal with Arthur and Helene before I could go home.

***

The rest of the week passed without incident, and according to Martha, the police were no further forward with their investigation. At least I hadn't been called in for more questioning—the CCTV tape from Pizza Express must have checked out okay.

Oh, and Martha had asked Chris the cop out, and he'd turned her down, so he must definitely be gay, she said.

Arthur remained tight-lipped but grumpy, and

Helene's daily whining had turned into more of a sulk. I suspected she'd practised that pout in the mirror. Every day. For years.

Martha told me Mr. Weston had returned to work for a day before breaking down in the corridor where his daughter died. I thought Helene might try to use that to make me feel guilty, but evidently his tears hadn't been loud enough for her to hear, and she couldn't sense her father's presence and emotions in the same way as she could mine. Even now, I was still learning new things about spirits.

"Work going better?" Shannon asked on Friday evening.

"Yes, it is."

"But the police haven't caught that maniac yet?"

"Not yet."

"I'm still worried about you going to that place alone at night."

"I know, and I'm grateful for that, but I could get run over crossing the road."

"Don't say that." She crinkled her nose in that adorable way she had, reminding me why men like Dick lusted after her. "Did you see that story on the news about the girl who got a firework put through her letter box? She accidentally ended up in the middle of some sort of turf war."

"Near here?"

"The other side of town." Shannon's phone buzzed, and she smiled as she read the screen. "Ooh, I've got us dates for this weekend! Good ones this time, I promise. Lisa said she'd look after Aisling again."

Lisa was the seventeen-year-old daughter of one of Shannon's colleagues. Blessed with four younger brothers and two sisters, she'd babysit once a week for pennies as long as we supplied her with plenty of ice cream and somewhere quiet to study. Unfortunately.

"Do we have to go?"

"Come on, Rania. You'll never meet the One sitting at home with a book."

"But I don't want to meet anybody. I'm better off by myself."

"And yet you've never told me why you're so anti-men." Her brow furrowed for a second. "There's this new lesbian dating app..."

"No! I don't want to meet *anybody*, male or female."

"Fine. Be a spinster your whole life." She tilted her head to one side and gave me a lopsided smile. "But you'll come on Saturday, right? It's just a bit of fun. You don't have to marry the guy."

"I promised Mrs. Garrett downstairs that I'd do her shopping in the afternoon." She couldn't walk so well anymore, and I'd started helping her after she tripped over the steps with her wheeled trolley a few months ago.

"I won't arrange anything too early. Please?"

When the alternative was worrying about Shannon all night? I sighed. "Yes, I'll come."

Chapter 5 - Will

"DID YOU FIND the lost dog?" RJ asked.

"Yeah."

"Want a beer?"

"Yeah."

"Thought I'd order hookers tonight. You want one or two?"

"Yeah."

RJ slammed the lid on my laptop, ignoring my glare.

"What the fuck?" I growled.

"I'm the one who should be asking that question, Will. You've been on a different planet this evening. Girl trouble? That blonde from last night?"

No, well, yes. Valerie, the blonde, had messaged me three times today and called twice. She might have been hot in the sack, but I didn't need that kind of clingy.

"The blonde's history."

"Shame. She made good coffee."

"Why don't you ask her out, then?"

"Sloppy seconds? Not my thing, man." I moved to open my laptop again, but RJ kept his hand on the top. "What's up? Tell Auntie RJ all about it."

RJ was Randall James Wilkinson-Shields, my best mate since we'd got detention together on our first day of boarding school for putting a live frog in the French teacher's pencil case. Not our fault nobody locked the biology lab at lunchtime. Rather than become known as Randy the Third for our entire school career, he'd shortened his name to RJ Shields and played a lot of rugby to avoid claiming the "geek" crown for his love of computers.

And now he was my housemate.

Well, sort of. RJ's father had bought him the three-bedroom townhouse as a gift for passing his university entrance exam, while mine kicked me out of the house for choosing the police academy over a career in law, and I'd been camping out in RJ's spare room ever since. Eight years on, and we bickered like an old married couple.

And if I didn't talk to him, he'd change the Wi-Fi password until I did. I sat back in my chair and sighed.

"I got offered a new case."

"And? What's the problem? You need the work, yes?"

I did, so badly I couldn't afford to turn any job away. And that bothered me.

When I didn't reply, RJ drummed his fingers on the desk. "Cheating husband? Stolen lawnmower? Another missing pet? You know those are your favourite."

Yeah, right. I'd spent the past fortnight tracking down Muffy, my godmother's best friend's elderly poodle who'd taken fright at some fireworks and run off on her evening walk. Another little old lady had claimed ownership under the "finders keepers" rule, and I'd got caught in the crossfire as the two women hurled doggy treats at each other. Then Muffy bit me on the arm when I picked her up.

Now I had a bandage, a sore arse from the tetanus shot, and a potential nightmare of a new case.

"No, this one's a murder investigation."

RJ gave a low whistle. "Bit of a step up. Are you going to take it?"

"Not sure I've got a choice."

Muffy's "mother" might have given me a generous tip, but my bank account was still alarmingly empty. RJ lived a champagne lifestyle on a Cristal budget, while my finances ran to Prosecco at the moment. And only girls drank that.

But RJ always had my back.

"Skip the rent for a few months."

RJ had never asked me to pay in the first place, but my conscience wouldn't let me live there and contribute nothing. "Can't do that."

He shrugged. "Your choice. Go on, then, tell me about this murder."

I stared at his hand until he lifted it, then opened my laptop again. Not that I really needed to. The victim's green eyes were burned into my damn soul now.

"Helene Weston, twenty-eight years old and heiress to her father's business empire. Someone stabbed her two weeks ago at their company headquarters. The cops haven't got very far, and her Daddy's getting impatient."

"Sounds like he could be a demanding client."

"Yes, he does."

In the brief meeting I'd had with him today, called at his insistence at two p.m. on a Sunday afternoon, Mr. Weston had impressed upon me the need for results, and quickly. The only thing he wanted for

Christmas, he said, was his daughter's killer behind bars. And Christmas was just two short weeks away.

RJ rubbed one hand over his mouth in the way he did when he wasn't sure whether to say something or not. I waited him out.

"Without wanting to be insulting, how did he come to pick you?"

It was a fair question. My reputation wasn't exactly stellar—a hasty resignation from Hertfordshire Constabulary before I got fired had been followed by an internet hate campaign started by a spouse I'd caught cheating on her wealthy husband. She'd been a one-hit wonder with some pop song about lollipops, but in her short career, she'd amassed several thousand Facebook fans and twice that on Twitter. And now they all knew Will Lawson's private investigation firm was a crock of shit. RJ soon got her social media accounts shut down, but not before the damage was done.

"Chris Turner recommended me for the job."

"As in Chris Turner, the by-the-book asshole who got you kicked off the force?"

"That's the one."

"Why would he do that?"

"Because he hasn't got anywhere with the case so far, he reckons I won't either, and he wants to make himself look better."

"He'll roadblock you at every opportunity."

"He will."

And the stupid part of me still wanted to take the case, because if I could solve it, that would be the sweetest revenge possible against a man who'd contributed to my downfall. And Chris Turner wasn't much of a detective. He knew his way around every form, report, and protocol the Hertfordshire Constabulary threw at us, but actual police work was a pesky task he'd avoided wherever possible. He'd only got promoted because he'd worked out through diligent study and years of experience which arses to lick.

"Aw, shit. I know that look. You're about to do something stupid," RJ said, tapping at his phone. "Look, I can shift some meetings around and work remotely for a week. The chalet in Verbier's free. Let's take off for a few days, get in some quality time on the snow, and distract ourselves in the evenings with pleasant female company."

"I can't."

"Sure you can. You've still got your ski gear, right?"

I'd been tempted to sell it on eBay, but things hadn't got quite that desperate yet. And if I could solve this case...

"I need to do this, RJ."

He rolled his eyes and blew out a long breath, sounding remarkably like Valerie did last night when I told her I'd be busy with work for the foreseeable future.

But like I said, he always had my back.

"Tell me what you need."

And while I'd ignored my father's orders and leapt straight into a job he didn't approve of, RJ had been a little smarter. Smart as fuck, he'd studied law at the London School of Economics and Political Science, one of the city's leading universities, and still found time in the evenings to turn his hobby into a business. I'd fought with my conscience and turned a blind eye to his slightly less than legal exploits, and now he ran the country's most successful ethical hacking firm, testing cybersecurity for major corporations and prominent individuals. But he still did black-hat stuff on the side.

"Can you get me the police files on Helene Weston's murder? And anything you can find on her family and acquaintances?"

"I'll take payment in beer and pizza."

"Pepperoni?"

"You know me so well."

CHAPTER 6 - RANIA

MARTHA LOOKED SUSPICIOUSLY cheerful when I arrived at work on Monday. On Friday, she'd been moping about Chris the cop and his lack of interest in her, but now she snapped shut her compact and tucked her lipstick back into her handbag as I approached.

"Good weekend?" I asked out of politeness.

She crinkled her nose, reminding me of Shannon. "So-so. I tried to get my Christmas shopping finished, but the shops were mobbed, I couldn't find any pink wrapping paper, and some git of a parking warden gave me a ticket. Sixty quid! I was only five minutes over the time. Okay, fifteen, but there's supposed to be a grace period, right?"

"No idea. I don't have a car."

"But things are looking up today. Mr. Weston's hired a private investigator, and he's freaking hot. L-U-S-H." She glanced down at the desk. "He wants to talk to you, and we've pencilled you in for six o'clock, right after Aiden. You know, Aiden who always wears the nice suits? We figured that would be okay seeing as you're always here late."

"Tonight? What about cleaning? If I stay any later than usual, I'll miss the bus." And Shannon would freak out, and the dinner she'd promised to cook would get cold.

"Mr. Weston said it was fine for you to skip a few bits and leave at your usual time, same as all of us. Apparently, talking to the cops and the investigator takes priority over everything. Can't say I blame him. The guy's aged a decade since Helene's murder. Anthony's pretty much been running the company."

Ah, yes, Anthony Weston. The male version of Helene, with the same eyes and entitled attitude. What he also had that his sister and father didn't was a love of Scotch. He kept a bottle of the stuff in his desk drawer, and he didn't save it for special occasions. If his secretary's mutterings were to be believed, he sometimes started on the sauce as early as breakfast.

Which meant we needed Mr. Weston back at the helm, and fast, or the company would go down the toilet and none of us would have jobs anymore.

"Six o'clock, you say?"

"Same room as before. I'd take your slot if I could, just so I could stare at the guy for a bit longer." Martha hesitated then held out her lipstick. "Want to borrow this?"

"Thanks, but I'll pass."

Happy Monday, Rania. Thankfully, Martha hadn't asked how my weekend had gone, because I barely had the energy to lie. Aisling was teething, Saturday night's date had been predictably awful, and I'd suffered from nightmares every time I closed my eyes. Now, I stomped past Arthur on my way to collect cups, not in the mood to talk. Negotiate. Whatever.

"Had any more thoughts on my offer?" he asked.

I ignored him. Same with Helene when I got upstairs and she smugly informed me of the new investigator's arrival.

"I knew Daddy would do something. See, not everyone's giving up like you are."

Tears pricked at my eyes as I reached the cleaning cupboard and shut myself inside. Was it too much to ask to get some peace? And Helene knew nothing about me. I'd tried doing things her way, my *duty* as she called it, and that hadn't worked out so well either. All I wanted to do in England was to live my life like any other twenty-something girl. Go to work, get paid, eat, sleep, watch movies with Shannon, and maybe go shopping occasionally. I didn't want to talk to dead people. Not for the first time, I cursed softly in Arabic at whoever put this burden on my shoulders. Why me? I wasn't special. I wasn't strong.

But I *was* wasting time. I had an entire building to clean and another stupid interview to fit in before I could go home, and sitting on an upturned bucket feeling sorry for myself wouldn't change anything.

I picked up a duster and a can of polish and went to clean the executive offices.

***

"Rania Algafari?"

Aiden's interview must have been over quickly because the meeting room had been empty when I arrived. I'd settled onto a chair and waited, and now, at five past six, a dark-haired man slid into the seat opposite. Hopefully, my interrogation wouldn't take long either.

"Yes, that's me."

He offered a hand for me to shake. "Will Lawson."

Custom called for me to say I was pleased to meet

him, but I wasn't, so I kept my mouth shut. Petty, perhaps, but I didn't ask to be here.

"I understand from Lloyd Weston that you're the cleaner here at Daylesford Hall?"

"I am."

He studied me, in no hurry to ask his next question, and I had to grudgingly admit that Martha was right. Will Lawson had the cop beat hands down in terms of looks, but his eyes worried me. Perfectly normal from a quick glance, chocolate brown with flecks of gold, but the way they bored into my soul unnerved me. The tension that had ebbed away a little over the past week began buzzing through my veins again like a low current of electricity just waiting for someone to turn up the dial.

"What hours do you work?"

"I arrive between three and four, and I'm usually done by ten, Monday to Friday."

"Ever work weekends?"

"Rarely. Only if there's an event on and I get asked. I didn't work the weekend Helene Weston died."

The words rushed out, and I bit my tongue. Will's lips curved up at one corner, perhaps because he could sense my fear. Even the cops hadn't made me feel this uncomfortable.

On the surface, Will looked relaxed, but when I dropped my gaze, I noticed he had a habit of sliding his pen cap off and on with one hand. Off. Clicking it back on again. Off. On. He caught me watching and dropped it on the table.

"And Sunday evening? Where were you?"

"I've already told all this to the police."

He let out a short laugh, but there was no mirth in

it. "I'm not working with the police, so I'd be much obliged if you could tell me too."

Something about the way he said it, his cold tone, told me there was no love lost between him and local law enforcement, so in a way, I could empathise.

"I was on a date."

Will's jaw cracked.

"In Pizza Express, with a guy called Jack." I'd checked with Shannon now. She'd been paying slightly more attention than I had. "We left around ten, and I went straight home."

"I'll need Jack's contact information."

"I don't have it."

Now Will smiled. "The date didn't go well?"

"Could have been better." Like, if I'd stayed at home.

"Never mind. I'll check with the restaurant. A face like yours, someone'll remember you."

"What's that supposed to mean?"

"You're striking. You must know that."

I looked for a sign he was joking, but his face stayed serious, and I shifted uncomfortably in my seat. Men didn't pay me compliments, especially in the middle of official interviews. I had no answer, so I folded my hands in my lap and waited.

Will leaned back in his chair and adopted a more conversational tone. "So, what did you think of Helene?"

"Back when she was alive?"

He gave me a puzzled look, and I wanted to smack myself for saying something so stupid. Will Lawson made me speak first and think after with his long silences and prying eyes.

"Has your opinion of her changed now she's dead?"

Yes. Before, I'd been indifferent. Helene had been pretty, kind of unapproachable, someone to envy a little if I was honest. Now, I thought she was a whiny brat.

"Of course not. I barely spoke to her before she died, and I don't know much more about her now. But her father must be getting desperate to have hired you."

His expression went flat. Dammit, I'd put my foot in it again. "Thanks."

"I didn't mean it like that, honestly. I just thought that the police were already investigating..."

"The police are suffering from funding cuts, same as every other government-run agency. Lloyd Weston wanted someone who's more focused on his daughter's case."

"I guess with his kind of money, that makes sense."

"I'm interested in your thoughts. Why do you think somebody might have killed Helene?"

"How am I supposed to know? I'm just the cleaner." And even Helene herself didn't have a clue who did it.

"But I bet you see things. Hear things. Offices like this always have their secrets."

"Nothing that I'd consider pertinent to the case."

"Really? No politics and power struggles? Petty theft? Affairs? Closet romances?"

I thought back over my time at Weston Corp. There'd been a rumour about Lloyd Weston shagging his secretary, borne out by the fact that she'd quickly been replaced by a forty-year-old guy the day after Mr. Weston's wife threw a cup of coffee over her. Then said guy was fired a fortnight later after smoking pot on company premises. Not long after that, a salesman got marched out of the building with the contents of his desk in a cardboard box, followed by whispers that he'd been abusing his company credit card. And I'd found a pair of pink panties wedged down the back of the sofa in the break room one day, a frill of lace just visible sticking out from behind the cushions. But were any of those linked to Helene's death? Unlikely.

"You should try talking to Martha, the receptionist. She knows far more about that sort of thing than me. I understand she even has a Facebook group."

"I already spoke to her." Will grimaced. "I'd still be speaking to her now if there hadn't been a problem with the catering for tomorrow's lunch meeting."

Will's obvious distaste meant I smiled without meaning to, and he grinned back, all white teeth and boy-next-door sexiness with an edge of danger running under the veneer. The odd camaraderie mixed with a hint of pheromones made my heart give a nervous flip.

"Don't worry, she'll move on to someone else soon enough. Last week, she had her sights set on one of the policemen. Uh, Chris Turner?"

"She's not Chris's type." Will's grin disappeared.

"You know him?"

"Our paths have crossed."

"In what way?"

"Doesn't matter."

Funny how he wasn't so keen on talking when it was me asking the questions, wasn't it? He picked up his pen again. Lid off, lid on, lid off, lid on.

"Out of everyone, you're here the latest at night. Have you ever seen anyone hanging around? Or felt anyone?"

"Felt anyone?"

"Intuition's often underrated."

Didn't I know it? My gut had got me out of more sticky situations than I cared to think about over the years. That and whispers from helpful spirits.

But I shook my head.

"Who else tends to work late?"

"The sales department. Sometimes the accounts team if it's a month-end. But it's rare for anyone but the Westons to be here after seven thirty."

A memory popped up, of the time I'd gone to collect Anthony's Scotch glass and caught him watching porn on his computer, dick in hand. Luckily, he'd been too busy concentrating on his happy ending to notice me.

"What?" Will asked. "You're smiling?"

"It's nothing."

"Let me be the judge of that."

"Fine. One member of the management team likes to watch porn when he thinks everyone's gone home. But I don't see how that could possibly connect to Helene's murder."

"Anthony?"

My silence gave him his answer.

"Thought so."

"How did you know?"

"He seems the type. Plus his girlfriend's screwing around with her tennis coach, so I don't suppose he's getting much at home."

I choked a little, and Will's grin came back, smug, as if he was pleased with himself for shocking me.

"You didn't know about that part, huh?"

"No, and I didn't *want* to know."

"You're an interesting girl, Rania. Every other woman in this place laps up gossip like it's her lifeblood."

"I'm not sure what you expect me to say to that."

He shrugged one shoulder. "Me neither. I guess I find it refreshing. Makes me curious about what makes you tick."

Another silence followed, long, painful even.

"Aren't we supposed to be discussing Helene Weston?" I asked.

"You didn't seem too keen on that, but now that you mention it..."

I let out a long breath because I'd fallen right into a trap again. "But I don't know anything. Really, I'd tell you if I did, just so I could get out of here."

He held up both hands. "I'm not holding you prisoner."

"No, but if I don't cooperate, I bet that would get back to Mr. Weston."

That lopsided shrug came again.

"Okay, the only person who's come across as odd since the murder is one of the salesmen. He asked if I was staying on my own in the evening, and when I said I was, he told me to be careful."

"That's it?"

"The way he said it, it sounded like more of a warning. Look, you were the one who talked about intuition."

"I did. Any idea of his name?"

No, but I gave Will the details I did have, including which desk the guy sat at.

"Nothing else?"

Perhaps because I was tired, or perhaps because I was too busy concentrating on the gold flecks sparkling in Will Lawson's irises to think straight, I came up with the idea of mentioning Arthur. After all, he couldn't keep complaining if I'd turned his case over to a professional, could he?

"There was another death here a while ago. I doubt they're connected, but..."

Will raised an eyebrow then flicked the cap off his pen entirely. "A murder? Nobody's mentioned that."

"It went down as a suicide."

"But you don't believe that?"

It was my turn to shrug.

"How long ago did it happen?"

"Uh, twelve years. Something like that."

"How do you know? Your personnel file says you've only been in the country for four, and nobody else I've spoken to has mentioned it."

Stupid, stupid Rania. This was why I shouldn't try to hold a sensible conversation when I'd barely had any sleep for three days.

"I guess I must have heard a rumour."

"Why do I get the feeling you're holding something back?"

"I don't know, okay? I've answered all your questions, I'm behind on my work, and while I'm very sorry that Mr. Weston found Helene's mutilated body in this building because no father should have to go through that, her death wasn't anything to do with me."

My chair juddered across the carpeted floor as I pushed it back, ready to leave, but Will didn't move. Instead, he fixed me with those dark, bottomless eyes, and the intensity of his gaze heightened the fear I'd been fighting against for the past two weeks.

What just happened?

Chapter 7 - Will

RANIA ALGAFARI. I'D read her personnel file, thin though it was, and even looked at the fuzzy photo that accompanied it, but nothing prepared me for meeting the girl herself. Woman, I should say. There was nothing childlike about the curves hidden under her clothing, although she still managed to project a strange innocence that made me want to beat every other man away with a stick.

And she was nervous.

Whether from meeting me or due to the recent events at Daylesford Hall, I couldn't tell, but every time she swallowed, my eyes fixed on the delicate lines of her neck.

Between her jeans, her dark-red polo neck, and the shapeless cardigan she wore, almost every inch of skin was covered, yet she still managed to be more attractive than any other female in the building. No make-up, and her thick brown hair, so dark it was almost black, was tied back without any ceremony. The only nod to decoration was the necklace she wore, an abstract gold piece on a chain that she tucked inside her top when she saw me looking at it. After that, she kept her eyes fixed on the table, and I wanted to wind my fist around that plait and force her head up to meet my gaze.

My cock began twitching the moment she sat down,

which was totally inappropriate.

Behave, Lawson.

Even though the police had already cleared her, and I'd read about her alibi in the file RJ had liberated for me, I asked her questions anyway because I wanted to hear her talk. Those lips. Thick and full, I could imagine them...

Fuck, now she was staring at me. *Say something else, Will.*

"So, what did you think of Helene?"

"Back when she was alive?"

What the hell was that supposed to mean? Rania's brow crinkled, and the light caught on the dark circles under her eyes. Tired. She was tired and struggling to think straight, and I felt bad for taking up her time when she still had work to do. But not so bad that I stopped questioning her. Then she insulted me without meaning to, and bastard that I was, I pushed her to confess she'd caught Anthony watching porn one evening. Jacking off, if her disgusted expression was any indication. Disgusted by the act itself, or because it was Anthony and he was an alcoholic prick?

My gaze drifted down to her hands. No ring on her finger. Did she have a boyfriend? Surely she must. Which meant I shouldn't have been imagining the little gasp she might give if I kissed her senseless, then...

"Aren't we supposed to be discussing Helene Weston?" she asked.

Discussing Helene was the last thing I wanted to do, especially with a girl who was way at the bottom of the list of suspects, but Lloyd Weston was paying me.

"You didn't seem too keen on that, but now that you mention it..."

And then Rania had surprised me. Another death in this building? Lloyd Weston hadn't mentioned that, and neither had anybody else. More to the point, how did Rania find out?

I had another task for RJ, and also an excuse to talk to the delectable Miss Algafari later this week. A treat indeed. I was tempted to offer her a lift home tonight, just to spend a few more minutes in her company, but as a man who prided himself on his ability to get inside people's heads, I struggled to get a read on her. And I didn't want to scare her off.

No, I'd wait.

At least, that was my initial plan, and then everything changed.

"Why do I get the feeling you're holding something back?" I asked her.

"I don't know, okay? I've answered all your questions, I'm behind on my work, and while I'm very sorry that Mr. Weston found Helene's mutilated body in this building because no father should have to go through that, her death wasn't anything to do with me."

At first, I got caught up in her adorable indignation, but then her words sank in.

Shit.

"Helene's mutilated body? Care to elaborate?"

Rania paused, halfway out of her chair. "I don't understand," she whispered.

"Sit."

She sat slowly, as if her natural desire to resist was fighting against a need to keep her nose clean at work, and she looked far from happy about it.

"None of the information released to the public has mentioned Helene's body being mutilated, so I'm curious as to why you think it was."

The colour drained from her face, leaving those shadows under her eyes darker than ever.

"I'm not sure why I said that."

But I was. Because she *knew*. That sentence had rolled off her tongue without a second thought, as if she'd said that winter was cold or sugar was sweet.

"What would you say if I told you Helene's breasts were cut off?"

Nothing. She said nothing, but I didn't miss the momentary flicker of confusion that crossed her face.

"Or her eyes were gouged out?"

The confusion turned to fear. Ah, now we were getting someplace. But where did Rania glean that particular snippet of information? The police files had made it clear that the details of Helene's injuries were to be held back from the press. Only the investigating team and of course Lloyd Weston knew the truth. Little facts like that were often kept secret to ward off copycats and set traps like the one Rania had just fallen into.

And I hadn't even set it on purpose. Pure, dumb luck.

But now Rania was on her feet. "I'm done here. You said you couldn't keep me."

I waved towards the door, the momentary spark of attraction I'd felt fizzling out as I struggled with the revelation that Rania knew more about this crime than she was letting on.

But *how* was she so well-informed?

***

"Spell that name for me again," RJ said.

"A-L-G-A-F-A-R-I."

For reasons I couldn't fathom, I felt like a shit for raking through Rania's life. I'd done it a thousand times before, so why was she any different?

"I'll run a few search programs," RJ said. "What's for dinner?"

"Pizza?"

"Pepperoni, and get me some chicken wings, would you?"

"Let's go out for a change."

RJ stared at me. "Hold on. Did you just seriously suggest the two of us go out for pizza? Have you turned into a girl? Do you want me to bring flowers and candles while you unload all your angst?"

"Shut up, man. No, I need to check Rania's alibi. She reckons she was at the pizza place on the high street, but there's something off about her whole story."

"That's why you're having me dig into her background?"

"Why else?"

"I just assumed you were interested in her and wanted to check for skeletons. She looks like your type."

"How? I usually go for blondes with no strings attached."

"For a good time, yeah. But those aren't the ones who stick. Think about it. Secretly, you prefer the innocent, vulnerable type so you can go full caveman."

True, maybe, but I didn't want to think about it. "What are you? A fucking agony aunt?"

"Just an observation."

"Says the man whose last date left when he got his

iPad out between the main course and dessert." And worse, she'd taken my date with her.

RJ looked up from his computer for a second. "She did?"

"If you don't take a break from that computer and come out for food, I'll unplug the damn thing. You've already had to get glasses because of it."

"Unplug it if you like. I've got an auxiliary power supply."

"I'm serious."

RJ got to his feet and turned off the screen. "Fine. But if you hold my hand, I'm hiring an all-male dance troupe to perform at your next birthday."

Just to wind RJ up, when we got to the restaurant, I asked the purple-haired waitress to seat us at a quiet table and bring a bottle of rosé. RJ glared at me as he changed the order to two beers. The waitress giggled and eyed up his Porsche keys, and I predicted she'd be sitting beside him in the passenger seat at the end of the evening. At least when he ditched me like that, he always forked out for my cab fare.

And I had more important things on my mind.

It didn't take me long to spot the manager, sitting at a quiet table as she checked over the evening's bookings on her tablet. I left RJ chatting up his new friend as I headed over.

"Do you have a minute?" I asked.

She opened her mouth to say no, but I smiled, and that changed to a nod of her head. The smile worked every time. Three years of braces from the best orthodontist money could buy was paying off in adulthood. It almost made the nicknames I'd endured worth it. Metal mouth. Zipper lips. Tinsel teeth. Kids could be cruel, and the little shits at my first boarding school were the worst. I'd been happy to get expelled, but my father hadn't shared that joy. Fortunately, RJ had been by my side all the way.

"How can I help?" she asked.

I offered a hand for her to shake, careful to hold onto hers for just a second too long and end with a little squeeze. Her cheeks flushed nicely pink.

"Will Lawson. I'm a private investigator, and I'm hoping to check an alibi for a lady who dined here a couple of weeks ago."

"Is this the same woman the police were asking about?"

"Very likely."

"I'm not really supposed to give out that information without the proper paperwork."

"I don't need to take anything with me. Just watch your security video and ask a few questions. After you get off, if you like. We could do the questions over drinks."

Even as I spoke the words, I thought back to what RJ had said earlier about me having a type. From the manager's predatory grin as she checked the clock above the bar, she definitely wasn't it. No vulnerability there whatsoever, just focus and determination.

She was more of a cougar, and I'd just volunteered to be her prey.

Chapter 8 - Will

I'D NEVER FELT guilty leaving a woman's bed in the morning before today. Since my last serious relationship ended, I hadn't been interested in more than one night, and I always made that quite clear up front. And I didn't feel guilty over the blonde sprawled out across the mattress, snoring softly.

No, I felt guilty because while I was pounding into her last night, I hadn't been able to stop thinking about a certain brunette who may or may not have been involved in plotting a murder.

I knew now that she hadn't been there at Daylesford Hall in person. Rania may not have looked directly at the camera on her way in or out of the restaurant, but the curves were all hers, and the manager remembered the unusual necklace she'd been wearing.

"Gold, fancy, looked like some kind of puzzle piece," the woman said.

"Can you describe Rania's demeanour?"

"Quiet. She barely spoke, and as soon as she finished dessert, she left with her friend and gave me the money for their half of the meal on her way out. Good tipper, though."

"So she didn't enjoy herself?"

"Sure didn't look that way. Why? Is it important?"

"Professional curiosity."

Professional my arse. I'd buried my face in the blonde's pussy to avoid further questions, and now I was sneaking out of her place like a damn burglar.

RJ was already at his computer when I got back, the big desktop he'd built from scratch and was constantly upgrading. He always kidded that it could give NASA a run for its money. At least, I think he was kidding.

"Good night?" he asked.

"The best," I lied. "What happened to the waitress? I thought you were onto a sure thing there."

"I had her tucked into bed by midnight, then I came home to do your shit. You can thank me with coffee."

I sighed and headed for the kitchen, mainly because I needed caffeine too. Sleep hadn't come easy last night. RJ worked odd hours, and half of his diet consisted of coffee, which meant we had a complicated Swiss Jura machine that cost him over two grand. It ground the beans to order and frothed milk at the touch of a button. Who needed Starbucks?

I made us both espressos and carried them through to his home office, once the third bedroom but now full of gadgets whirring away.

"Go on then, what have you found?"

"Your girl's an interesting one."

"She's not my girl."

Why did that feel like a lie? Even RJ gave me a "yeah, right" look.

"Rania Algafari, twenty-four years old, Syrian citizen, granted refugee status in the UK three years ago. She arrived from a camp in France a year before that as part of a deal to spread asylum seekers around Europe. She's got another two years before she needs to either leave or apply to stay permanently."

"They can't send her back, surely? There's nothing left out there."

"I'm just telling you the rules."

"Okay, I get it. What else?"

"She lives with a girl called Shannon Doyle and her daughter, Aisling. Shannon's a year younger and left County Kildare in a hurry five years ago. I'm still trying to get to the bottom of that. Anyway, they've been sharing a flat for the last two and a half years. Why do you want to know all this? Is she a suspect? Or are you trying to work out where she might like to go on a date?"

"I'm not entirely sure." Where Rania was concerned, my brain refused to function properly.

"Because most girls would rather you got to know them through conversation and quality time in the bedroom, not by having an admittedly genius hacker go through their records."

"I mean, I don't know whether she's a suspect. She's got an alibi for the murder itself, but she knew Helene's eyes had been gouged, and I can't work out how. Lloyd Weston swears he didn't talk to anyone but the police, and if they've got a leak, how come the only person who knows about it is the office cleaner?"

"Could she have stumbled across the body before Weston did?"

"The timings don't fit. She was still out for dinner when Weston called it in."

Helene had died at nine, and her father rang 999 at ten when he stopped at the office to pick up a contract to read through. His secretary had printed it out for him to take on his train trip to Manchester the next morning.

"Maybe Rania was an accomplice? How did the perp get into the building?"

"Perp? Have you been watching *CSI* again?"

RJ threw a pad of Post-it notes at me, followed by a pen when I ducked. "Just answer the question if you want any more help."

"There was no sign of forced entry. The old security system registered what time the doors opened and closed, but not who went through, and Helene had turned off the alarm when she arrived."

"If they needed a swipe card to get in, then surely that narrows it down to employees?"

Oh, if only it were that simple. "Not quite. Nineteen visitor passes have gone missing in the last six months alone, along with twelve employee passes. They never got deactivated in case they turned up again. Plus, there's a back door leading to the basement that still uses an old-fashioned key. Nobody's kept track of who's obtained those over the years, and of course, someone could have got an extra one cut."

"Or what if Rania lent her card to somebody?"

"What would her motive have been? She says she barely knew Helene, and everyone I've spoken to says she didn't get involved in office life. She came in, cleaned, then went home again. Most people didn't even know her name."

"What do you always tell me? Most crimes are motivated by sex or money. Maybe she needed the cash. From her address, she doesn't have a lot of it."

No, nothing about her screamed that she had money to splash around. Although the manager at Pizza Express said she was a good tipper. Routine generosity, or a reason to celebrate that night?

Or something else? "She dates occasionally. Any sign of a more serious relationship recently?"

RJ shook his head. "No. And... Never mind."

"What?"

"It probably doesn't matter."

"Tell me."

He swivelled in his seat until he was looking at me. "You won't like it."

"I'm a big boy, RJ. Just fucking tell me, okay?"

"As part of the medical assessment Rania had to go through under the resettlement programme, the doctor noted evidence of repeated rough sex and sodomy. She denied rape but refused to talk about it any further."

Shit. Of all the things I might have suspected... I wanted to hide her away from the evil fuckers who'd hurt her, but as soon as I had that thought, I shoved it away. I couldn't afford to be thinking like that, not when there was a question mark over her involvement in Helene's death.

"Noted," I said through clenched teeth. "But we still can't rule out a sexual angle. How about Helene's boyfriend? Anything there?"

I'd interviewed him myself. Derek, the dull-as-fuck lawyer who headed up Weston Corp's legal department and seemed to spend more time playing golf with Lloyd than romancing the man's daughter. When I'd asked about the last time he saw Helene, he actually got out his calendar to check. They'd had dinner the previous Tuesday, and no, he didn't stay over because he had a breakfast meeting the next day. What kind of dullard couldn't manage to show his girl a good time and still turn up for croissants in the morning?

"I'm not sure he's got the imagination to organise a crime like that."

"Appearances can be deceiving. Maybe he and Rania had a thing going?"

I spat espresso, luckily back into the cup. The thought of Rania with that fool turned my stomach. "I can't see it."

"Another bit on the side?"

"He doesn't seem the type, but I won't write him off."

***

I was on my third cup of coffee by the time I sat down in Lloyd Weston's office for our first proper update meeting. This was the part I hated most about running my own company—the schmoozing. The richer the client, the more face-to-face time they wanted, never mind that while I was talking to them I wasn't investigating anything.

"So, how's it going?" he asked.

AKA, what am I getting for my money?

I gave him a précis of my interviews yesterday, glossing over my suspicions about Rania. I didn't want to play up her involvement until I had a better idea of what was going on. It bothered me that I couldn't get a handle on her personality, even if my cock had its own thoughts on the subject.

"What's your next step, son?"

I may have been thirty-five years younger than him, but I still found it patronising when he called me that. Had he been anyone other than a client, I'd have set him straight. And I bet he wouldn't have called Chris

Turner "son," either. The power of a warrant card.

"I have half a dozen interviews left, and I need to do some more research into people's backgrounds, but I was hoping you could help with a few questions."

"About my daughter?"

"Among other things, if you're up to it."

His hands shook as he reached into his desk drawer and came out with a hip flask. Only once he'd taken a generous slug did he nod.

"Anything to see my daughter's murderer behind bars."

"Firstly, I need to ask about Derek."

"It wasn't Derek. He loved my daughter."

"At the moment, I can't rule any leads out. That's why you brought me in, after all. To be a fresh pair of eyes."

Lloyd reached for the flask again, thought the better of it, sat back in his chair. "What I'm about to say doesn't go any further than this room, you understand?"

"Of course."

I only ever talked to RJ, and he knew how to keep his mouth shut.

"You may have noticed my son has...problems."

Yes, I'd smelled one of them on his breath at ten o'clock in the morning. "The drinking?"

Lloyd shoved his flask back into the drawer and slammed it. "It started out as a tipple with lunch, and before I realised it, he was drinking Scotch for breakfast. We've tried everything—rehab, bribery, even a minder. But he just can't help himself. That doesn't leave Weston Corp in a very good position, and I was grooming Derek to take over the company alongside

Helene. Not only is—was—she my daughter, she was an excellent marketing director. I know what you're thinking. That statistically, most murders are carried out by someone close to the victim, but trust me, you're on a hiding to nothing with Derek."

Well, Lloyd Weston was the client. And given that he was the one who'd hired me, he had little incentive to steer me in the wrong direction. I'd defer to his judgement for now. Which brought me onto a more sensitive subject.

"My next question is about your daughter, and what was done to her eyes."

Weston deflated before me. "I've been thinking about that too. Why? Why would somebody do that to her? Was it symbolic? A message? Or they genuinely didn't want her to see something?"

"I can't give you an answer to that yet, and it's an important piece of the puzzle, but my question was actually regarding who might know about it."

"I haven't told a soul, not after the police asked me not to. Even my wife. She'd be distraught if she found out. Why?"

"Just something for me to be aware of. One final question, and this one goes back a few years. I heard a rumour there may have been another death in Daylesford Hall. A suicide?"

"You must mean Arthur Brady. The man threw himself over the second-floor balcony one evening."

"Any idea why?"

"Not at first. His wife said he'd been stressed lately, and that led to us establishing our employee well-being program. We were the first company in the area to do that. A relaxation room in the basement, yoga, Pilates, that sort of thing. Every member of staff also has access to a twenty-four-hour guidance helpline staffed by trained counsellors. That's Arthur's legacy."

I'd seen the relaxation room when Martha showed me around. Beanbags, a pool table, some weird sleep pod that looked as if it came out of a sci-fi movie. Martha reckoned they were considering a flotation tank for next year.

"You said 'at first.' Did something else come to light?"

A huff escaped Lloyd's lips. "Yes, it did. A month later, one of the other finance staff noticed several large unauthorised payments had been made from the main bank account. We traced the funds to offshore accounts, but that was as far as we got."

"And you think Arthur took the money?"

"He must have known transactions that size would get picked up in the quarterly reconciliations and panicked. We tightened procedures right up after that."

"Did the police have any luck finding the money?"

"We didn't tell them. The chances of retrieving it would have been slim, I suspect, and I had no desire to drag a grieving widow through a criminal investigation. No, Weston Corp swallowed the loss."

"That was...kind." I wasn't sure I'd be so forgiving, but then Lloyd Weston was from a different generation.

"We'd just picked up some lucrative contracts, and it seemed like the right thing to do. Do you have any more questions?" He glanced at his watch. "I have a call at ten thirty, but if you do, I'll have my assistant reschedule."

"Not today."

"Same time on Wednesday?"
"It's in my diary."

CHAPTER 9 - RANIA

I FELT RATHER than saw Will Lawson, his eyes burning into my back as I dusted the light fittings in the biggest conference room. I turned slowly, and sure enough, there he was, leaning against the doorjamb.

"Nothing wrong with your intuition," he said.

I didn't want to talk to him. I didn't even want to think about him, so I swivelled back around and resumed my dusting. He had nothing on me. Nothing. My alibi would check out, and all he could accuse me of was an overactive imagination and a slip of the tongue.

"You're just going to ignore me?"

I nodded. "That was my plan."

"We need to have another chat."

Wonderful. I could hardly refuse, but what should I say? The rules were so difficult to understand here in England. Back in Syria, it was simple. You got captured, you got tortured, and you kept your mouth shut until you escaped or died.

"You want to talk tonight?" I asked.

Will yawned, covering his mouth with his hand, and shook his head. "Tomorrow. I need some sleep, so you get a temporary reprieve."

Was I supposed to thank him? He was waiting for me to speak. "What time?"

"Six?"

"Same place?"

"Unless you feel like talking over dinner."

He was joking, right? But his face stayed impassive, and I struggled to get a read on him. Will Lawson, the newest star of my nightmares, and the man who'd given me many sleepless nights since our paths first crossed. Why couldn't he just crawl back under his rock and leave me alone?

"I don't have much of an appetite when you're around. I'll meet you upstairs."

I breathed a sigh of relief, an exorcism of my anxiety, as he backed out of the door and closed it behind him with a *click*. Gone, but not for long. I took a moment to look around as I willed my heart to stop racing. Despite its deceased inhabitants, I loved this old building with its juxtaposition of modern furnishings and period features. High ceilings with fancy mouldings offset by modern lights hanging down—a collection of lime-green spheres for this room. Soft music in the waiting area, comfy sofas I wished I could curl up on. The rich aroma of coffee drifting from the kitchen no matter what time of day it was.

Daylesford Hall had its own soul, a kind one, unlike the stark office buildings I'd worked in when I first arrived in England. In some ways, it reminded me of the traditional Arabic house I'd grown up in on the outskirts of Aleppo's old city, a series of interconnected rooms set around a sheltered stone courtyard. My bedroom had shared the same high ceilings, edged with intricately carved stones I imagined a wizened old craftsman chiselling by hand hundreds of years before. Summer evenings were spent under the delicately fragranced jasmine tree in the courtyard, reading, eating, and listening to the calls to prayer, while in winter, I'd loved to play chess with my father.

Until he died. I lost my innocence then. The first black soul I banished was the man who took my father's life, and I hadn't even reached my thirteenth birthday.

A tear rolled down my cheek, and I swiped it away. If I started crying, if I dwelled on the life I'd once had in Syria and what it turned into, I'd never stop.

"Don't think about it, Rania," I whispered to myself.

I forced myself to finish cleaning the room, making sure to dust thoroughly so I could skip that tomorrow. By the time I finished with Will, all I'd want to do would be to crawl home and weep. Or stick pins in the Voodoo-Will doll I'd go out and buy if he didn't leave me alone after that.

"What's wrong?" Arthur asked as I strode past him on my way to get the vacuum cleaner.

"Nothing. Can't you leave me in peace for one night?"

He held up his hands. "Sorry I asked."

And of course, Helene heard me coming. The perfect end to a perfect evening.

"What's happening?" she asked. "Has the private investigator found anything?"

"How should I know?"

"By asking? I heard Daddy say to Derek that the man's been questioning people."

"He has. And you've already got me into trouble with him."

"How?"

"Because..." Of my own stupidity, and I didn't want to admit that. "Because he thinks I know more about what happened to you than I do."

"Why?"

"I may have let slip about your eyes."

Her hands came to her face involuntarily, and her breath hitched. I waited a second for her to pull herself together. Please, no more sobbing.

Luckily, she opted for insolence. "So?"

"Nobody apart from the police is supposed to know what happened to them, and now I have to keep avoiding his questions. It's awkward."

"Well, just answer them."

"So easy for you to say, Miss—"

"Who are you talking to?" Will asked from behind me.

I turned slowly, one painful degree at a time. Oh, how I wished I'd been blessed with the power of teleportation rather than the ability to see dead people. I could transport myself to an uninhabited desert island and spend the rest of my life alone, living off mangos and coconuts while practising my palm frond-weaving skills.

"Uh, myself? I get lonely sometimes."

Now I'd crossed the line from slightly kooky to borderline insane. *Welcome to the asylum, Will.*

"Why don't I believe you?"

"Look around. There's nobody here."

Will walked towards me, but he didn't stop when he got close. No, he kept coming, forcing me to back into the wall, where he caged me in with his arms.

"Get off!"

The bastard smirked. "I'm not touching you."

Helene started laughing, which wasn't funny.

"And you can be quiet," I snapped.

"Still talking to yourself?" Will asked.

Helene laughed louder.

I put my hands on my hips, which might have looked intimidating if Will hadn't been totally focused on my face.

"Fine. I'm talking to Helene. Is that what you wanted to hear?"

He dropped his arms, and while I could have taken the chance to escape, my legs had other ideas, and I slithered down the wall to the floor. And worse, Will dropped to one knee in front of me, the hard lines of his face softened by concern.

"The worrying thing is, I think you actually believe that."

"Think what you like. It's true."

"It's crazy."

"For you, maybe. For me, it's normal. I just wish it wasn't."

Helene had stopped laughing now, and her expression turned smug. "Finally, we're getting somewhere."

"Enough!"

Will reached out and squeezed my hand, and while I'd normally have snatched mine away, I knew he wouldn't hurt me. Not physically, anyway.

"Do you want me to call someone? That friend you live with? Shannon?"

"Is any part of my life still private?"

"I'm only doing my job."

"And I'm only trying to do mine. It's not my fault I got stuck between you and a brat who thinks everyone should jump when she snaps her fingers."

Helene glowered to the best of her ability with her

face the way it was. "I earned my place at Weston Corp, I'll have you know. Just because my daddy owned the company didn't mean I filed my nails all day like that receptionist. What's her name? Martha? Did you know she was sleeping with the finance director? Talk about punching above her weight. I'm only surprised his wife didn't find out. They weren't very discreet."

I squashed my hands over my ears. "Please. Stop with the gossip."

Will peeled my hands away. "I thought women liked to gossip?"

"Not this one. I like to come to work, do my job in peace, then go to bed alone."

"Normally, I'd find that refreshing." He moved his gaze lazily down my body. "But what a waste."

"I think he likes you," Helene said. "Goodness only knows why."

I finally came to my senses. "I'm done here. You..." I pointed at Helene, then remembered she couldn't see me. "Helene. Stop asking me to sort all your problems out. And you..." Will rocked back as I poked him in the chest. "Leave me alone. Unless you can come up with any evidence that I've committed a crime, which you can't because I haven't..." Not in this country, at least. "Stay out of my life."

He offered a hand to help me up, but I ignored it and clambered to my feet.

"I'm finishing the cleaning, and then I'm going home. You two can chat amongst yourselves."

***

I thought Will really had left, at least until I walked of

out the front door at Daylesford Hall with the burglar alarm chirping behind me and tripped over him. He was sitting on the wall next to the car park, legs outstretched as a persistent drizzle fell from the cloudy sky.

"You need to be more aware of your surroundings," he said. "When you get angry, you miss things."

"Which part of 'stay out of my life' did you not understand?"

I'd got two steps past him when he stopped me with three words, softly spoken.

"I believe you."

My world ceased spinning as I came to a dead halt. "What did you just say?" I whispered.

I heard him get up, then felt him close the distance between us. His warm breath puffed on my ear.

"I believe you."

"I don't understand."

"Neither do I. But I can't work out how else you would have known about Helene's eyes. I know you weren't there, and everything I've found out about you says you're a loner who lives hand to mouth with no ambition to change that, but you've got an altruistic streak that makes you care for others. Your roommate, her kid, and the old lady who lives downstairs, for example. And if you weren't involved as an accomplice, that only leaves one explanation..." He gave me a lopsided smile, shadows playing across his lips in the gloom. "Reckon I've gone crazy now too."

"Are you playing with me?"

"Not in the way I'd like to be." His smile flattened. "Shit. I shouldn't have said that. You bring out the worst in me."

Ignoring that last comment, now I didn't know what to think. But two things were certain: there was a murderer on the loose, and Will Lawson wouldn't leave me alone until I'd given in and talked to him properly.

"Fine. You ask your questions, and I'll answer them truthfully. But I can't help it if you don't get the answers you're hoping for."

"Fair enough. I can't ask for more than that. Dinner?"

I stared at him.

"Drinks?"

I kept staring.

"Can I at least give you a ride home?"

That seemed to be the least painful of his suggestions, and at least I wouldn't need to walk to the bus stop in the rain.

"You can drive me home, but no detours."

His grin came back, and I bit my lips to stop myself from returning it. He may have been annoying as hell, but he was still frustratingly attractive too.

"Deal," he said.

CHAPTER 10 - RANIA

WILL DROVE A BMW, slightly scuffed around the edges, and he shoved an old sweatshirt and a pile of candy wrappers off the passenger seat so I could get in.

"Kinder Eggs?" I asked, picking one up.

"Guilty secret. I like to build the toys when I'm on stakeout."

"How old are you? Six?"

"Twenty-six, actually."

He ambled around to the driver's side and slipped behind the wheel, and the car started with a barely restrained purr.

"I don't suppose I need to give you my address?"

He tapped the satnav built into the dashboard. "Already programmed in. You realise that building's a health-and-safety violation waiting to happen."

"Is there any other area of my life you want to criticise?"

He grimaced. "Sorry. I just hate to think of you living in a place like that."

"Why would you even care?"

He shrugged. Mr. Eloquent. Will seemed to be good at asking the questions, but not so great at answering them. I wasn't a suspect, so surely he could offer some insight rather than this entire process being one-sided? After all, I didn't want to be there and I'd made that obvious.

"As I only live a fifteen-minute drive away, why don't you start with the questions related to Helene's murder?" I suggested, reaching for the seat belt. The car rocketed forward just as I clicked the catch shut. "Okay, ten minutes if you're going to drive like that."

"Let's start with the obvious—has she told you who killed her?"

"She doesn't know."

"Seriously?"

"Someone grabbed her around the neck and jabbed her with a needle. The next thing she knew, she was looking down at her own body."

"She was drugged?"

"That's what she thinks."

"It's not in the police report. Not yet, anyway. They're still waiting for the rest of the forensics results."

If Will planned to question every one of my answers, this was going to take a long time. Especially when he was the one with dubious information.

"You've seen the police report? I thought that would be confidential."

It wasn't entirely a surprise that Will had access to inside information. He didn't strike me as the type of man who did everything by the book.

And now he smirked. "I'm not supposed to have seen it, so I'd appreciate if you'd keep that part quiet."

"Did Chris Turner give it to you? Or the older cop? I forgot his name."

"No, neither of them. Chris Turner wouldn't piss on me if I was on fire unless he'd filled out the correct form in triplicate first."

"Then—?"

"I got it from another source, who shall remain nameless."

"And Chris Turner? It doesn't sound like you get on so well."

Not that I could blame Will entirely for that. Chris Turner had given off nasty vibes during my interview, and Will undoubtedly knew him better than I did.

"I thought I was supposed to be asking the questions?" Will said.

"If you want me to talk, there's got to be a bit of give and take."

"I wouldn't piss on Chris either. Happy now?"

"Oh, deliriously."

"For a foreigner, you've sure mastered sarcasm well."

How dare he? What did my origins have to do with this case? I unclipped my seat belt. "Stop the car."

He kept driving and even sped up a little.

"Now!"

"No. You agreed we'd talk."

"That was before you insulted me. I may not have lived in England for long, but I've been speaking English since I was three. My father thought it was important to learn a second language, and my childhood nanny came from Essex."

"Really?"

"Syria wasn't always at war, you know. It used to be a beautiful place to live. And since I came to this country, I've tried everything to fit in, including speaking like you people, but every time I set foot outside the flat, I'm still treated like a second-class citizen because I look foreign. Yes, I'm a refugee. But I didn't ask for my entire family to die and my home to be destroyed, and in the time I've been here, I've put more money into your benefits system than I've ever taken out."

I was breathing hard by the time I'd finished, having spilled out words I'd never said to anyone but that I'd been secretly longing to get off my chest for years. And Will didn't snap back at me. Instead, he drove on in silence, leaving me to regret my outburst because he really didn't deserve to be the target of anger I'd been storing up for far too long.

A minute passed. Two. Three. Will lifted his foot off the accelerator, and the car slowed. Sixty... Fifty... Forty...

"I'm sorry," we both said.

I focused on the dashboard in front of me as the car slowed to a halt in a lay-by a couple of miles from home. *Airbag inside.* The words suddenly became fascinating. Will clicked on the interior light and leaned across, then popped open the glovebox and reached inside.

"Here." He dropped a Kinder Egg into my lap and kept another for himself. "Peace offering. Did you know these were illegal in the US for years? Even though you could buy an assault rifle in Walmart."

"They were? Why?"

"Apparently, the authorities thought people might get confused and eat the toy." He shook his head. "More people choked on hot dogs, and the toys are probably more nutritious than those as well."

I peeled the foil back, hungrier than I cared to admit. My nanny used to bring me these when I was a kid, although the chocolate mostly melted before I got the chance to eat them. I still remembered the collection of tiny toys lined up on my windowsill, high above the jasmine tree. What did I have today? I pulled the two halves of the chocolate apart and popped open the capsule hidden inside. A racing car. I got a racing car. Will leaned over and peered at it.

"Cute. Want to swap for a polar bear?"

"Because you think you're Lewis Hamilton?"

"More that you can be a little frosty."

"Here, have the car if it means that much to you." I glared at him, and too late, I caught the twinkle in his eyes. "I did it again, didn't I?"

He sighed and held out his hand. "How about we start afresh? Will Lawson, private investigator and lover of children's chocolate who puts his foot in his mouth far too often around a certain brunette."

I couldn't help a giggle escaping. What was wrong with me? I never giggled. But I did put my hand into his. "Rania Algafari. Cleaner and seer of dead people who gets tetchy around men who make her nervous."

"Shall we do the questions now?"

I popped a piece of chocolate into my mouth, chewed, and swallowed. "Just get them over with."

"When did you first see Helene's...ghost?"

"Ghost... Spirit... Soul... They're all the same thing. The first day I went back to work after the murder."

"In the hallway she was in today?"

"Exactly the same place. The spirits can't move."

"Okay." His deep inhale said he still had a hard time believing me. "And what did she say?"

"She was upset, understandably. And once she realised I could see her, she demanded that I find the person who murdered her and...and...do the same to them."

"Drastic. But like you said, it was probably an understandable reaction."

How much did I tell him? My mother had shared the curse, and since she died, I'd never spoken to another living person about the Electi. Well, apart from Shannon, who pretended she hadn't heard any of it.

"Helene had her reasons."

Wrong thing to say.

"Which were?"

"You'll think I'm crazy."

He stared at me for a beat, no words necessary.

"You already think I'm crazy."

He didn't bother to deny it, but who could blame him? The story I was about to tell would have sounded farfetched even in a novel.

"Helene wanted me to kill her murderer because then her soul would be set free."

"Free?"

"To live on Earth again."

Will rolled his eyes but nodded anyway. "And what would happen to the other guy? He'd take her place?"

"No, a soul taken by one of the Electi gets banished. Or so the story goes," I added quickly. "Helene's spirit guide told her all about it."

"That's what you are? An Electi? That means 'chosen' in Latin, right?"

So Will had been well educated, then. My mother taught me basic Latin as soon as I could talk, but few people today still spoke it. A dying language used by a group whose existence revolved around death. Fitting.

"Yes. We've been around for longer, but I don't think there was a proper term for us back then."

"Us? How many?"

"Four."

"Like a club? Do you sit down and chat about these poor lost souls over drinks?"

"I have no idea who the others are. I only know the legend because it was passed down through my family."

"Haven't you ever tried to find them?"

"How? If they're anything like me, they won't exactly publicise their abilities."

"I guess that makes sense. So, what happens to these banished souls?"

"Who knows? I didn't make the rules."

In fact, it was quite fascinating. Time and time again, I'd watched the darkness rise up from a person's body before being scattered in every direction by an unseen force. The force that lurked within me. A force that I both loathed and feared.

Dust to dust.

"What did you tell Helene?" Will asked, interrupting my memories.

"Well, of course I said I couldn't do it. Then she had a rethink and decided jail would be adequate."

"Seems like we've both got the same goal."

"No, my goal is to spend my days babysitting Aisling and watching bad television, clean Daylesford Hall in the evenings, and sleep at night."

"How's that working out for you? The sleeping thing?"

He reached out and lightly traced the skin under my right eye with a fingertip. Little tingles spread through my cheek.

"Not so well," I admitted.

"Me neither. I want to solve this case, perhaps more

than any other."

"Why? Helene might have been rich and pretty, but she's got an attitude problem."

"Not because of her. Because I've heard a rumour Chris Turner's after a promotion and he wants to solve it too."

Ah, and we were back to Chris Turner. "What did he do to you?"

We were also back to not answering.

"Look, you've raked over every detail of my life—the least you could do is to be a little forthcoming in return."

"He got me fired."

"Oh."

"From the police."

"I didn't know you were in the police."

"That's because you never asked. All we've done so far is argue. We might as well get married and be done with it."

Another giggle. Seriously, where were they coming from? "What happened?"

"It's a long story."

"Well, as you don't seem to be taking me home..."

Will blew out a long breath, and mist crept across the inside of the windscreen. Spooky. Kind of fitting, considering our reason for being here tonight.

"It was a couple of years ago. We were dealing with a disturbance at a nightclub, and the guy at the centre of it was a first-degree shit. He'd beaten his ex-girlfriend to within an inch of her life and got off on a technicality. So we dragged him out the back door, and I may have dropped him down a flight of steps."

"Well done."

"All Turner had to do was keep his mouth shut and say the guy tripped. But no, he reported me, embellished the details, and got me booted off the force."

"Why?"

"I reckon it was because I used to take the piss a bit because he always insisted on doing everything by the book. Following procedure to the letter, even when it was written by imbeciles with no idea of what goes on in the real world."

"Evil doesn't follow the rules. I learned that back in Syria. Ceasefires got broken, people got shot, bombs got dropped. My parents both died. Nobody listened to reason, and everyone had their own agenda."

This time when Will reached for my hand, it wasn't for the formality of a handshake. Instead, he sandwiched it between both of his, then rubbed his thumb gently over my knuckles.

"I'm so sorry you went through that. And also that you've been treated badly in England. Nobody deserves to go through that."

I swallowed hard. People being nice also made me uncomfortable because they usually had an ulterior motive.

"I just want to move on."

A squeeze of my hand, and this time, little crackles of electricity buzzed up my arm. But before I could process that, Will let go and started the car engine. Warm air blew out of the vents and caressed my face.

"I'm sorry for everything I did this evening. I'll take you home. Here, you can have the polar bear too." He reached out and closed my fingers around it.

"What about your case?"

"I'll work it the old-fashioned way. Somebody must have seen something."

"Arthur did," I blurted.

Will's head snapped around. "Arthur? Arthur... Shit. The guy who took a dive off the balcony. There's another ghost?"

"At the bottom of the stairs in the waiting area. He's mostly cranky."

"What did he see?"

"Helene's killer, or so he says. He won't tell me who it was unless I solve his murder, and guess what? I don't have a clue where to start with that either."

I could almost hear the wheels spinning in Will's head.

"But it gives us another option. We only need to solve one of the crimes, and then we can catch Helene's killer."

"We? What happened to taking me home?"

Will leaned back in his seat and closed his eyes. "Sorry. I got carried away again."

While he wasn't looking, I took the chance to study Will more closely. Fine worry lines marred his forehead, and the dark circles under his eyes were worse than mine. Plus, now he knew some of my secrets, and he hadn't laughed at me or tried to have me committed.

"I'll help you," I said. "Just with talking to Arthur and Helene. No more."

Those brown eyes popped open, dark yet shiny in the dim glow.

"Are you sure?"

"I wouldn't have offered otherwise. And I haven't mentioned Arthur's deal to Helene, so do me a favour and keep quiet about that."

If she found out, she'd try to interfere, if only to give me an earful every time I walked past.

"I will, and thank you." He flashed that smile, just for a second, and my heart skipped. "I don't suppose there are any more ghosts lurking?"

"Only two. One never speaks, and Lucy at the front gates didn't see anything useful."

I'd found a few minutes to talk to her late last week, but she'd been more interested in the prospect of snow coming. Vehicles and details and strangers and death weren't priorities in Lucy's life, and I felt a little envious. Stupid, really.

"Nobody coming or going?"

"She saw cars, but her observational skills aren't good. The most I could get out of her were colours—white, blue, several dark 'boxes on wheels' as she calls them, and a cherry-red one that I think was Helene's. Walkers tend to park on the verge inside the gates, so the others could have been anyone. And if I were planning a murder, I'd have come via the network of footpaths, not driven in and risked somebody remembering my registration number."

"Good points. Do you want a job?"

"What, and give up the glamorous career I already have?"

Will put the car into gear and pulled out into traffic. "Time we both got home. I'll do some more research tomorrow and meet you at Daylesford Hall in the evening. Is six o'clock still okay?"

"I can't talk to the spirits until everyone else has gone. I don't think I need to tell you how crazy I look otherwise."

"I'll wait for as long as it takes."

He pulled up outside my building, and a neighbour who was outside smoking stared at the BMW with undisguised curiosity. The car park rarely saw anything classier than a beat-up Nissan Micra.

"See you soon," Will said.

I closed the door and he drove off, leaving me standing among the potholes clutching a tiny polar bear and a plastic racing car so tightly the edges dug into my palm. I didn't know why they mattered to me, but they did.

CHAPTER 11 - WILL

TEN MINUTES AFTER I got home, I hadn't even taken my shoes off, and the can of beer RJ dropped on the coffee table in front of me remained unopened. I needed a clear head. Or maybe I didn't. After all, I was totally sober and I'd just had the most surreal evening of my life.

Rania could see ghosts? More specifically, Rania could see—and talk to—Helene Weston?

I wasn't sure what I'd been expecting when I pushed her, but certainly not that.

If the whole story was even true. But she spoke so earnestly, and the only other explanation—that she was deeply involved as an accomplice—didn't sit right either. And then there was Arthur.

Before things went any further, I had to verify Rania's story, and there was only one way I could think of to do that.

"RJ, I need another favour. Two, actually."

"Does it involve accompanying you to an all-female jello-wrestling match?"

"No, but if you're into that, I'm sure I could arrange it."

"Then it'll have to wait for a couple of hours. I've got a video conference with a potential takeover target in Japan in fifteen minutes."

That explained RJ's odd attire—shirt, tie, and suit jacket on the top, boxer shorts and comedy socks on the bottom. Despite appearances, RJ was a successful businessman, and when he wasn't messing around in his home office at odd hours of the day, he ran Wonderland Enterprises out of a three-storey building five minutes' walk away from our home in Enfield.

But computers were his first love, hacking was his second, and despite the cloak of legitimacy he now wore, he'd never switched his black hat out for white entirely.

"Want me to order pizza for when you're done?"

"Make it Chinese tonight, would you?"

I put my hands together and bowed as I shuffled backwards out of the room with his laughter following. Forget the clear head. It was time to open that beer.

Three hours passed before RJ got back into the police database, alternating between typing furiously and forking chow mein into his mouth. I'd been picking at my food, and now it had gone cold.

"What is it we're searching for?"

"Back to Helene Weston first. I want to take another look at her autopsy results. Have the toxicology results come back yet?"

More tapping on the keyboard. "Pass me a spring roll?"

We skipped over the photos this time and went straight for the reports. Lo and behold, another batch of lab results had arrived. Helene's blood showed traces of fentanyl.

"Isn't that a painkiller?" I muttered, but RJ was already consulting Dr. Google.

"It's an opiate, fast-acting, and a hundred times

more potent than morphine. Also used in anaesthesia, and recreational drug users sometimes take it instead of heroin. Says here three milligrams of fentanyl will kill an adult male, compared to thirty milligrams of heroin."

"Helene had twenty-one nanograms per millilitre in her bloodstream."

RJ studied the screen in front of him again. He'd always been the chemistry geek at school while I was more into biology.

"So, if she hadn't bled out from the stab wound, she'd most likely have died from an overdose. Not much in the way of defensive wounds. Looks as if the drug hit her hard and she never got up again."

And Rania had been right. I sat down on the chair next to RJ's desk with a bump and stared at the noticeboard behind him, covered with scrappy pieces of paper filled with years' worth of scribbles.

The implications of Helene being drugged went far beyond a simple murder. Despite what I'd said to Rania earlier, I still hadn't entirely believed her story. But now? Either she really could speak to the dead, or she was playing me like a fucking maestro.

"Can you look up another case? Arthur Brady. Died about twelve years ago, and it went down as a suicide."

"Is this connected to Helene?"

"I don't know. But it happened in the same building, so I'm not ruling anything out."

And insinuating a connection was better than admitting the truth—that Arthur's ghost might still be hanging around at Daylesford Hall.

It took a few minutes for RJ to wade through the files, and I got up to stare over his shoulder when

Arthur's appeared on-screen. My feet fidgeted of their own accord. What was that about? My colleagues on the force had nicknamed me "high roller" because of my poker face, but I couldn't seem to get rid of the weird buzz running through me where Rania was concerned.

I forced myself to focus on Arthur instead. Brown hair that was greying at the edges and receding a little in the middle, gold-framed glasses, thin lips. He could have been anybody's grandfather. Nobody passing him on the street would have given him a second glance.

"Arthur Frederick Brady, aged fifty-two when he died. Looks older. He dove off an internal balcony at Daylesford Hall and broke his neck on impact. Died instantaneously."

"Who found him?"

"The cleaner. Isn't that girl you had me check out the other day also a cleaner?"

"I think that's just a coincidence. What does the rest of the report say?"

"The cops interviewed all the staff, but Arthur was the last person left in the finance department that night. Walked out of his office on the top floor and boom: he jumped two storeys. Didn't even bother to finish his coffee or turn his computer off."

"They didn't find that odd?"

"Odd enough to ask questions. But there were no signs of a struggle, and the cleaner was vacuuming the back staircase when it happened. Everybody heard the noise."

"Who else was in the building?"

"A handful of sales staff, plus Lloyd and Anthony Weston. They'd stayed behind for a meeting on overseas expansion. There's a note here that Anthony's breath smelled of alcohol."

"Sounds about right."

"There was also a broken window next to the basement door, which nobody can explain."

I skimmed over the remainder of the information. RJ had a rule when he did me favours like this—no printouts, no screenshots, no downloads. Just in and out. The police had questioned Arthur's family, and his wife said he'd been distant lately. Secretive. There'd also been an argument with a neighbour over a scratched bumper. A proper stand-up row. Apparently, the guy thought Arthur had reversed into his car, but Arthur denied all knowledge. And of course, I already knew about the missing money from Lloyd. Signs of a fragile mental state? Or was Rania right and Arthur had a helping hand?

Only one way to find out—I'd have to take Rania up on her offer to channel the dead.

I glanced down at the beer beside me, my second of the evening. It was no good. Tonight, I needed something stronger.

Chapter 12 - Will

RANIA HAD CHANGED her hair when I saw her the next evening. A high ponytail instead of a plait, and I wasn't sure which style I liked best. Truthfully, neither of them. I wanted to see those dark tresses tumbling loose around her shoulders, or better still, spread out over my naked chest.

At least, that was what my cock thought. My head told me that lusting over Rania was a very bad idea indeed.

"You're early," she said, glancing at her watch.

"By ten minutes. Traffic was lighter than I thought."

I neglected to mention the hour I'd spent hanging around at home, just waiting until I could leave.

"Do you have far to come?"

"The trip takes about forty-five minutes."

"Oh."

She bit her lip, and I wished she were biting mine. *For fuck's sake, Lawson. She's not your type.*

But what was my type? I'd had two failed relationships, one with the kind of girl my mother wanted me to date and the other with a cop groupie, although I hadn't quite realised the extent of her tastes at the time. Since then? More one-night stands than I cared to think about and some quality time with my fist.

"There are still other people in the building," Rania said. "You'll have to wait until they leave."

"How about I give you a hand?"

Her eyes widened in surprise. "What? No, you couldn't... It's not your job."

"And helping me isn't your job either, but you're still going to, and seeing as I'm planning to drive you home again tonight, it's in both of our interests to clean this place quickly."

"I can take the bus."

"You can, but you're not going to."

Now she put her hands on her hips. "Are you always this bossy?"

"You're welcome. Where's the hoover?"

A couple of the salesmen gave me odd looks as I shoved the vacuum cleaner around the reception area. What? Hadn't they ever seen a man cleaning before? Probably they left all that to the little woman at home. Or a cleaning service, like RJ did. Someone came in three times a week, and I made a mental note to be less messy. We should buy the lady a Christmas present too. Chocolates or something. I didn't even know her name.

Rania walked past with a tray of cups, flicked her eyes upwards, and mouthed, "Two left."

Hurry up, assholes.

Another half hour passed before they sauntered by, ignoring me like I didn't exist. Was that how they treated Rania too? As though she were invisible? No wonder she sounded so bitter about life in England.

I turned off the vacuum cleaner and watched from the window until two sets of flickering headlights moving down the drive showed our last two friends had departed for the evening, then I went to find her. She was on the top floor, stacking paper towels into a cupboard.

"Ready?" I asked, and she jumped.

"Don't sneak up on me!"

"Sorry. Next time, I'll phone first."

"You don't have my number."

"Want to bet?"

Her mouth set into a thin line. "What? Bothering me here wasn't enough, so you had to go full-on stalker?"

I shrugged, and she clenched her teeth.

"Old habits die hard."

And so would I if she didn't quit with the righteous indignation. Something about the way her eyes flashed got parts of my anatomy inconveniently fired up.

I turned, making a mental note to wear tighter underwear tomorrow. At least I wasn't wearing sweatpants, or everything would have been on show. I felt her following, soft footsteps mixed with the delicate swirl of perfume. A floral scent. Jasmine?

"Who do you want to speak to first?" she asked.

"Helene."

I knew more about her than Arthur, so if Rania was playing a twisted game, I'd find it easier to tell.

Rania stopped, and I did too, gesturing along the corridor.

"Is she here?"

"You just put your hand through her chest."

I drew my arm back like I'd been burnt, and Rania laughed.

"Don't worry. She can't feel you, and you can't hurt her."

Well, this was awkward. I gave the empty space a

little wave. "Hi."

"She says hello. But remember, she can't see either of us." Rania touched a finger to the corner of her eye.

"I'm Will Lawson. Mr. Weston—your father—hired me to look into your death."

I waited as Rania listened and nodded.

"She says you haven't done a great job of it so far if you're here asking her for pointers."

"Really? She said that?"

"I told you she was a brat." Helene must have said something else because Rania narrowed her eyes. "You are. And until you wanted me to help, you barely acknowledged my existence."

I touched Rania on the arm. "Let's not argue, okay? It won't get us anywhere." Then to Helene, "Can you think of a reason why anybody would have wanted to kill you?"

"No," Rania said.

"That's it? No?"

Rania shrugged, a "see what I'm up against" gesture. "Helene, it seems unlikely that someone randomly broke in on the off-chance they'd find somebody here, and seeing as they brought a syringe of something—"

"Fentanyl," I said.

Rania raised an eyebrow, and I nodded.

"—fentanyl with them, they probably planned the attack. Which means there must have been a reason for it. Have you upset anyone recently? I mean, more than usual?"

Rania winced, and I imagined her getting an earful.

"Helene had a small disagreement with her hairdresser in the week before she died. She asked for a shoulder-length bob and got... Well, I'd say that was still shoulder-length." A pause. "Apparently, it should have been left an inch longer."

"Any disagreements with Derek?" I asked.

"No, nothing. Derek was very easy to get along with. They agreed on everything."

Having met Derek, I suspected Helene voiced her opinion and the man went along with it for an easy time. He'd only come to life when I asked him about Weston Corp, and it was clear that work was his priority. Marrying Helene would have secured his place in the business. Would he have risked everything and killed her before that? I couldn't see it. Even during our interview, he kept stopping to answer emails before excusing himself to attend the company yoga session at five thirty. "Now, more than ever, it's important for employees to let go of their stress," he'd said.

"Who benefits financially now that you're gone?" I asked Helene. "Did you have life insurance?"

"Of course she did," Rania said. "It all went to her mother and father."

"Nothing for Derek?"

"Not that she's aware of. Her father planned to transfer some of his shares as a wedding present, but that never happened."

"Who'll get the shares now?"

"Probably Anthony. Or maybe her father will give a percentage to Derek anyway. They get on well."

"I have to ask this—do you think Derek was faithful?"

"The idea of him sleeping with someone else... No, she can't see it happening. He got more turned on by the stock market than sex." Rania held up a hand. "No,

I should tell Will. He won't mention it to anyone else. You can trust him."

"What?"

Rania struggled to keep a straight face. I could see from the way her lips quirked up at the corners, and her eyes danced as they cut back to the empty air opposite us.

"She says Derek needed pharmaceutical help in that department. The little blue pills. And he hated taking those because they gave him a rash on his..." Rania's cheeks went delightfully pink. "You know."

"Okay. So we can probably rule Derek out. How about Anthony?"

"Anthony was a good salesman when he was sober, but that hasn't been often recently. Her father promised things would get sorted out."

"Helene, did the two of you get on okay?"

"As well as any siblings. The odd argument, and she wasn't happy he drank so much, but nothing irreparable."

"What about clients? Competitors? This company does some big deals."

"Helene only looked after sales and marketing. She didn't sign any contracts. The men dealt with that side of things."

"What if somebody wanted to cause a distraction? Make your father and Derek take their eye off the ball?"

"It's possible. Maybe. But Helene still doesn't have any idea who would do that."

I leaned back against the wall, turning the new information over in my mind. Either Helene wore rose-tinted glasses when it came to others' perceptions of her, or we'd missed something big. I needed to talk to her father again, and also Anthony. Drink did funny things to people's minds, and I had to consider the possibility he'd graduated to something harder. Back when I was a PC, I saw an addict throw his six-year-old daughter out of a window because he thought she'd turned into a lizard. LSD. And with new designer drugs hitting the streets every month, the problems were only getting worse.

"I need to look into things." And talk to Arthur.

Rania took the hint. "Let's head downstairs. You can check through your notes while I unload the dishwasher."

I took a couple of steps towards the stairwell as Rania paused and closed her eyes, her lips tightening again. "Look, I can't stay here all day, every day, just because you're bored, Helene. I'll see you tomorrow."

In the waiting area, I sank onto one of the sofas while Rania remained standing. Hmm. They weren't as comfortable as they appeared.

"Where's Arthur?"

Rania pointed at the bottom of the stairs.

"Can he see me?"

She nodded.

I couldn't exactly shake the man's hand, so I settled for a nod in his general direction. "I'm Will Lawson. Lloyd Weston hired me to investigate his daughter's death, and I understand you might be a witness?"

My knee began to bounce, and I rested my hands on my leg to keep it still. This case was going to steal my sanity.

Rania tilted her head to one side then smiled. "He says you look damned uncomfortable talking to thin air. Like you're starting to question your own mind."

"He's got that right." I cleared my throat, which had been getting drier throughout the evening. What I wouldn't have given for a coffee. Or better still, a shot of vodka. "Rania said you wanted to cut a deal."

"He does."

"But all we've got is your word that you saw the murderer. How can we be sure that you really did? I'm not busting a gut hunting for two culprits only to find you were mistaken."

Another pause.

"He says that as a gesture of good faith, he'll tell us that the killer was wearing a blue jumper, and he knows it was the killer because the front was covered in blood when they left. He reckons the forensics people will have found blue fibres on the body. Did they?"

"The police are still waiting for half of the reports to come back."

"Really? But on *CSI*—"

I shook my head. "Forget what you see on TV. It takes weeks for the lab to send anything, even if you put a rush on it."

And we didn't have time to wait, not with Lloyd Weston's Christmas deadline looming. What would Arthur have to gain by lying about the fibres? He'd know that we'd quit right away if the forensics report came through with different results.

Rania must have read my mind. "Arthur, if I find you haven't told the truth, I'm never speaking to you again. You can spend eternity alone." She turned to me. "He swears he's being honest."

"I'll start some preliminary work, but I'm not committing to anything until the lab results come back. And Arthur has to promise us his full cooperation. He can start by explaining why he stole money from Weston Corp."

Rania listened, and when she shrank back, I stood up and went to her side.

"What is it?"

"He says he doesn't know what you're talking about, and he never took a penny from the company." She winced again, obviously getting an earbashing. "Ever. He prided himself on his honesty."

"So, why does Lloyd Weston think he did?"

"Isn't it obvious? Somebody else took the money, framed Arthur, then killed him."

CHAPTER 13 - RANIA

EVEN THOUGH WILL had helped me with the cleaning, I still felt drained as I climbed into his car after work. Although I'd never admit it to him, I was glad I didn't have to trek to the bus stop, especially since it was raining again. Yet another thing I missed about home—the long, hot summers followed by moderate winters where I didn't need to wrap up like a mummy every time I stepped outside. The novelty of everything being grey wore off years ago.

"What are your thoughts on Arthur?" Will asked. "Reckon he's telling the truth?"

"Yes, I think so. He didn't act shifty when he answered, and when you mentioned the stolen money, he looked shocked at first, then he got really angry. And more than that...it was like everything slotted into place for him. I've been talking to him since I started at Weston Corp, and until today, he's always wondered why somebody would want to kill him."

"His wife said he'd been secretive before he died. He had an argument with a neighbour too."

"Arthur's never mentioned that. I can ask him tomorrow if nobody's around."

"I really appreciate you helping like this."

What was I supposed to say to that? Custom said I should be polite, as was the British way, with a "no problem" or a "don't mention it." But I wasn't feeling very charitable towards Britain at the moment.

"I just want this whole affair to be over."

"Hmm... An affair. Do you reckon Arthur could have been having an affair?"

I choked a little. Arthur? "I don't think he's the type. His idea of a dirty weekend was probably doing the gardening."

That got a laugh out of Will, and a grin. I'd missed those grins.

"You want to pick up something to eat on the way back?"

"Shannon always cooks in the evenings. How about you? Is somebody cooking for you?"

I still knew next to nothing about Will. For all his flirting and inappropriate comments, he could have a girlfriend waiting for him at home. Lucky cow. *No, Rania. Not lucky.* Obviously very patient to put up with Will and his bossiness.

"I'm not great at cooking," he admitted. "And neither is my housemate. We usually live on takeout."

"Your housemate?"

"RJ. We went to boarding school together."

"I thought that in this country only the posh went to boarding school."

"Now who's being judgemental?"

"Sorry." After the number of times I'd grown upset about people judging me, I should have known better.

"You don't think I'm posh? I suppose I should take that as a compliment."

"Of course not. I mean, you're not, are you?"

"My father's a doctor, as was my grandfather on his side, and my mother's heiress to a cosmetics empire."

"My father was a doctor too," I said softly. "A neurosurgeon."

"What? But how did...?" Will trailed off.

"How did I end up penniless in England? I'd rather not talk about it. Let's just say war is a great leveller."

Tension bloomed between us, that knot in my chest growing ever more tangled until my stomach stepped in with a loud gurgle. Will reached over, opened the glove compartment, and dropped another Kinder Egg into my lap.

"Here. This should keep you going until you get home."

Dammit, I could handle bossy Will and I could handle irritating Will. I could even handle flirty, inappropriate Will. But sweet Will would be my undoing.

"Thank you."

"Don't mention it."

In a master stroke of timing, I stepped from the passenger side of Will's BMW just as Shannon walked out of the bin storage area on the far side of the car park. Her eyes lit up as she came closer and peered through the driver's window.

"Who's this?" she asked as I hastily slammed the door.

"Uh, just somebody who works at Weston Corp."

Please, Will, just leave. But it was too late. He was already halfway out of the car before I could drag Shannon back inside.

"Shannon? I've heard so much about you."

Liar. I hadn't told him a thing. He'd researched it all on whatever dodgy databases PIs used to invade people's privacy. But even if I'd told Shannon that, I suspected she wouldn't care. Not when he gave her *that* smile and bent to kiss her cheek.

"Will Lawson."

She took his proffered hand and turned pink when he held onto it for a beat too long. "Shannon Doyle. So, you're a friend of Rania's?"

"Something like that."

Oh, Will. To me, "something like that" meant that Will was the man who overstepped his boundaries to ingratiate himself with my flatmate. I wasn't sure what the phrase meant to him, but Shannon interpreted it as "the man who Rania wants to get to know better."

"We're just about to have dinner," she said. "Would you like to join us? There's plenty enough for three." Even me shaking my head violently behind Will's shoulder didn't stop her from talking. "Nothing fancy—just a pasta bake with bread-and-butter pudding after."

Will's expression turned smug as he twisted to look first at me, then back to Shannon. "That's very kind..."

Please say no, please say no, please say no.

"I'd love to join you."

Shannon clapped her hands together. "*Fáilte.* I'll set another place at the table."

As she strode on ahead, I grabbed Will's arm. "Now that you've basically invited yourself around for dinner, please do me a favour and avoid mentioning anything to do with ghosts."

"Shannon doesn't know, I take it?"

"No, she does. It just freaks her out, and every time the subject comes up, she goes on about me needing counselling for days afterwards."

"My lips are sealed."

"And stop looking so pleased with yourself."

"I'm having dinner with two pretty ladies. Of course I'm pleased with myself."

I marched off after Shannon, putting on a show of frustration. But secretly? I didn't hate the idea of sharing a meal with Will as much as I should have.

***

"Plenty for everyone," Shannon said as she slid a big earthenware dish onto the table.

Pasta, tomato sauce, vegetables, and a crispy topping made from bread and cheese. Pretty much every meal we ate had bread in it somewhere because Shannon got to take home rejects from the line at work every day. All those loaves that were a little burnt or a bit wonky got given to the staff.

"I hope you like carbs," I muttered to Will.

"They're the cornerstone of my diet. RJ installed a gym downstairs in the garage when we both started getting fat."

So that was where he got his abs from. Not that I'd been looking or anything.

"It's so nice of you to drive Rania home," Shannon said. "It puts the heart crossways in me every time I think of her in that place alone."

"Mr. Weston's installed a new security system," I reminded her.

"But that doesn't cover the driveway, does it?"

"No, but—"

"And the maniac who killed your boss's daughter is still walking free."

"What's that saying? Lightning doesn't strike in the same place twice?"

"I was watching the Discovery Channel the other day, and that actually happens quite often."

"It doesn't matter," Will said. "I'm planning to bring Rania home each day until the guy gets caught."

"Excuse me?" When had he been planning to tell me that? "I don't need a babysitter. I've lived through a lot worse."

"Yes, and it was awful," Shannon said, lip quivering. "I can't bear to think of you getting hurt again."

I tried one more time. "But I don't finish work until late."

"It's no trouble."

Shannon reached over and patted his hand. "Thank you. We both appreciate it. And I'd be happy to make you dinner any night you like."

Oh dear. I'd walked right into that one. Shannon and Will chatted away like old friends for the rest of the meal, and either he'd spent several nights researching Irish folklore and traditions when he found out my best friend was from County Kildare, or he had a genuine love of the Emerald Isle. They didn't stop talking until Aisling cried out from Shannon's bedroom and she rushed through to settle her daughter.

"So, you're running a taxi service now?" I asked.

"I prefer to think of myself as a chauffeur. Much more exclusive." His voice softened. "I promise I won't get in your way. If I'm not actively working in Daylesford Hall, I'll just show up to collect you at the end of your shift."

"But why? You don't live anywhere near here."

He cupped my cheek in one hand, and I resisted the urge to shy away.

"Because, Miss Algafari, I like you."

He liked me? In what way? I mean, I liked ice cream, but I didn't get the urge to drive forty-five minutes out of my way every night to pick it up.

But I couldn't ask because Will was already on his way out the door.

"See you tomorrow," he said, waving before it clicked shut behind him.

Sure. If I managed to get any sleep at all.

CHAPTER 14 - WILL

FOUR HOURS' SLEEP, three cups of coffee, two dreams of Rania, and one happy ending in the shower when I still couldn't get her out of my head. That was my morning. And now I was sitting in Lloyd Weston's office for an update on progress, trying not to yawn.

"I need to see details of Helene's finances," I said. "Money's the motive behind a large percentage of murders, and I'd like to check through her bank statements and credit card bills to see if there are any clues there."

"But I've already given all that information to the police."

Of course he had. But the chances of Chris Turner cooperating in any way weren't just slim, they were anorexic.

"The police have procedures to follow, and unfortunately, they can't hand over any evidence being used in an ongoing investigation. If you can give me duplicates, I'll be able to dedicate more time to combing through them than the police can."

"Very well. I'll have my secretary make copies of everything. How far back?"

"Let's start with two years."

"And how are the interviews going? I understand you've spoken to most of the staff?"

"I have, but I've got little to go on so far. Helene generally seemed to be well-liked." I mentally crossed my fingers. I mean, nobody hated her. "And the other staff respected her contribution to the company."

"If anybody obstructs your investigation, you let me know, you hear? I won't stand for it."

Lloyd put his head in his hands. He seemed to have aged a year every day since I'd met him. Helene might have been a brat, as Rania put it, but there was no doubt how much her father loved her.

"I'll inform you right away. Looking at another angle, I understand the police are still waiting for some of the forensics results?"

Might as well give the illusion that Chris and I had been talking, even if all I wanted to do was punch him in the mouth. But Lloyd didn't bite.

"That bastard drugged my daughter! Drugged her then destroyed her face. She had the prettiest eyes. They were the first thing everybody commented on. Her whole wedding was going to be themed around them. Green dresses for the bridesmaids, green table centrepieces, green ribbons on the Rolls Royce. Now I'll never get to walk my beautiful girl down the aisle."

This was always the part of police work I'd hated most—seeing the effects of crime on those left behind. I'd never been very good at comforting grieving relatives, but I'd still done a better job of it than Chris Turner, who had all the empathy of a brick despite carrying a spare handkerchief around just in case anyone cried, probably because he'd read to do so in a fucking manual somewhere.

"I'm sorry for your loss. I understand how difficult it must be."

Lloyd stared past me, out of the window at the lawns and woods beyond. Although part of the grounds had been converted to a car park, the rest had been left as it was a century ago.

"Every morning, I wake up and think this has been a nightmare. *Hope* it's been a nightmare. I can't believe I'll never see Helene again. She didn't live far away, did you know that?"

I nodded.

"Some people say it's difficult to work with family, and with Anthony... Yes, there's an element of truth in it. But Helene was good at her job. I'd never have found anyone better to look after the marketing side of things. And now she's gone... I don't know what to do."

"It's okay to feel lost for a while. Nobody expects you to have all the answers right away."

"I guess I'm just used to being the one in control. Who expects to survive their children?"

"Take some time to grieve. Has the funeral been arranged yet?"

"We're... We're waiting on her body to be released. End of the week, they said, once the forensics results are all in."

At least he'd answered my earlier question. I'd get RJ to take another look at the database on Friday, not least because I needed to find out whether Arthur was telling the truth about the blue jumper.

"If there's anything I can do to help, then let me know," I offered. "I know it's not in my job description."

"That's kind of you, son."

"And I won't drop this until we catch the person who killed your daughter. You have my word on that." I stood, knees cracking like a fifty-year-old's. This job would be the death of me. "Can I make you a drink? Tea? Coffee?"

"I've got a secretary for that. You just get out there and find that bastard."

Easier said than done. As promised, Lloyd's secretary got me Helene's financial documents, and I borrowed a meeting room on the top floor to go through them. The woman had six bank accounts, a trust fund, investments in shares, bonds, and even an interest in a bloody racehorse.

At least we could rule a dispute over the nag out as a likely motive—a search showed that the gelding, who went by the unfortunate name of "Hoof Hearted," had come second to last in both of his races.

Taxi fares, weekly deliveries from Net-a-Porter, visits to the hairdresser, the beauty salon. How many manicures did a lady need? The only items that stood out were regular visits to the Lanefield Park Hotel and Country Club. Every month starting a year and a half ago, then every fortnight. Dirty weekends with Derek? I pulled up the calendar on my phone and checked the dates. Wednesday evenings. Always Wednesday evenings.

The police had taken Helene's computer, but companies this size generally shared networked calendars, and I was curious about what she claimed to be doing on those days. She could have marked those appointments private, of course, which would give RJ more work to do, but instinct told me otherwise. If Helene had been trying to hide something, nothing would arouse more curiosity in a place like this than blocking out information.

I headed back downstairs to Lloyd Weston's office, where his assistant was reading a magazine. In my pre-Rania days, I might have given the slim brunette a second glance, but now she did nothing for me. I glanced at the title of the magazine before she shoved it into a drawer. *Fish-Keeping World*. Hmm. Different.

"Do you have access to Helene's calendar?"

"Uh, yes?"

"Can I take a look?"

"I guess."

She called the program up on her screen, then hovered at my elbow while I sat in her chair. No, that wasn't irritating in the slightest. I fished her magazine out of the drawer and waved it at the sofa on the far side of the room.

"Why don't you sit and read this until I'm done?"

"Mr. Weston might not like that."

"Is he still here?"

"He has a meeting until three."

"Well, I won't tell him if you don't."

She retreated, leaving me to study a list of appointments that tallied to the bank statements. Days filled with business meetings and the odd beauty appointment, evenings split between awards dinners, nights out with Derek—mainly to restaurants with fancy French names—visits to the salon, and meals with friends. I quickly scrolled through all the Wednesdays.

Dinner with Carla.

Movie with Samantha.

Drinks with Felicia.

Art exhibition with Pandora.

Helene rarely scheduled Wednesdays with the same

people, and not once did she mention the Lanefield Park Hotel. Just for good measure, I checked Derek's schedule. Every Wednesday, he went to the Hertfordshire Business Forum's weekly networking evening.

With the secretary still engrossed in koi carp or whatever, I noted the contact details for each of Helene's Wednesday "dates" for follow-up, then closed the application.

"Thanks for your help."

She smiled brightly, back to corporate mode. "You're welcome!"

Back upstairs in the meeting room, I closed the door out of habit. There was no telling who was listening in, or as I now knew, whether they were alive or not. One of the easiest cases I ever solved involved half a dozen valuable paintings that disappeared from an auction house. After I'd questioned the auctioneer's assistant, I went to the john and happened to stop outside his office on the way back, just as he asked his partner in crime whether he should move the loot. I'd laughed all the way to the bank with that one.

But Helene's murder? There was nothing funny about this case.

***

Rania arrived at four, and I beckoned her into my meeting room before she could start work.

"Don't you think people will find the amount of time we're spending together odd?" she asked.

"Nah. If they think anything, they'll assume we're having some quick and dirty fun."

I waggled my eyebrows, but she didn't smile. No, she wrapped both arms around herself and took a step back.

"Hey, it was just a joke. I didn't mean it, okay?"

"It's not funny. I don't want people thinking of me that way."

Shit. Trying to work out Rania's moods made comforting the grieving relatives seem easy. I thought back to what RJ had said about her medical tests. Rape. Sodomy. The defiling of a beautiful woman from the inside out. No, joking about her sex life made me an insensitive bastard.

"Five minutes. I just need to run a few things past you. Nobody'll even notice you're in here."

"Fine. Five minutes. Then I need to get on with the cleaning. On my own."

Was this about last night? Maybe I shouldn't have told her I liked her, but it was hardly a declaration of undying love, was it? Mental note—tread even more fucking carefully around this girl. Dealing with Rania was more nerve-racking than walking on Fabergé eggshells.

"Helene's been spending an awful lot of time at a hotel not too far from here."

"Why would she do that? She had a house. Quite a nice one, according to Martha."

"The question I want to ask isn't so much why, but with whom?"

"Oh." A pause. "Oh!"

"Yes. Oh."

"Helene was cheating on Derek?"

"On the Wednesday before she died, her calendar said she was meeting her friend Carla for dinner. They went to school together. When I spoke to Carla, she said Helene was out with Felicia from her spinning class. Felicia thought she was with Carla."

"And this is connected to her murder?"

"I don't know. But I am curious as to why Helene didn't mention it to her friends."

"And let me guess? You want me to ask her?"

Now I brought out the grin. It usually made women fall at my feet, and although Rania might have stumbled on occasion, she remained firmly upright.

Her answering smile was tight.

"I'd appreciate it," I said.

She sighed but nodded. "When everyone else has gone."

***

Judging by the way Rania grimaced, Helene didn't like my question about her Wednesday night escapades. I waited for a moment, presumably for the shouting to stop.

"The sanitised version," Rania said once she'd taken a couple of deep breaths, "is that it's none of our business."

I waved my hands at the air, as irritated by Helene upsetting Rania as by her withholding facts. Facts I could ferret out. Apologising to Rania for what I was putting her through would be more difficult. If I'd had limitless funds, I'd have flown her out to Tahiti and installed her in a beachside villa for the duration.

"In case you hadn't noticed, we're trying to solve your murder here. Your entire life is our business. I'd quite happily take Rania home so we could spend the rest of the evening drinking eggnog and watching The Sound of Fucking Music, but I promised your father I'd find out who killed you. Who were you with?"

"She said it doesn't matter, because he'd never have hurt her."

He. Now we were getting somewhere. "And by 'he' I take it you don't mean Derek?"

Rania shook her head.

"Good grief. Normally, couples wait until after the wedding to start shagging other people."

Silence. More silence.

"She's sulking," Rania whispered.

"Not saying anything?"

"No."

Well, wasn't that a miracle? Usually, it was hard to get her to shut up.

"Let's leave it for tonight. I'll help you finish here and take you home."

This evening, I gave Rania a Kinder Egg as soon as we got in the car, hoping for a smile. She didn't disappoint. My exes had required gifts of jewellery and handbags to keep them happy, and even then I usually managed to buy the wrong colour or style. Rania simply wanted chocolate and toys, it seemed.

For years, I'd found it difficult to live with myself after the bust-up with my father. After being raised to believe in the importance of material things, to have it all stripped away had been hard. But I still couldn't bring myself to give in and bow to his wishes. And now, sitting next to Rania, I wanted to be the one to make her happy, and I knew that would only come by breaking through the barriers she threw up and finding out what made her tick, not by throwing money at her.

"I hope Helene wasn't too much of a bitch to you."

"For somebody so posh, she sure knows a lot of nasty words."

"If she went to a private school, that doesn't surprise me. The first thing I learned there was how to swear in three different languages."

"Which were?"

"French and German as well as expanding my vocabulary in English."

"I speak a little French, but not German."

"Germany's nice this time of year. Full of Christmas markets."

"I never really celebrated Christmas until I came to England, but Shannon likes to have a tree, and she's cooking a turkey for dinner."

"My parents went all-out when I was a kid. Even when we flew to the Caribbean for the holidays, we still had a mountain of presents and enough food to feed a small town."

"Are you coming for dinner tonight?"

"Do you want me to?"

"Shannon said you were invited every night."

"That doesn't answer my question."

She took so long to answer, I thought she wasn't going to, but when she mumbled a quiet, "Yes," I wanted to punch the air.

But I couldn't afford to scare her off. Just thinking of her past sickened me, and I hated to imagine what she'd been through.

"Then I'm coming for dinner."

CHAPTER 15 - RANIA

WILL LOOKED OUT of place sitting at one end of the tiny table in our dining area. I couldn't say dining room because our flat just wasn't that big—all we had was a gap between the back of the sofa and the door to the kitchen. And only two proper chairs. Shannon sat lower than us on the fold-up stool she'd taken to some fancy outdoor opera with Slick Dick. Will had offered her one of the proper seats, but she'd insisted that as he was the guest, he should use the good furniture. That was Shannon all over.

Today, she served up chicken in breadcrumbs with colcannon, followed by treacle tart. It always amazed me how many dishes she could cook, but she'd been brought up by a grandma who knew a thousand and one recipes for potatoes, and then she'd begun experimenting herself as soon as she was old enough.

"Tastes great," Will told her. "Better not tell RJ, or you'll be needing to buy another one of those fold-up seats."

"Who's RJ?" Shannon asked.

"His housemate," I told her.

"Oh, do you live near here?"

As usual, Shannon took over the conversation, one which veered from living arrangements to local restaurants, but I didn't mind. It gave me the chance to listen to Will's voice and watch his face as he spoke, without facing the pressure of having to think up answers. Something told me my usual evasive tactics wouldn't work with him.

And I wasn't sure I wanted them to.

Will was the one man I could see breaking through my walls, and that both scared and tantalised me. Something had woken inside, a buzz different to the tension that usually tied my belly up in knots, and I hadn't yet fathomed out what to do about it.

But at least with Shannon making Will promise to come back tomorrow because she was making spaghetti with meatballs, I had time to think it over.

"Thanks, sweetheart," he said, kissing Shannon on the cheek when he got up to leave. "I look forward to it."

She giggled, then rushed off to the kitchen.

"Are you coming to Daylesford Hall in the day again tomorrow?" I asked.

He shook his head. "I want to pay a visit to Arthur's widow."

"She still lives around here?"

"According to land records, their old house is still in her name. It's a ten-minute drive from Weston Corp."

"Do you need company?" I blurted before I could stop myself.

"You want to come with me?"

"Well, uh, maybe. It depends what time. I mean, I have to look after Aisling in the morning while Shannon's at work, and—"

He pressed a finger to my lips. "We'll go in the afternoon. Just tell me what time to pick you up."

Heat from his touch seared my skin, and I took a

step back to regain my senses. "Two o'clock. I can do two o'clock."

"I'll be here. In the evening, I'd like to have another chat with Helene. See if she's calmed down yet."

"Okay," I whispered.

"See you tomorrow."

***

Skirt? Trousers? What did a girl wear for private investigating? I picked up one of my only two dresses, a black jersey number, and shoved it back into the closet. What was I thinking? I needed to wear trousers because Will would take me straight to work afterwards, and I'd probably have to stay in the car while he talked to Arthur's wife, anyway.

But I still put on a jumper a little tighter than I'd normally wear and made sure my hair was tidy. It needed a cut, really. Something else to add to the "when I can afford it" list.

Will handed me another Kinder Egg as I climbed into the passenger seat.

Another chink of light shone through my armour.

"What's the plan?" I asked, fingers peeling the foil off chocolate I was too nervous to eat.

Why was I so unsettled? I'd been shot at, attacked more times than I cared to remember, survived crossing the Mediterranean in an overloaded, sinking dinghy, and travelled across two continents without feeling this edgy. Probably because I'd been numb inside back then. I'd accepted I was going to die and been as surprised as anyone when I lived.

"I'll do most of the talking, but feel free to jump in if

you have any questions."

Oh, so I was coming inside. "Want some chocolate?"

He kept both hands on the wheel, but half turned with his mouth open. I broke off a chunk and fed it to him, resisting the urge to shudder when my fingers brushed against his lips.

Get a grip, Rania.

By the time Will pulled up outside the nondescript bungalow, my heart had slowed enough that it no longer rattled my ribcage, I'd forced down half the chocolate, and I'd built a toy dragon.

"Ready?" Will asked.

No. "Yes."

He opened my door, and I got out and followed him along the path. Weeds grew through the cracks here and there. The rest of the garden had been paved over, and I recalled Arthur once telling me about his greenhouse and all the prizes he'd won in the local horticultural society's competitions. Probably he wouldn't be too happy about the lack of greenery.

Will rang the doorbell, and I stood by his side as a middle-aged woman answered.

"Virginia Brady?" he asked.

"You want next door, only she's Virginia Roxburgh now. I just rent the house from her."

"Next door?"

She pointed to the almost-identical house to the left, one which had a caravan parked in the front garden.

"Thanks for your help."

"She married the neighbour?" I murmured as we headed down one path and up the next.

"Looks like it. Bernard Roxburgh's the man who accused Arthur of denting his car."

"And if Roxburgh married Arthur's wife, could that have given him a reason for wanting Arthur out of the way?"

Will flashed me a smile. "Do you want my job?"

This time, an older lady answered the door, but before Will managed to get a word out, she tapped a finger on a laminated sign: *No cold-callers.*

"Whatever you're selling, we don't want any."

Will disarmed her with a grin, and I was glad to see it wasn't just me he had that effect on. "We're not selling anything. My name's Will Lawson, and I'm a private investigator. This is my partner, Rania."

Partner?

"Why are you here? Is it about the missing cats?"

"I'm afraid I don't know anything about missing cats."

"Two from this street and three from the next, all in the last two months. The ladies at bingo think there's a catnapper on the loose. But if it's not because of the cats, why are you here?"

"I was hoping to have a quick chat about your ex-husband."

"What? Arthur? But he's been dead for over ten years."

"I'm aware of that, but some new information—"

"I don't want to hear it. My husband killed himself, did you know that? Whatever problems he had, he didn't care enough to share them. No, he took the coward's way out and left me right in the lurch instead."

"As I was saying, some new information has come

to light. It's possible Arthur's death wasn't a suicide."

She'd opened her mouth to speak again, but at Will's words, she closed it and turned a few shades paler.

"What do you mean? What information?"

"I'm afraid a lot of it's confidential at the moment, but I wanted to get an idea of Arthur's state of mind at the time. Whether he'd been having any problems at work, that sort of thing."

She opened the door a little wider. "I suppose you'd better come in."

As we took our shoes off at the front mat, a thin man with a sallow complexion came down the stairs.

"Who's this, Virginia? I didn't know we were expecting visitors."

"Detectives. About Arthur. They say he might not have committed suicide."

The man's expression turned grim. "Have you been upsetting my wife?"

"That wasn't our intention."

"Walking in here, twelve years after the man's death. Have you no shame? She went through enough hardship back when it happened."

"I can only imagine how difficult it must have been. It's a good thing you were around to help her."

"Are you insinuating something?"

"Not at all. I'm just saying that everyone needs a hand when they're down."

Virginia pressed her fingertips on her new husband's arm. "Calm yourself, Bernard." Then to Will, "I told the police at the time that Arthur had no reason to do what they said he did."

"You mentioned he'd been secretive?"

She sighed. "Let's talk in the lounge. Would you like tea?"

"We'd love a cup."

"Bernard, would you be a dear?"

She led us into a living room decorated in shades of pink. A vase of freesias sat on the windowsill—did the former Mrs. Brady enjoy gardening too, or had Arthur and her new husband shared the same hobby?

"Please, take a seat."

She waved us over to the back of the room, where two grey leather sofas faced each other with a wooden coffee table in between. I took a seat next to Will on the smaller two-seater while Virginia perched on the one opposite right next to... Well, I didn't know, but from the cheesed-off expression on her pale face, I suspected I was going to find out.

"About time you got here," the spirit said. "Twelve years, I've been waiting. Twelve years since that good-for-nothing husband of mine smothered me so he could move his other woman into our house."

Oh, hell.

Virginia sighed again, and I got the impression it was a habit. She still hadn't got her colour back, and her hands twisted in her skirt as she spoke. "You were asking about Arthur being secretive?"

Will nodded, giving her room to speak.

"I think I know why, but I didn't find out until three months after he died. He'd booked us a cruise. One of those fancy all-inclusive ones around the Med for our tenth wedding anniversary. And then he took his life before that and left me on my own. He'd been depressed, and the police said people often do the unexpected."

"Was he on medication?"

"The doctor gave him pills. I forget which ones. Do you really think it could have been...what? An accident? Murder?"

"It's an angle we're looking into."

"Virginia," Mr. Roxburgh called from the kitchen. "I can't find the tea strainer."

"Excuse me a second," she said.

While she crossed the room to the serving hatch cut through to the kitchen, I scooched closer to Will and whispered in his ear.

"The first Mrs. Roxburgh is sitting next to the second Mrs. Roxburgh, and she's not happy."

It took a few seconds for Will to process that. "I thought you could only see the dead if they were murdered?"

"That's right."

Virginia came back before I got the chance to elaborate.

"Where were we?"

For once, Will was lost for words, but I'd had practice at this—pretending to ignore the dead while at the same time holding a conversation without looking like a lunatic.

"It's possible Arthur had some assistance falling over the balcony. Did he mention problems with any of his colleagues?"

"I don't understand why you're looking into this now?"

"There's been another death at Daylesford Hall."

Will squeezed my leg in a silent thank you. Ordinarily, that contact would have made me squirm, but when he took his hand away, I found myself wishing he'd left it there.

"We can't be sure of anything at the moment, Mrs. Roxburgh," Will said. "It's just a possibility. Only one step on from a rumour, but we have to follow up every angle."

Mr. Roxburgh walked in with the tea. The cups rattled as he slammed the tray down on the table between us, but Virginia smiled at him.

"Thank you, Bernard."

The other Mrs. Roxburgh glared. "He never used to make me tea," she said.

"The bottom dropped out of my world when Arthur died," Virginia said. "I still remember every detail of that day. I spent the afternoon in the garden, tidying up the rose bushes. Bernard drove me crazy with his lawnmower all afternoon."

"It was having engine problems, as I recall. Water in the fuel."

"I'd not been inside fifteen minutes when the police knocked on the door. I could hardly believe it when they said Arthur was dead. In fact, I didn't believe it. I thought it was a joke. I didn't know what to do, so I went around to Bernard's because he lost his Primrose not long before and I thought he might understand."

The first Mrs. Roxburgh—Primrose—glowered at him. "Understand? That jackass helped me on my way. Any normal husband would have called an ambulance when his wife had an asthma attack, but he held a pillow over my face instead."

"I was watching *Antiques Roadshow* when Virginia knocked on the door. I'd only just taken my shoes off," Bernard said.

Primrose tutted. "Lazy, as usual. That man never

lifted a finger around the house. If he wasn't making a mess, he was sitting in front of the TV with his feet up."

"So you'd been in the garden together for the whole afternoon?" I asked.

"Yes," Virginia said. "Bernard helped me to sharpen my shears, even though he's never been big on horticulture."

"It was my wife who insisted we have the lawn," he said. "We've replaced it with decking now."

I refrained from rolling my eyes when Primrose started up again. "Decking! What sort of heathen puts decking in a garden? A tasteful patio is acceptable, but all that newfangled wood? I always told Bernard we'd put that in over my dead body, and now look—he's done exactly that. And why are you just sitting there, staring? You're one of those chosen ones, aren't you? You're supposed to be on my side."

I was beginning to see why Mr. Roxburgh might have wanted to hold a pillow over Primrose's face.

"Still," Will said. "You must miss your wife, especially if she died suddenly."

Bernard grimaced for a brief second, then quickly schooled his features into a more appropriate expression. "Of course, although she wasn't always the easiest woman to get along with."

Oh, how I longed to stick my fingers in my ears.

"Me, difficult to get along with?" Primrose snapped. "I wasn't the one who spent the entire weekend fly fishing instead of fixing up the house. Bernard left me with all the housework to do. He got home late almost every day, and I barely had enough time for my Women's Institute commitments. But now you're here, you can do your duty and show him who's boss."

No, I could take a deep breath and try not to lose my temper with a woman who made Helene look saintly.

"Virginia, going back to Arthur—did he mention any issues at work?" I asked.

"No, nothing. He didn't really talk about his job. It was all numbers, and truth be told, it bored me to tears."

"We really appreciate your time today."

"Will you keep me updated if anything else comes to light? I've spent so many years blaming Arthur, and if he was a victim too..."

"You'll be the first to know."

Thankfully, Will took the hint and got to his feet, pausing to shake Bernard's hand and smile at Virginia again.

"Hey! Where are you going?" Primrose demanded.

I ignored her.

"You can't just leave!"

Yes, I could.

And as we walked out the front door, Will kept his hand lightly on the small of my back. A gesture of... thanks? Camaraderie? Possession?

Whatever it was, it made me shiver, but at the same time, I liked it.

"I'm dying to know what went on in there," he said as he opened the car door. "Excuse the pun."

"The next Kinder Egg you buy me had better come with earplugs."

CHAPTER 16 - RANIA

"SO, EARPLUGS, HUH?" Will said once we were in the car with the doors closed. "The first Mrs. Roxburgh?"

"I know I'm supposed to side with the deceased, but honestly, if I'd had to live with that woman, I'd have wanted to bump her off too."

"That bad?"

"She'd have nagged Bernard to death if he hadn't got in first."

Will leaned back against the headrest and groaned. "I used to be an officer of the law. Really, I should report it if I suspect a murder."

"And what would you say? The woman died over a decade ago, and there's unlikely to be any evidence left. Besides, you'd ruin Virginia's life again."

He let out a long breath, then reached over and squeezed my hand. "I'm beginning to see why your job's so difficult. Not cleaning. Your...purpose. It's not all black and white, is it?"

I shook my head. "Some people kill because of circumstances—they have little choice. Others snap under pressure or lose concentration and make a mistake, then truly repent. And some of the spirits are real assholes."

Will's laughter made me smile too. "Speaking of assholes... We still need to talk to Arthur and Helene."

A groan slipped out. "Just when I thought today couldn't get any better."

"Sorry. You did good in there, by the way. Would you be offended if I said you were wasting your life as a cleaner?"

Would I? When I was a little girl, I'd wanted to be a surgeon like my daddy. But my mother had other ideas, and I'd sunk into a dark, dark place. Then war came, and I'd lowered my ambitions to survival and a quiet life, pure and simple.

But was Will right? Could I be more?

"No, I'm not offended."

He dropped me off outside Daylesford Hall at four p.m., and I felt a bit guilty that I didn't speak to Lucy so often nowadays. Would it be crazy to ask Will to stop one evening on the way out so I could have a chat? Probably. Assuming, of course, that he was serious about his intention to pick me up every night, something I still felt guilty about, even if Shannon was over the moon. I'd caught her looking at bridesmaid dresses on her phone this lunchtime.

"I'll be back around seven," Will said. "I need to pick up more Kinder Eggs."

"That takes three hours?"

"I have to get proper food as well. RJ never buys groceries, and if I don't go to the supermarket, he'll live on pizza." Will reached out to tuck a stray lock of hair behind my ear. "Stay safe."

I'd officially lost my mind. In less than a week, I'd gone from fiercely independent to checking my watch every five minutes to see if it was time for Will to come back yet.

It was the situation, I told myself. That was all.

We'd been shoved together in stressful circumstances, and it was perfectly natural to feel off-kilter.

And perfectly natural to hope he'd kiss me on the cheek like he did with Shannon when he came back. Right?

But he didn't.

When he walked into Daylesford Hall at a quarter to seven, I wished I could turn back time and retract all the "don't breathe my air" vibes I'd thrown off when I first met him. Then he might show me the same affection as he did my friend. But I couldn't, so I had to accept the consequences.

"Where's my Kinder Egg?" I asked, going for playful then panicking in case I sounded greedy.

"In the car, along with your earplugs. Is anyone still here apart from us?"

"No, the last person was Anthony, and he left fifteen minutes ago after he'd paid a visit to the men's room to sponge something off his trousers."

Will made a face. "Porn again?"

"Either that or he dropped coconut ice cream in his lap and it melted."

"Nice. Do you fancy tackling Helene or Arthur first?"

"I already spoke to Helene. She said if we kept fixating on her hotel trips—her words—she was never speaking to us again. I thought that sounded like a good deal, so I asked her how they found the room service."

Will burst out laughing, and for a moment I was reminded of the girl I could have been if *circumstances* hadn't caught up with me. Happy, confident, maybe slightly snarky if I cared to admit it, which I didn't.

"And what did she say to that?"

"Nothing. She folded her arms and faced the wall. But don't worry, she hasn't got anyone else to talk to, and she gets lonely easily. She won't keep it up. But tonight, I suggest we talk to Arthur."

"I wasn't planning to tell him about his wife and Bernard."

What would it achieve? It would only upset a man who'd spent the last twelve years trapped by his own misfortune. "I agree."

Now we were looking into his death in earnest, Arthur became a little less curmudgeonly. I loved that word. Gemma, my old nanny, taught it to me many years ago in one of my English lessons. I'd called my father that on occasion, and he'd taken it in good humour.

"Arthur, can you give us information on who else would have had access to the bank accounts?" I asked.

"Something tells me that money's part of the puzzle," Will added. "Who else worked with you in the finance department?"

"There were five of us, but I haven't seen any of them around for years. Paul Nelson, the financial controller, he died two or three years after me. I heard some of the staff talking about it."

"Natural causes?" I asked.

"Heart attack. He was fond of a fry-up, was Paul."

So I couldn't find him and ask any questions. "Paul Nelson was in charge, and he's dead," I told Will. "Who else?"

"Davinder Singh did the management accounts. Young chap, right out of college. Always struck me as conscientious. Nervous of Claire, though, which was hardly surprising."

"Claire?"

"Claire Chapman, our credit controller. We never had a problem with bad debt, because Claire offered to visit and collect the cheques personally if they were late."

"Davinder Singh," I said for Will's benefit. "Nervous. And Claire Chapman, scary. You said there was one more person?"

"Celia Marr looked after the bank reconciliations, more or less. Since the banking went online, she struggled a bit."

"And who had access to the account?"

"All of us except Davinder."

"The final person was Celia Marr," I told Will. "Everyone could access the bank except for Davinder."

"What authorisation was needed to make a payment?" Will asked. "Did it need two signatories?"

"Just one. Theoretically, we were supposed to print out details of each transaction and have Paul approve them, but he was off sick so often it didn't always happen."

I relayed the information to Will.

"So, we've got three people to track down. I'll see whether Lloyd Weston can help, but I have to tread carefully because his priority's Helene. I can hint at a possible connection, but it'll be difficult because there really isn't one apart from a proposed information exchange with a dead man, and I'm not even going to try explaining that."

"Celia's most probably retired," Arthur said. "She always said she'd move up north to live near her son and grandchildren when she started drawing her pension."

"How far up north?" I asked. "Do you know where?"

"He lived in the Lake District."

Apart from a suggestion to wear body armour when we spoke to Claire, Arthur couldn't help much more. And I was tired. Will too, most likely, seeing as he'd had farther to travel.

"If you think of anything else, I'll be back tomorrow," I said.

"I know you think I'm callous for doing this. Holding back, I mean." Arthur's shoulders slumped forward. "I remember Helene when she was a little girl, coming to work with her father. She wasn't a bad kid. But there's no other way for me."

"I understand. We all have to play the hands we're dealt."

***

We were two minutes from the flat when my phone rang. Shannon.

"Is something wrong?" I asked.

"No. Yes. Not with me. Are you coming home soon?"

"We're almost there."

"Thank goodness. Can you sit with Aisling for the evening? Bethan from work called in tears—her boyfriend's just dumped her, and she's threatening to drown herself in vodka. I need to go over there and pour it all down the sink or we'll be a person short on the early shift tomorrow."

"Sure. Is Aisling in bed?"

"Fast asleep. And dinner's in the oven."

Another reminder of why getting involved with a man was a really, really bad idea. I glanced across at Will as I shoved the phone back into my pocket.

"Everything okay?" he asked.

"One of Shannon's friends is having man trouble."

"Do I need to apologise on his behalf?"

A bubble of laughter escaped. "That won't be necessary. On the plus side, she's already made dinner."

"That's a relief. For a second, I thought I might have to take you out somewhere flashy."

"And after I'd dressed up too."

Shannon ran out the door as we walked in, blowing a kiss to Will on her way past. "Lifesavers! See you later."

And then we were alone, apart from a two-and-a-half-year-old child who usually slept all evening. I checked in on her quickly, tucked into her cot-bed in Shannon's room, and she didn't stir.

"Spaghetti and meatballs, just like she promised," Will announced. "Reckon the meatballs have bread in them?"

"Definitely." It stretched the meat a little further on our limited budget. "But they always taste good."

"I'm sure they do. What's your favourite food, Rania?"

"I don't have one." Not in England, anyway.

"Everyone has a favourite food. Chocolate?"

I shrugged.

"Pizza?"

"That's *your* favourite."

"No, it's RJ's. I prefer cheeseburgers. Hmm... Cake?"

"If you must know, I like kibbeh, but I haven't eaten it since I came to this country."

"What's kibbeh?"

"A Syrian dish made from bulgur wheat and minced lamb. Or beef, sometimes. My mother used to make it with onions and pine nuts in the middle."

"What happened to your parents? Do you mind me asking?"

"Yes."

"Sorry."

He cast his eyes downwards and twirled spaghetti on his fork, and I felt guilty for snapping.

"My father died when I was twelve, then my mother died when I was sixteen."

"Shit. I shouldn't have brought it up."

"I've... It's... Talking about my old life is difficult. Some days, I wish I'd never left Syria."

"Was staying an option?"

I dropped my cutlery. "No. And that makes being here even more frustrating. I'm not welcome in England, but the people here don't understand that I never wanted to leave my home in the first place. If I'd stayed, I'd be dead, and the spirits... Will, they were everywhere. Thousands and thousands of tethered souls, begging me for help wherever I went. On and on and on and on. I barely slept, I couldn't think, and I never got a moment's peace."

He shoved his chair back and came to crouch at my side, holding both of my hands in his. "I'm so sorry. I wish there was some way I could turn the clock back."

"There is no back, only forward." My voice dropped to a whisper as the lump in my throat grew. "The last night I spent in Aleppo, I nearly didn't see morning.

Death came so, so close. As soon as the sun rose, I started running, and I didn't stop until I reached France."

He shook his head. "Inside, you're still running."

How did he know me better than I knew myself? A tear ran down my cheek, and he wiped it away. I didn't protest when he scooped me up and carried me over to the sofa, cradling me in his arms while I sobbed into his shirt.

"I want to help you to stand still," he murmured, and that only made me cry harder.

Tears of relief, because I'd finally found my anchor.

CHAPTER 17 - WILL

IT DAMN NEAR killed me to leave Rania yesterday evening. I'd wanted to crawl into bed beside her and hold her for the rest of the night. But I'd done the gentlemanly thing, and when her eyes began to close, I'd tucked her in then backed out of the room and waited for Shannon to come back. Lucky the baby didn't cry, because I wouldn't have had the first clue what to do.

"Is Rania in bed already?" Shannon had asked.

"She was tired."

Shannon wrinkled her nose. Cute, but whereas once my type had been warm and female, I'd refined it lately to something more specific.

"I kind of hoped you'd be in there with her."

At least she got that and was on my side. "That makes two of us, but I get the impression Rania's had a difficult past."

"She has. I think her time in Syria must have been awful. I've seen all the pictures on the news."

"Of Rania?"

"No, of Syria. Rania never talks about the specifics."

"What? Never?"

"Nope. She's... Don't get me wrong, I love that girl to death, but she can be a little...different."

"The ghosts thing?"

"She told you about that?" Shannon sounded surprised.

I nodded. "She mentioned it. You sound as if you don't believe her?"

"Well, it's cr— Not an easy thing to believe."

"How do you explain it?"

"I saw one of those myth-busting programmes once, about mediums. How they're perceptive to their surroundings and use careful statements to make you think they're psychic."

Could that be Rania? I'd thought so at first, but she knew too much. Either she was genuine, or she had better connections than I did and rivalled RJ with her computer skills.

I made a non-committal noise. "One thing that struck me as unusual is that she doesn't spend half her life on social media."

Shannon laughed. "I've tried to get her on Facebook, but she refuses. I guess she doesn't know that many people, so it doesn't matter much to her. And she doesn't even own a computer."

So much for that idea.

"Unusual. Did you get your friend sorted?"

Shannon crinkled her nose again. "I talked her out of the vodka, but she still wants to take a baseball bat to his car. The asshole dumped her by WhatsApp, for crying out loud."

"An asshole indeed. Maybe Rania's right to avoid all that stuff."

"No, she's not. Because you'd never be that callous, would you?"

***

Rania at least had a phone, so I sent her a text message when I woke up. Nothing heavy, just a quick line to say good morning.

I got zilch back.

Which left me stewing as I stood over RJ's shoulder, watching while he tried to break into the Lanefield Park Hotel's computer network.

"You're gonna have to give me time, buddy."

"It's a bloody hotel, not NASA. How difficult can it be?"

"Yes, it's a hotel, but I've had years to finesse my way into the good stuff. Back doors, malware, that kind of thing. You're asking me to go in cold here. Reckon I'll try emailing one of my little worms and see if any of the fish bite."

"And if they do?"

"It'll open a door wide enough for the Trojan Horse to ride in. Look, just call her and put us all out of our misery."

"I don't want to scare her off."

RJ glanced sideways at me. "What happened to the old Will? Mr. 'If the blonde doesn't want to have fun, there's always the brunette'?"

"Rania's different."

"As in 'blows your mind as well as your cock' different?"

"The first part, definitely. No idea about the second."

"You mean you haven't...?"

"No."

"But it's past the third date. That's the chick rule, right?"

"Technically, we haven't had the first date yet."

"Then what have you been doing every evening? You said you were having dinner with her. Was that just a ploy to avoid my skills in the kitchen?"

In the kitchen, RJ had a skill, singular. And I'd only witnessed it once, thankfully, when I'd arrived back earlier than planned one evening and found him fucking a redhead over the counter.

"Aw, honey, I'm just not that kind of guy. And it wasn't a proper date—her flatmate invited me in to eat with them when I dropped her home."

"Threesome? Nice."

"Piss off. You've got sex on the brain. Anyone would think you weren't getting any either."

RJ cleared his throat. "Make me a coffee while I send these emails, would you?"

Bullseye.

***

Rania still hadn't replied when I left for Daylesford Hall at eleven for a pre-scheduled catch-up with Lloyd Weston. Except when I arrived, he was nowhere to be seen, and his secretary adopted a look of panic when I walked in.

"Oh, er, Mr. Lawson! I meant to call you, but I... things... I forgot. Mr. Weston's ill today."

"Nothing serious, I hope?"

"His wife said it was a migraine, but I think it's a broken heart. He hasn't been the same since Helene died."

All of which meant I'd trekked out to Weston Corp early for nothing. I could have stayed at home with good coffee and a handy punchbag in the gym if trawling through online records looking for missing members of the finance team got too frustrating.

But since I was here, I might as well make the best of it.

"Do you have a meeting room I can borrow?"

"I'm sure I can find one."

"And I need to track down the current whereabouts of a few ex-employees. Are you able to help?"

Seeing as the boss was out and he didn't pay her to read magazines about fish, she should have plenty of time.

"I-I-I've only been here for two months."

"Then I'm sure you'll know exactly who to ask for assistance. Mr. Weston's keen to get this case cleared up as soon as possible."

She swallowed hard. "Of course. Just tell me what you need."

By mid-afternoon, my new friend Kayleigh had found me Celia's address from her friend who administrated the company pension scheme, but struck out on Davinder and Claire. From what Arthur said, I'd have been surprised if anyone had kept in touch with the dragon lady.

But no matter. I'd got a lead on Davinder myself, from LinkedIn, and I'd find Claire too. Davinder, it seemed, had grown from his experience at Weston Corp and become the financial controller of a small but successful architecture firm. His offices were just down the road, but when I called, his PA informed me he was at a conference in Newcastle and wouldn't be back until Monday. Who went to a conference in Newcastle? My father always attended forums in Paris or Rome, the events chosen more for their locations than their subject matter.

But still, I'd made some progress, and it turned out Kayleigh made a mean cup of coffee, which was an admirable quality in any woman.

I was on my fifth Americano and wired as hell when my bladder made its objections known. Bollocks. I'd been sitting there for five hours, and Rania would have arrived by now. My knees cracked as I got up and headed for the john.

Except before I got there, I heard a raised voice coming from the room next-door-but-one.

"Leave me alone!"

"Miss Algafari, you realise if you don't provide a satisfactory answer, I'll just keep coming back."

Chris Turner, and he had Rania in there. I'd shoved the door open before I stopped to think about what I was doing.

"Sorry, my mistake, Turner. I heard a distressed female and my mind screamed 'sexual assault.' And we both know how difficult those cases are to prosecute without witnesses, don't we?" The bitterness I carried inside leaked out in my voice, and Rania turned to stare at me.

"Well, obviously there's no assault, so you can get... leave us to continue."

"I'm not continuing," Rania said. "Not when you try using threats over my immigration status to get me to give you answers I don't have."

"Miss Algafari—"

"Are you charging her with anything?" I asked.

"No."

"Taking her to the police station? Because you

know she's entitled to a lawyer if you do that. You like to do everything by the book, right?"

"Under the Police and Criminal Evidence Act, I'm entitled to question any person from whom I think useful information can be obtained."

"She's already told you she doesn't know anything."

"And you're obstructing a police officer in the course of doing his duty. Police Act 1996, section 89."

Turner folded his arms, and I wanted to wipe the smug grin off his face.

"Bullshit. I'm merely assisting a member of the public."

"Enough!" Rania said. "I've said over and over that I didn't see Helene Weston cavorting with a man in the evenings. Whether you choose to believe that is up to you, but I'm done here."

She walked out, leaving me with Turner, and I forced myself to unclench my fists before I took a swing at him. If his red face was any indication, he felt the same way.

"Some thanks I get for recommending you for this job, Lawson."

"We both know why you did that."

"Maybe I felt sorry for you after what happened with Marco Renton."

"Right."

"And then Susanna dumped you when you lost your job. That couldn't have been easy."

"I don't care about Susanna anymore."

"Really? But you were engaged to her."

"I've moved on to better things."

Turner looked from me to the door Rania had just walked out of, and I could almost see the wheels turning. He might have been a prick of the first order, but he wasn't totally useless as a detective. Only about ninety percent. Shit.

"Ah, I get it. The cleaner. That's why you came steaming in here to defend her."

"You don't know what you're talking about."

"Really? Deny it, then."

I couldn't. I might have bent the truth on occasions, but I couldn't lie outright.

Turner gave a mocking laugh. "I must admit, I expected better. Oh, how the mighty fall. You've gone from living it up in high society to slumming it with a refugee."

I came so fucking close to knocking his teeth out. The only thing that stopped me was the strangled sob from outside the door, and I realised Rania had heard the entire conversation. Footsteps receded along the corridor, and I took off after her with Turner's sniggers echoing behind.

"Rania, stop!"

She didn't, and then she pulled that favourite chick trick and ran into the women's toilets.

I stood outside the door and sucked in a breath. They had stalls, right? It wasn't like the men's where we let everything hang out at a urinal. And I knew then that I'd chase that girl to the ends of the earth, so barging into a ladies' restroom wasn't a problem.

Sniffing came from the end stall, and I used my penknife to unlock the door from the outside, praying Rania hadn't decided to take a leak as well as cry. No, she was sitting on the closed toilet lid with a wad of tissues in her hand, and at the sight of her so upset I almost went back outside and sent Turner over the balcony to join Arthur.

"You shouldn't be in here," she said.

"I'll leave when you come with me."

"I can't." Another sniffle. "I'm not going outside like this."

I shoved the door closed behind us and leaned on it, hands in pockets, going for relaxed even though I was wound up tighter than a virgin's pussy.

"Don't listen to Chris Turner. He only said what he said to bait me." And it fucking worked.

The outer door opened and heels clicked across the tile. I couldn't say anything more with an audience, so I took a chance and squeezed Rania's hand in mine, relieved beyond words when she didn't snatch it away.

For goodness' sake, hurry up and pee, woman. What had she been drinking? A bloody river? Finally, the toilet flushed, water ran, then the hand dryer blasted and the interloper pissed off.

"I'm so sorry." What else could I say? Because I was. Sorry Rania had been forced to leave her home, sorry she'd got involved in this case, and sorry men like Chris Turner considered her a second-class citizen.

"It's not that I haven't thought those things about myself... I guess it just stung to hear him say them out loud."

"But he's wrong. You're as much of a person as I am, and more of a person than he is. I am *not* fucking slumming it." Another tear rolled down her cheek, and I wiped it away with my thumb. "Look, come for dinner with me tonight. Not something Shannon cooked. I want to take you to a fancy restaurant where neither of us has a clue which fork to use and try to decipher the menu with you."

Half a minute went by, and it felt like a lifetime.

Then she shook her head, biting her lip in a way that made my cock twitch even as my heart sank. *Will, you sick asshole.*

"Can I get out? Please?"

What could I do but let her past?

The door slammed behind her, and I locked myself in the stall again, hoping for some insight into the female mind. What made those grey cells tick? Because right now, between Helene and Rania, I was fucked if I could work it out.

Chapter 18 - Rania

TALK ABOUT SLEEPLESS nights. At three a.m. I almost resorted to Shannon's vodka. Two days ago, I thought I'd found my anchor, but now I realised *I* was the anchor and I'd drag Will down with me if I kept taking advantage of his good nature. No matter what he said.

And last night, he hadn't said anything. After I'd left him in the bathroom, he'd disappeared, and I'd been ready to walk to the bus stop when I found him sitting outside the door of Daylesford Hall in his BMW. Since it would have been rude to walk right past him, I'd climbed into the car, but like earlier in the day when he'd sent me a text message and I hadn't known what to say in reply, I'd kept quiet, and he hadn't spoken either.

Part of me—the grown-up child who still believed in fairy tales—wanted to tell him I'd been stupid when I turned down his dinner invitation, because the idea of going to one of those upmarket places just once in my adult life held a morbid appeal. And I couldn't deny I craved his company. I even had a dress I could wear—a black strapless number Shannon had treated me to when she insisted I go on a double date with her and Slick Dick and one of his friends.

But I'd got out of the car and walked into the flat

alone, ignored Shannon's questions about why Will hadn't come in to eat with us, and gone straight to bed.

***

At five thirty in the morning, her usual time despite it being Saturday, Shannon walked in with a cup of coffee, Aisling toddling along behind her.

"Okay, you've had time to wallow in self-pity. What's wrong?"

"Nothing."

I reached out for the coffee, and she held it out of reach.

"Fine. Everything."

"On a scale of one to Slick Dick?"

I grimaced at the comparison. "Maybe a three?"

She handed over the mug, and I sipped gratefully.

"Go on, tell me. I thought you and Will were getting on so well. What did he do?"

"It started when one of the cops who first interviewed me wanted to ask more questions. I know Will doesn't like him, so I'll admit I didn't go out of my way to be helpful, but he kept asking me who I'd seen Helene spending time with in the evenings, and I never saw her spending time with anyone."

"So tell him that."

"I did, and he put me on a guilt trip. Gave me this lecture about how if I wanted to stay in England, I needed to act like an upstanding citizen and assist with upholding the law."

"Sounds like a real asshole."

"He is, and he wouldn't let it drop. Then Will heard part of the discussion and came barging in."

Shannon's voice turned dreamy. "Aw, your knight in shining armour."

"Well, sort of. He and the cop had words, and I got out of there while I could, but I waited outside the door for Will."

"I'm not seeing the problem here?"

"The cop told Will he was slumming it with me. And even though he isn't with me, exactly, he can do better. He doesn't talk about his past much, but I know he went to a private school, and the cop said he came from high society."

Plus he had built-in manners and a voice that wasn't exactly posh, but definitely well-spoken, especially compared to mine. I'd spent hours practising my English, talking aloud to myself or sometimes Aisling, and I still hadn't managed to strip away my Middle Eastern inflection completely.

Shannon rolled her eyes. "Who cares where he came from? It's where he is now that matters, and he's been chasing after you all week. It's clear he cares."

"I get that, but one of us has to put the brakes on this...this thing." I took a gulp of coffee to cover up the fact that I was getting sniffly again. "Anyway, it doesn't matter. He asked me to go out for dinner with him, and I said no."

"Have you lost your mind?"

"Most of the time it seems that way."

Between ghosts and murders, unsuitable men and my wayward heart, I felt even less in control than usual.

"Call Will and tell him you weren't thinking straight. Blame it on your period. That excuse works for everything with men."

"I am not calling Will Lawson to talk about my period."

"Well, think of a better story. You two should be together. I know it."

***

My phone buzzed mid-morning, and I grabbed it off my bedside table. I'd tried getting up, but it didn't work out. Everything was grey. The sky outside, my mood, and the white shirt I'd accidentally left in with the darks when I put the laundry on yesterday morning. Thoughts of Will had been distracting me again.

And now he'd sent me another message.

Will: The forensics results came in. The lab found blue fibres under Helene's fingernails. Wool mixed with acrylic. Just thought you might want to know.

I did want to know. But I still wasn't sure what to say. For a moment, I envied those teenagers who walked around with their noses buried in their smartphones, communicating exclusively in the modern equivalent of hieroglyphics.

Rania: Thank you. I'll see you on Monday.

I hit send before I could chicken out, then immediately regretted it because my message sounded as though I didn't want to speak to him for two days. The needy part of me wanted to type out a follow-up, but that might have encouraged him to do something impulsive.

Like drive over and kiss you?

No! The thought both thrilled and scared me.

So, I stayed in bed watching a terrible movie until Mrs. Garrett from downstairs phoned and asked me to walk to the supermarket with her. I foolishly figured it would do me good to get out of the flat, but the old lady took one look at me and her expression turned sympathetic.

"What's up, love?"

"Nothing."

"Ooh, there is. Normally you've got such a pretty face, but this morning it looks like a smacked arse."

Tell me again why I helped this woman?

"Really, I'm fine."

"Is it that handsome young man you've been coming home with for the last few days? Did you have a bust-up?"

I forgot Mrs. Garrett saw everything. She spent her days sitting by the window at an old card table with a cup of herbal tea, stroking her cat, Bigly. I often thought that she'd have made a great Bond villain if she were fifty years younger.

"No, not a bust-up. Just a small awkward moment."

She patted me on the arm. "Life's full of awkward moments, dearie. You don't live to my age without seeing your fair share. The only way to get over them is to think of them as learning experiences and move on."

"I hurt him," I whispered.

"Then that means he cares."

But I did too, perhaps more about Will than myself, and I wanted to do what was best for him.

CHAPTER 19 - RANIA

I HAD A hundred goes at writing another message to Will on Sunday, and my finger hovered over the call icon more times than I could count, but in the end, I decided I'd be better off speaking to him face-to-face. I wasn't great at deep and meaningful conversations at the best of times, and I needed to see his expression to work out what he wasn't saying as well as listening to what he was.

There was no sign of Will's BMW in the car park as Geri, the yoga teacher, held the door of Daylesford Hall open for me. While I felt like death, she looked perky in hot-pink leggings and one of those artfully draped tops that showed more than they hid. She'd even tied tinsel around her ponytail.

"You look tense," she said. "You need to relax more."

"I'm finding that difficult at the moment."

"I've got a class starting at five thirty. Why don't you join us? We're working on breathing and flow this week."

I slipped past her, grateful to be inside out of the cold.

"Tempting, but I start work as everyone else finishes."

"Maybe another week?"

"Maybe."

Er, how about never. How did she stay so perky? Thankfully, Derek wandered past and saved me from further conversation as Geri scooted over to him, eyes bright.

"Derek! Have you got a moment to discuss my idea for a new class? Lots of people'll be making New Year's resolutions, so I thought we could do something on a 'new year, new you' theme."

"Excellent, excellent..."

They disappeared around the corner, and I veered in the opposite direction, even though it meant walking past Arthur, who looked as if he wanted to talk but understood I couldn't because two visitors were sitting on the sofa next to him, engrossed in a sales brochure.

That meant I got a free pass all the way to the cleaning cupboard on the second floor.

And nearly had a heart attack when I yanked the door open.

"What the hell are you doing here?"

Will looked a little rough around the edges, far from his usual smooth self as he sat on an upturned bucket.

"Waiting for you."

"But how...? Your car isn't outside."

"Another warning light came on, so I had to take it to the garage. I borrowed RJ's."

"Oh."

"Oh? That's all you've got to say? I gave you time to cool off after Friday, but you can't keep avoiding me."

"I'm sorry." I bit my lip, stuck for what to say next. "Did you come this whole way just to say that?"

He sighed, long and drawn out. "No, I had a meeting with Lloyd Weston."

"How did it go?"

"Could have been better. The man's lost his daughter, and he's sick too. Coughing and spluttering all over the place. I tried not to touch anything, but it made me want to drink a bottle of that alcohol hand sanitiser just in case."

"I don't suppose he's going to have a great Christmas."

"No, I don't suppose he is. And when I asked a few questions about Arthur, he wanted to know why I was looking into a twelve-year-old suicide rather than his beloved daughter's murder."

"What did you tell him?"

"That two deaths in the same building was unusual, so I had to consider the possibility of a connection."

"Did he believe that?"

"He just huffed and reminded me I was here because of Helene."

"If only Arthur wasn't so stubborn."

Will hooked one arm around the backs of my legs and pulled me closer. "Reminds me of somebody else I know."

I looked down as he smiled up at me, his face level with... No, I shouldn't even be thinking about that. Not that I'd ever experienced that pleasure, but I'd read about it. And with Will touching me, my brain went all frazzled again.

"I need to get to work."

"And I need to visit a potential new client. But I'll be back later to pick you up. Is Shannon still offering dinner?"

I nodded.

"Stay safe."

Then he was gone, and I sank onto the bucket in his place, legs shaking. I'd become so much more fragile since I left Syria. Back then, the need to survive had overridden everything, but now I had time to think and analyse, and the more I thought, the more confused I got about everything.

Simple answer: don't think.

Clean. I needed to clean.

By the time I heard a car pull up outside in the quiet of the night, Daylesford Hall was sparkling. I'd even polished the bannisters. And whatever car Will was driving, it didn't purr quietly like the BMW. Low, black, and mean-looking, it certainly wasn't a family hatchback.

"What is it?" I asked as he climbed out to open the door for me.

"A Porsche 911. RJ likes his toys."

I could see that. It felt like climbing into a spaceship, if a spaceship were done out in tasteful leather and chrome. I breathed deeply. The car reeked of money.

"Still got that new-car smell," Will said. "He's only had it a couple of weeks."

"And he doesn't mind you driving it?"

"RJ doesn't get precious about things like that. But if I touched one of his computers, he'd chop my fingers off."

"Thanks for the warning. If I ever meet him, I mean."

"You'll meet him tomorrow. I need to travel to Nottingham to speak to Celia Marr, so he'll be picking you up in the evening."

"Honestly, there's no need for that. I can catch the

bus."

"You can, but you won't be."

Now the stench of testosterone mixed with the pungent aroma of the leather, and in the confined space, Will's determined presence threatened to overwhelm me. At least we'd be home soon. Shannon could help to balance things out a bit.

Except... "What are all those lights ahead?"

We'd rounded a bend on one of the narrow country lanes that led between Daylesford Hall and Enderby village proper, and stationary cars stretched ahead as far as the eye could see.

"No idea. Does it often back up here?"

"I've never seen a traffic jam in the whole time I've worked for Weston Corp, unless you count the occasions when the bus got stuck behind a tractor."

"Well, it's not going anywhere."

And neither were we, because now more cars had driven up behind us, so we couldn't reverse either. I leaned to the side, trying to see around the next bend, but it didn't help.

"Now what?" I asked, hating the hint of panic that crept into my voice. "I need to get home!"

"What's the hurry?"

"Uh... Shannon's cooking dinner. It might burn."

He patted my phone in the pocket of my jeans. "Then call her. If you know how," he added under his breath.

I deserved that.

"I'm sorry," I said, fumbling with the phone. It fell into the footwell and skittered away under my feet. "I just never know what to say to you."

"So saying nothing is better?"

I shrugged.

"I don't need War and fucking Peace, Rania." He leaned back and closed his eyes. "Shit. I didn't mean to say that. I can be an insensitive bastard at times, but I'd never intentionally hurt you."

"I know that."

"Well, that's two of us who don't know what to say."

The silence was more painful than talking. So I tried.

"What you said about liking me and taking me out for dinner... I understand what you want, and I can't."

"What do I want?"

Oh, hell, did he seriously want me to put it into words? He cupped my chin, his fingertips hot against my skin, and turned my head to face him.

"What do I want, Rania?"

That gentle pressure remained, and he ran his thumb over my bottom lip, making me shiver. Beads of sweat popped out on my spine as my body responded with a weird mix of fear and anticipation.

"You want me to go out on a date with you. Kiss you. More..."

"More?"

"Sex," I whispered.

"And is that so awful?"

"I'm damaged goods."

"I'm not exactly perfect myself."

"Really? Because you look pretty damn faultless from where I'm sitting."

I screwed my eyes shut—as if that would somehow erase my words, the start of an admission I didn't want to let out because the consequences made me shudder —but not before Will had hit me with that grin again.

"Nice to hear you say that." His words vibrated through my chest with a heavy purr. "But you're mistaken. I'm just as screwed up as anyone else. I grew up in boarding school because my parents were too busy to look after me, when I was eighteen they disowned me because I joined the police instead of following in my father's footsteps and going to law school, then at twenty-four I got fired from the police for throwing a man who liked to beat up his girlfriend down the stairs. Now, in a good month, I make enough to pay the rent."

"I'm sorry."

"There's no reason for you to apologise. So you see, I may have the public school accent and drive a car that's a relic from my past and live in a decent house—which RJ owns, by the way, not me—but I've messed up more times than I care to think about. For the last two years, I've been clinging to the hope that my business would take off, and it hasn't. I'm so damn tired, Rania. And for the first time since my ex-fiancée ditched me, I've met a girl I want more than a meaningless fuck with, and I don't want to let her go."

"I still don't have a clue what to say."

"Then don't say anything. But please, give me a chance. I'll mess up, I always do, but I'll try to make it right in every way possible."

"You barely know me."

"Then let me get to know you."

His voice took on an edge of desperation, and after what he'd told me, I owed it to him to let him into my past. Not all the way in—that was a dark path and one I'd walk alone—but enough for him to understand why I couldn't be the girl he dreamed of.

"I didn't want to leave Syria. It was—still is—my birthplace, my home, and a country that gave me so many good memories growing up. But the night I almost died there, I knew it was time to go."

A police car drove past on the wrong side of the road, blue lights flashing, which kind of explained the traffic jam. But I didn't stop talking. If I didn't tell Will this stuff now, I probably never would.

"I was nineteen. My parents were dead and the whole of society had collapsed, so I had to fend for myself. Do you know how many jobs there are in Aleppo now, especially for women? None. So I fought, because if I fought, I got fed, even though both sides were as bad as each other."

Will reached over and gripped my nearest hand in both of his. "Rania, if you don't want to—"

I shook my head, cutting him off. "I'm not proud of what I did. But watching a black soul leave a man's body... It rises up then scatters like the wind snatched it away, even on a still day. And then some of the spirits leave with it, but they just fade away. Disappear like a grain of sand in the desert. But every time I freed a handful, the ones left behind yelled even louder for me to help them too."

I could still hear them now. The terrible wailing. Pleading, cajoling, threatening...

"And I still stayed. Partly because I didn't know anything else and partly because I was scared that wherever I ended up would be just as bad. Then the building I was sleeping in one night got bombed, and I nearly died in the fire. Everything left that could burn, did burn, and the doorways collapsed, and people were screaming, and I couldn't get out—"

Or breathe. I couldn't breathe then, and I couldn't breathe now. Memories of the smoke swirling around as I stumbled through a ruined building lit only by flames made me choke until Will wrapped an arm around my shoulders and bundled me closer.

"But you did get out, and now you're here. I won't let anything bad happen to you, I promise."

He twirled my hair around his fingers, an oddly soothing sensation, and it reminded me of the way my mother had stroked my head as she cuddled me on her lap when I was little. I leaned into his touch as I continued, even though what happened afterwards would probably disgust him.

"Yes, I did get out. And that night I took off for the border. Mostly on foot, sometimes in trucks if I could hitch a lift. But staying in that part of the world wasn't an option. So much death." I shuddered. "I decided to go to Europe, but I needed money for that. So I sold the only thing I had left."

"Yourself," Will whispered.

I nodded, unable to speak for a few seconds, but he didn't let me go. If anything, his grip got tighter.

"Sometimes, I wish I'd died in Syria." Often, in fact. "So you see, for me, sex isn't a pleasurable thing. It's something to endure, and it hurts. And the rest of the stuff? I have no idea. Men didn't kiss me. They just took what they wanted and threw some euros down afterwards."

Will didn't look as surprised as I thought he would, or as horrified, but his voice still cracked when he spoke.

"I'm not giving up on you, Rania. You've seen the ugliest parts of human nature, but you're still beautiful.

And I want to take you on a date."

"You do?"

"Yes, I do. I want you to put on a pretty dress and smile and laugh and eat those kibbeh things you like. And then I want you to fall asleep in my arms because even if we don't do more than that, you've got under my skin and I never want you to leave."

Dammit, the tears were coming again. Tears for the life I'd lost and the people I'd never see again, but also happy tears because Will hadn't run screaming into the night when he found out what I'd done.

"I think I'd like that too," I told him.

We must have sat there for another ten minutes, not saying anything, just living in the present and thinking about our pasts and our future. Together. Our future together.

But then the people in the cars around us began to get tetchy, and slamming doors and raised voices brought us back to reality.

"What do you think is going on?" I asked.

"No idea. I'll call RJ."

"How will that help?"

"RJ has ways of finding out everything."

Will used the Bluetooth system in the car so I could hear the whole conversation. RJ picked up after two rings.

"Tell me you haven't crashed my car."

"That'd be hard to do since we haven't moved in the last twenty minutes. I was hoping you could shed some light on that."

"We? Are you with that girl who's made you go all mushy?"

Will smiled. "I am, and she can hear every word

you're saying. Rania, say hello to RJ."

"Hi."

"Rania, my friend has told me so much about you. Apparently, you shine with the light of a thousand suns and radiate the beauty of a field of unicorns."

"Shut up, asshole," Will growled at him.

RJ chuckled in response. "Where's this traffic jam?"

Will described our location while I mused over this evening's events. If Will was serious, I'd have another person in my life. Somebody living to talk to other than Shannon. Weird, but I kind of liked the idea.

RJ came back two minutes later. "Okay, ahead of you is a motorway bridge, and there's a dude standing on the edge threatening to jump. The motorway's closed too, and that's backed up for miles."

"Any indication of when it'll clear? Are you listening to the police scanner?"

"Nope. Some morbid freak's streaming it live on Facebook. Oh, hold on... The dude's climbing back over the railing. You should be good to go in a few minutes."

"Thanks, buddy."

"Are you coming home tonight?"

Will paused, and despite what I'd said about wanting to fall asleep in his arms, the automatic stiffening of my spine told me I wasn't ready.

And he must have realised that.

"Yeah, but not until later. I'll eat dinner with Rania and her friend first."

"I won't wait up."

When RJ ended the call, I reached my left hand up to squeeze Will's, still resting as it was on my shoulder.

"Thank you."

"I mean it, beautiful. I'm in this for the long haul.

We'll do whatever you feel comfortable with, but walking away and never seeing you again isn't an option for me." He brought my hand to his lips and kissed my knuckles. "So you'd better work out how to reply to a text message."

"Okay."

"I'm serious. Even if you only write a couple of words. Because if I get twenty-four hours of radio silence again, you'd better believe I'm coming to find you."

I did believe it, and the thought made me warm inside.

Chapter 20 - Rania

AFTER WHAT I'D just told Will, dinner should have been an awkward affair, but when traffic started moving again, he turned on the radio, fiddled with the buttons until he found a station playing rock, and didn't press me with further questions. But he did leave one hand resting on my leg. I'd never studied his hands before, but as we passed under the street lights, I took in his long, nimble fingers and soft, unblemished skin. Elegant hands. A surgeon's hands, not unlike my father's. I curled my fingers around Will's and glanced across at his face. He was smiling.

By the time we got home, my heart had stopped trying to escape from my ribcage, and as we walked through my front door, the delicious aroma of Shannon's lasagne brought my appetite back. She swore it was her grandma's special recipe, but as her grandma came from County Kildare the same as she did and not Italy, I suspected it might have come from a cookbook.

And while we ate, I somehow managed to have a reasonably normal conversation about the merits of cats versus dogs followed by a debate on the usage of solar power. Wonderful in principle, but England needed some sun before it would be a viable option.

How could Will act so normal?

Inside, I was a goofy mess.

And when Shannon headed off to her room, leaving me alone with Will and a whole lot of nervous anticipation, he stepped closer and wrapped his arms around my waist. Not with his body pressed against me or anything, but just...nice.

"Are you okay?" he asked. "After earlier, I mean."

"Yes. No. I think so. Most of that stuff, I've never told to anyone."

"And I'm honoured that you trusted me with it." He leaned forward so his forehead rested against mine. "And though I'd love to stay here with you all night, I meant what I said. I'm in this long-term, and I'm not going to push you."

Those words only made me want to push myself. But not tonight. Tonight, I needed to think.

Will shifted, running his thumbs up my back in a barely there caress before pressing his lips to my cheek. Not a quick peck like he gave Shannon, but a lingering touch that set my skin aflame. I nearly, so nearly, turned to offer him my own lips, but I couldn't. Not yet.

"I'm not sure I'll be back at a sensible time tomorrow, but RJ's going to pick you up," he said. "And I'll message you, so you'd better get thinking up some answers."

"I'll see you on Wednesday?"

"Nothing could keep me away. Dinner again?"

"Yes. I'd like that."

"I don't know where Shannon gets all her energy from—working early, looking after a kid, then cooking in the evening."

"She usually grinds to a halt by the weekend and sleeps for most of it. I get Aisling duty." Last weekend had been the exception.

"You don't mind?"

I shook my head. "When I first came here, Shannon was the one person who treated me like a human being rather than a parasite. The government gave me a little bit of money, but not enough to live on, and she helped me with food and clothing. So not only do I adore Aisling, I'll do anything for Shannon."

Will smiled, chuckling softly. "You sound fierce when you believe in something, did you know that?"

My cheeks heated. "No."

He brushed his fingers across the pinkness. "I like it. One day, I hope you'll get fierce about me."

If Will kept chipping away at the bricks around my heart, then yes, I'd say that was quite likely.

***

Even though I knew Will wouldn't be around on Tuesday, that didn't stop me from missing him. But his messages helped.

They started the moment I got up, the screen already flashing on my phone when Shannon called out that she was leaving for work.

Will: Morning, beautiful. I'm going to make this easy for you, so we'll start with a simple question. Pancakes or Full English?

What was he talking about? We always ate toast because Shannon got the bread for free. And Will couldn't take me out for breakfast because he wasn't here. Was it a trick question?

I left it too long to reply because a follow-up message arrived.

Will: I just want to get to know you. And maybe one day, I want to take you out for breakfast too.

Oh. Okay, it was like the cats-or-dogs discussion. I could do this.

Rania: Pancakes.

Half an hour later, my phone lit up again.

Will: Good choice. Summer or winter?

Rania: Summer. Always summer.

Despite what I'd said to Will about Aisling being adorable, at the moment she was going through the tantrum stage and determined to prove me wrong, as evidenced by the wail from the living room. I dashed in from the kitchen just as she burst into tears.

"What's wrong, sweetie?"

She pointed at Taffy. "Bad cat!"

"What did he do?"

"Take dolly."

Oh dear. I peered over the sofa and saw Aisling's Disney Princess doll with a ripped dress and teeth marks in her face. This called for diversionary tactics.

"Why don't we do drawing?"

Quick, where were the crayons? They might have been messy, but no messier than Aisling bawling her eyes out.

"No drawing. Park."

Oh, the little monster already knew how to bargain.

"We can go to the park after lunch."

"Now."

I was still wearing my pyjamas. "Drawing first, then park after lunch."

I should have known better than to argue with a two-and-a-half-year-old. She snatched Princess and hurled her on the floor, then ran into her bedroom and tried to throw herself on Shannon's bed. I say 'tried' because she had to scramble up there first, and it didn't have quite the same dramatic effect. It took ten minutes of coaxing to get her sitting at the table with paper and crayons, and another twenty minutes before I managed to retrieve my phone.

Will: Looks like I'd better start saving up for our trip to Tahiti. Day or night?

Rania: Night.

I liked the shadows because I could hide in them. That and the people who went out at night didn't usually want to hang around making idle conversation. Fifteen minutes passed before Will sent another question, and by then I'd googled Tahiti on my phone, first to find out where it actually was and second to drool over all the pictures of the tropical paradise.

Will: Bananas or strawberries?

Hmm... I quite liked both, but—

"Rarrrrrrni!" Aisling still couldn't say my whole name. Or scream it.

"What? What's happened?"

"Thirsty."

My phone rang an hour later, and I cursed under my breath in case the noise woke Aisling. She'd fallen asleep on the sofa as I was hunting for her mittens, so I'd breathed a sigh of relief and left her there.

"Hey," I whispered, slipping into my bedroom and pushing the door closed.

"Just checking you haven't quit on me."

"I spent the last fifteen minutes scrubbing crayon off the table."

His chuckle hit me in my chest, a pleasant tingle that spread through my limbs and warmed every part of me.

"Aisling?"

"I didn't get the urge to emulate Jackson Pollock myself."

"You know who Jackson Pollock is?"

"I did get educated in Syria."

"Shit, I'm sorry. That came out rude. I just know so little about you, and I want to know everything."

"My mother was an artist."

Well, sort of. She'd certainly been creative, but she'd only painted for a hobby. One of my biggest regrets was that I didn't have a single one of her paintings left. All that talent had been lost along with her life.

"You keep surprising me."

I took a deep breath. "Picasso or Van Gogh?"

"Picasso. There's a peculiar beauty in imperfection. Tell you what, it's your turn with the questions this afternoon. I'm just about to go in and talk to Celia, so wish me luck."

"Good luck."

"I'll call you when I'm done."

He did call, an hour later, right after Shannon had arrived back and tiptoed past her sleeping daughter. I was off duty for the day.

"Well, that was a waste of time. Celia couldn't tell me much about Weston Corp, other than to suggest I wear a flak jacket when I visit Claire."

"Same as Arthur."

"Yeah. Claire left a month before Celia retired, and apparently the entire office had a party. Lloyd Weston even bought cakes for everyone."

"A momentous occasion. I'm pretty sure he hasn't

done that since I've been there." Because I'd have noticed when I had to clear up all the dirty plates and crumbs.

"Well, if she twists my balls off, I might need a shoulder to lean on tomorrow. Wish me luck."

"Good luck."

I wasn't sure what made me more nervous—the thought of Will getting emasculated by the dragon lady or worrying about his friend picking me up. Talking to one stranger per month was my limit—any more pushed me out of my comfort zone—and I'd already had Chris Turner and his sidekick to deal with as well as Will. My quota was full.

Later that evening, I heard rather than saw the Porsche pull up outside Daylesford Hall again, and I hurried out the door before RJ had the chance to turn off the engine. He grinned at me as I slipped into the passenger side.

"Yeah, I can see why Will's lost his mind over you."

"Sorry?" The British were always sorry, and I'd adopted the expression too.

RJ pulled away smoothly, faster than Will drove. "Since he met you, he's bailed on pizza more times than I can count, knocked back a very nice blonde, and at the weekend, he was checking his phone like a girl."

"Not this girl. He gets annoyed at me because I don't always reply."

"Not annoyed. More...worried."

"I didn't mean to worry him. I guess I'm just nervous." About being with Will, and also about not being with him.

"Don't be. He likes you, and he's a good guy. Trust me. I've known him since we were twelve."

"He said you went to school together."

"Schools, plural. We got expelled from one and his father shit a brick."

"Yours didn't?"

"My father was pretty hands-off. I told him which new school I'd be attending, and he wrote a cheque. But listen to me, going on about the past when I haven't even introduced myself." He held out his right hand, crossing it over his left, which he kept on the steering wheel. "RJ Shields."

I reached out to shake. "Rania Algafari."

"A pretty name for a pretty girl." He quickly shook his head. "Good thing Will didn't hear me say that. He'd probably turn prehistoric and start beating his chest."

Which shouldn't have made me smile, but it did. Since my parents died, I hadn't had anyone to look out for me apart from Shannon, and damn if it didn't feel good to have another person in my corner.

"Satnav says go right here," RJ said. "Is that the best way? I've never trusted it since it sent me the scenic route through Wales. I got to this gate, which seemed odd, but hey, we were in the country, so I opened it and drove through. Then I got to another gate. And another one. And another one. Eighteen fucking gates. It was dark by the time I got to the last one, and I trod in cow shit."

That set me off giggling, and with the ice broken, I confirmed that turning right was indeed safe, and we chatted all the way back to the flat. And then I remembered what Will had said about living on pizza and thought I should make an effort to be sociable.

"Do you want to come in for dinner? My flatmate

always cooks, and... Is that weird? Inviting you in?"

"Who knows? But I'll take you up on the offer because I'm sick of takeaways."

"You don't cook at all?"

"Last time I looked in my oven, the shelves still had the protective plastic on them."

"Oh. Okay."

For me, a takeaway was a treat to be afforded a couple of times a year, not a diet. But I led RJ up the stairs and into the flat, where Shannon's eyes widened.

"How do you manage it?" she hissed. "I've swiped left on the whole of Tinder and you walk in with two hotties in two weeks."

"Shannon, meet RJ. He's a friend of Will's."

"Not a replacement for Will?"

RJ laughed. "No, I'm not a replacement for Will. Not if I value my life."

But he still pulled the same moves, dipping to kiss Shannon on the cheek. She turned redder than her Christmas jumper, a knitted affair with reindeer marching across it. And with good reason. RJ may have had blond hair and blue eyes to Will's brown and brown, but he still looked every inch like a model on his afternoon off—handsome but a little scruffy around the edges.

"We've got enough dinner for three, haven't we? RJ doesn't know how to cook."

"I'm sure I can make it stretch."

From the gleam in Shannon's eye, she'd have run to the twenty-four-hour supermarket, bought fresh ingredients, and rustled up something from scratch otherwise. At least, until RJ dropped his Porsche keys on the table in our tiny hallway. She peered at them, eyes narrowed.

"What car do you drive?"

"A Porsche 911."

He sounded proud, and rightly so. From what Will said, RJ had worked hard to buy it. But Shannon tossed her hair over her shoulder and harrumphed.

"Oh. I see. Well, I'd better dish up dinner."

She spun around and stomped off to the kitchen, leaving RJ looking confused.

"Did I say something wrong?"

"Not exactly."

"Then why is she banging pots together like my testicles are between them?"

"Her ex used to drive a Porsche. It didn't end well. And you perhaps want to avoid mentioning investments, your vacation homes, your net worth, and the number of celebrities you've met. Just a tip."

"Uh, okay. For the record, my family only has one vacation home, and I don't know any celebrities."

I gave him a smile I hoped was encouraging. "Then don't worry—she'll come around."

She didn't. Firstly, RJ got relegated to the fold-up stool. Then I had to make all the conversation while Shannon remained as frosty as the ice cream she slammed down in front of him for dessert. You can't imagine how grateful I was when his phone rang, and he looked as if he shared my sentiments.

"Excuse me a minute," he said, dashing out to the hallway, only to come back seconds later, holding out his mobile. "It's for you."

I pressed it to my ear.

"You're not answering your phone again," Will growled.

I closed my eyes. Oops. "I left it in my jacket pocket, and then I got distracted."

"By what?"

Shannon had retreated to the kitchen, out of earshot, but even so, I got up and headed into my bedroom. "Shannon's been mentally flaying RJ."

"What? Why?"

"She saw his Porsche keys. I forgot to warn him she really doesn't like wealthy guys."

"That's a refreshing change."

"Maybe, but it's kind of awkward being at the dinner table with them. I hoped she'd have mellowed a bit by now. I mean, it's been over three years since her Porsche-driving ex was on the scene."

"Aisling's father?"

"Yes."

"But she sees her daughter every day. That's a pretty strong reminder."

"I guess. How did your visit to Claire go? You survived?"

"Good and bad. I'm just about to start the trip back. Celia was right—Claire's an absolute bitch—but she also told me that Celia was too stupid to remember the internet banking logon and password, so she used to keep them written on a Post-it note in her desk drawer."

The implications of that sank in. "So anybody could have got hold of them and made those transactions?"

"Seems that way. She didn't even hide them, according to Claire. The details were all there, sitting on top of her tray of pens and paper clips."

So we were no further forward, and possibly even a few steps backwards. Suddenly, I wanted to crawl under the duvet and sleep for a week.

"Will we see each other tomorrow?" I asked, covering a yawn with my hand.

"Now I'm picturing you with your mouth open. Sorry. Inappropriate." Will paused. "Yes, I'll be there tomorrow. I need to speak to Davinder first, but I'll come in the afternoon."

I never knew how to end a conversation with a man. The whole "you hang up, no, *you* hang up" thing popped into my mind, and I snorted by accident.

"Er, yes, bye. Better go."

I hung up as Will was still laughing on the other end.

CHAPTER 21 - WILL

"I HEAR YOU got an earbashing last night," I said to RJ as he sat at the breakfast bar, eating a bowl of Rice Krispies. The antithesis of the CEO of a 300-million-pound-turnover company, which was what he'd be in an hour once he'd put his suit on.

He blew out a long breath. "That woman's like Leanan Sidhe."

"Leanne who?"

"Leanan Sidhe. A beautiful Irish vampire who seduces a man, ruins him body and soul, then leaves him so depressed he dies a slow and painful death."

"Aren't you being a tad dramatic?"

"Man, she snapped every time she talked to me, but all I could think of was those pink lips wrapped around my cock."

I roared with laughter. "Good luck with that one, buddy."

"I like a challenge."

"A challenge is climbing Mount Everest or learning to skydive. Going after a woman scorned is more like suicide."

"Tell me everything you know about her."

***

RJ moved his first meeting so I could brief him on Shannon, and when I left, he was heading for his computer. Was the way to a woman's heart through her Facebook profile? Or in RJ's case, through her banking details, her medical records, and cached versions of her online dating history?

I shook my head, chuckling to myself. The irony was that if Shannon had just sucked his cock last night, he'd have been bored with her by morning.

While my best friend took cyberstalking to insane levels, I headed off to visit Davinder Singh in his office. His assistant had cleared half an hour for me in his schedule, and had been at pains to point out how grateful I should be. What did she want? Flowers and chocolates for doing her damn job?

Still, I smiled and muttered the appropriate platitudes as she ushered me into a conference room that must have been decorated by a colour-blind toddler—all orange and purple and weird angles. The mission statement written in block capitals on the opposite wall read, *WE STRIVE TO BUILD LIGHT AND HAPPINESS INTO THE LIVES OF OUR CUSTOMERS.*

With fish-shaped lampshades and tables suspended from the ceiling? Okay then.

Davinder kept me waiting for five minutes before making an appearance. A thin man in an ill-fitting suit, he had a limp handshake that probably matched his dick. I knew he was in his early forties, but he looked ten years younger and that probably led to him getting steamrollered in the boardroom.

"Mr. Lawson, I take it?"

"Call me Will."

"Will. How can I help you today? My personal assistant mentioned something about Weston Corp? I haven't worked there for years."

"I've got a few questions about one of your ex-colleagues. Arthur Brady."

"Arthur who jumped off the balcony?"

"There's a possibility he was pushed."

I watched Davinder's reaction carefully, and his eyes widened in surprise. Surprise that Arthur might have been murdered, or surprise that I'd found out?

"His death always struck me as slightly unusual."

"How so?"

"There was an incident a couple of months before he died. Jessica from sales was running a marathon to raise money for the Samaritans, and Arthur would only sponsor her a fiver. Claire called him a cheapskate, and he muttered something about suicide being the coward's way out and how the victims should man up and face their problems rather than hurting those around them."

"Did you tell the police this?"

"I mentioned it, but they didn't do anything further. According to Lloyd Weston, they said it was an open-and-shut case. He gave everyone a half day off for the funeral, and that was that."

"I understand some unusual transactions came to light after Arthur's death?"

"Yes, six of them. Round sums, two at twenty-five thousand pounds, three at fifty, and one at a hundred."

Well, I could say what I wanted about Davinder's dress sense, but there was nothing wrong with his memory.

"And Arthur got the blame?"

"He did. Celia really should have spotted them earlier, and by the time we found the anomalies, Arthur had gone."

"Do you think he did it?"

"I think he could have done it."

"That wasn't what I asked."

Davinder shrugged. "There were a lot of people who could have transferred the money."

"You included?"

"Mr. Weston investigated this. I could have made five of the transactions, but for the sixth, I was on an eco-holiday in Patagonia without access to running water, let alone internet."

"Fair enough." I'd check that later. "And Arthur?"

"He was around, but he had no motive. Arthur was a creature of habit. His wife made him cheese sandwiches for lunch. They took a caravan holiday to Bognor every year. He owned five ties that he used to rotate Monday through Friday, and he drove the same Ford Fiesta the entire time I was with the company. What would he have spent the money on?"

"I don't know. Any medical bills?"

"Weston Corp provided medical insurance, and neither of his kids went to university, so there was no tuition to pay. It always baffled me."

"So, if it wasn't Arthur, who do you think did it?"

"I never worked that out, and I kept an eye, believe me. Nobody suddenly bought a new vehicle or flashed the cash or went on a fancy holiday. Whoever took the money, they had a plan for it, and I never worked out what it was. I guess that's why I didn't make a fuss back then."

"The other evidence all fitted."

"I also figured that if they killed Arthur to cover up a crime, they could do the same to me if I didn't keep my mouth shut. Now if you'll excuse me, I need to get back to work."

As I left Davinder's office, I began to wonder what sort of hornet's nest we were stirring up. What if Davinder was right? And what if whoever murdered Arthur found out I was looking for him? Or worse, found out that Rania was helping me?

I'd have to be more careful who I spoke to at Weston Corp, and no way would Rania be going near a bus again.

***

"I'm disappointed," Lloyd Weston said, in a tone that suggested he wasn't so much *disappointed* as really, really *pissed*. "It's Christmas Eve tomorrow, and we're still no further forward. What's more, I hear you've been asking more questions about that Arthur fellow than Helene. The man died twelve bloody years ago, and tragic though it was, the police have already concluded he took his own life."

"But—"

"No buts, young man. I'm paying your fees, and I want you concentrating your efforts on my daughter or I'll find somebody who understands priorities."

From "son" to "young man." I'd clearly been demoted. And while Weston's rant may have been justified, at that moment, he reminded me of my father and the tongue-lashings he used to give me about my choices in life. He hadn't so much wanted a son as a clone, a second Jack Lawson to pass his scalpel on to.

Growing up, every time my parents held one of their fancy parties to show off a ridiculously overpriced painting, or a new sports car, or knock back the exports from the vineyard they part-owned in France, his colleagues would thump me on the back and remind me I had some big shoes to fill. Except after I chose a pair of Vibram-soled patrol boots over handcrafted Italian leather brogues, I didn't get invited to those little soirees any longer.

That didn't make me lose any sleep.

But Lloyd Weston? He was a client, and I needed his cash.

"Yes, sir. Rest assured, I won't lose my focus."

He looked as if he was about to continue his tirade, but Kayleigh knocked on the door, and he glared past me.

"What is it?" he snapped.

"Sorry, sir, but Mr. Crowe from Datacorp is waiting in the boardroom."

Weston wagged a finger as he strode past me, heading for the door as Kayleigh hastily stepped out of the way.

"Find the bastard who took my Helene. Just find him, and fast."

I was dismissed.

Kayleigh offered a tentative smile. "You got off lightly, I reckon."

"You do?"

"Mmm-hmm. This morning, Anthony told him you were hoovering the reception area the other day instead of investigating, and Mr. Weston slammed his cup of coffee down so hard it broke."

Shit. "I was just helping someone out. I didn't

charge him for any of that time."

"Mr. Weston doesn't always think rationally."

Yes, in the future, I'd *definitely* have to be more careful. I could handle Lloyd being unhappy with me, but I didn't want him taking his anger out on Rania if he found out we were involved with each other. Not as involved as I wanted to be, not yet anyway, but like Kayleigh said, he might not be sympathetic to me spending my evenings attempting to woo a woman rather than hunting scum.

I headed for a meeting room and closed the door softly behind me, even though I wanted to kick it shut.

"Have you got any further with the hotel?" I asked RJ as soon as he picked up the phone.

"Huh?"

"The Lanefield Park Hotel. Helene Weston... Secret bookings... CCTV..."

"Ah, sort of."

"You spent the whole day cyberstalking Rania's friend, didn't you?"

"Not the *whole* day. I also fitted in a board meeting and two conference calls. And yes, I did look into your little problem, but the CCTV feeds aren't online. Looks like they're using a pretty antiquated system. If you want access, you'll have to get it in person, and I'd suggest you do that sooner rather than later because I found an email from their head of security telling the manager that they wiped the footage at thirty days."

And we were at—I did a quick calculation in my head—twenty-eight, with day thirty being Christmas Day.

"We need to get in there tomorrow."

"We?"

Yes, we. I couldn't do this alone.

"Where's your sense of adventure, mate?"

A plan. We needed a plan. I considered the options for a minute while RJ muttered comments about my sanity, or rather the lack of it, and came up with a possibility that had a chance of working. But my plan called for a couple of decoys, and there was only one other person I could ask.

Rania.

Chapter 22 - Will

WHEN I'D EXPLAINED my plan to Rania in the car last night, her long silence followed by a quiet, "There's no other way?" told me what she thought of the idea.

But here she was beside me, dressed in a hastily purchased shift dress that did everything for her ass and nothing to calm the half chub I got from looking at her wearing it. High heels, a string of fake pearls, a twinkling cubic zirconia ring, and RJ's Porsche completed the illusion of a young but well-to-do couple out for brunch.

The dining room at Lanefield Park could blind a man if he looked directly at the lights. Heavy chandeliers hung at intervals, glittering like the eyes of the gold-digging trophy wives hanging onto the arms of their geriatric meal tickets below. Rania's hand shook in my grip, but thanks to my parents' influence during my formative years, I'd had plenty of practice at putting on the snooty, entitled air required to dine in an establishment like this one.

"Table for two, sir?" the maître d' asked.

"I have a reservation under Lawson."

"Certainly, sir. Please follow me."

I should have booked in RJ's name—I bet a double-barrelled surname like his would have got us a top-notch table. As it was, we ended up in the far corner next to the kitchen with waiters walking past every twenty seconds, their steps silent on the plush carpet.

But no matter. The scrambled eggs and toast topped by artfully arranged slivers of smoked salmon were merely the entrée, and I doubted we'd be dining here again.

"Food okay?" I asked Rania.

She'd only taken a few bites.

"The food is fine."

Fine. A word to strike fear into any man's heart, but her answer didn't surprise me, not when her posture was stiffer than a corpse. I forked a mouthful of eggs into my own mouth, but Rania was wrong. It didn't taste fine at all. I might as well have been chewing RJ's three-day-old socks.

Usually, I got a thrill out of undercover work—the buzz of hiding in plain sight while I balanced on a knife edge between getting paid and getting caught. But today, with Rania dragged into the mess? I just wanted to take her home and spend the day watching lousy game shows while we cuddled on the sofa.

Yeah, cuddled. I wasn't normally the type, but with the right woman...

"I can't eat any more," she whispered, dropping her fork on her plate with a metallic clatter. "Can we just get this over with?"

I pinged a quick message to RJ: *In place?*

When he returned a thumbs up, I nodded. "Let's do it."

I braced my hands on my thighs, fingernails digging into my trousers, but the sting of her palm against my cheek still hurt like hell. Yes, I'd told her not to hold back, but the force of her slap still shocked me.

"You bastard!" she screamed.

The entire dining room fell silent, and light glinted off a thousand jewels as every head turned to stare at us. *So far, so good.*

"Who is she? Who?" Rania yelled.

"Loretta," I said quietly.

"Our *next-door neighbour*?"

I didn't say anything. I didn't need to. Everyone looked horrified enough as it was.

Rania leapt up, hand out. "Give me the car keys."

I got to my feet more slowly. "Why?"

"So I can go and pull her damned hair extensions out."

"Honey, you're not driving anywhere. You had two dry martinis for breakfast."

Gasps all around.

Rania flew at me, arms outstretched, fingers clawing at my pockets. I stumbled backwards into the next table, and I didn't need to look behind me to know I'd just knocked some posh woman's meal into her lap. The rattle of china and her outraged scream told me everything.

Her dining companion, too young and handsome to be her husband, stood and took a step forward.

"Do you realise—"

"Butt out. This is a private argument."

A woman at a nearby table snorted, but before I could glare at her, Rania made me double up with an elbow to the guts. Fuck! I almost brought the little brunch I'd eaten up on the carpet as I staggered sideways. Where did she learn to fight?

As she came in for another go, I managed to snake an arm around her waist, spinning and lifting at the same time so her legs flew out and kicked the tray out of a nearby waiter's hands.

Beautiful. I could have kissed her at that moment.

The maître d' shouted for security, and it was all I could do not to grin. *RJ, time to do your thing.*

Rania wriggled free and flung a bagel at me, followed by a salt shaker and a spoon. I ducked those, then got caught in the nuts by a flying saucer.

Her hesitation as I groaned gave me enough time to grab her again, and I started dragging her towards the door as she informed me and the rest of our dining companions exactly which body parts of mine she'd be chopping off when we got home. And poor Loretta— she'd certainly think twice before she shagged another girl's fiancé again.

The hotel's security guys came sprinting around the corner, all four who were on duty according to the rota RJ had found on their intranet. Now we just needed to keep them busy for a few more minutes.

I let Rania slip out of my grip again, and she did us proud by hurling a sugar bowl in my direction followed by a choice selection of obscenities.

An old lady sitting next to me cackled, pausing her round of applause to pass Rania a plate of toast.

"Try this, dear. I bet he'll think twice about letting it out of his pants next time."

Good grief.

The toast flew in my direction, hitting butter-side down as dictated by Sod's Law, and the security team skidded to a halt beside me.

"What's going on?" the tallest one asked.

"My fiancée's a little upset."

"Ex," Rania shouted. "Ex-fiancée."

One of the men made a grab for her, but she sidestepped neatly and bounced a croissant off his head.

"Sir, I'm going to have to ask both of you to leave the hotel."

I plastered on a smile. "Honey? You heard the man. We have to go home."

"I'm not going anywhere with you, you cheating bastard."

"Is that true?" the security guard asked. "You cheated?"

"It was an accident. If our next-door neighbour hadn't been sunbathing topless..."

Yes, I was a complete arsehole.

Security guy looked about as impressed with me as Rania did. "You'll need to discuss this elsewhere. Our guests want to eat their meals in peace."

"I'm enjoying the show," the old lady piped up, her diamond necklace glinting. "So nice to see a young lady with spirit."

The maître d' crouched beside her. "Lady Fordingham, we really can't encourage this."

"Oh, be quiet, Harold." Then to Rania, "You stick up for yourself, darling."

Rania took a couple of steps back, breathing hard, that thick, dark hair flowing around her shoulders. Was it wrong that I was just a tiny bit turned on? If she could show that much spirit in a fake argument, then I bet she'd be passionate in the bedroom.

A teaspoon to the chest shook me out of my reverie, and Rania quirked one eyebrow as if to say, *Hey! Have you forgotten what we're doing here?*

Time to grovel. "Sweetheart, please... Can we just

talk about this?"

Hands met hips, a pissed-off goddess. "Fine. Talk."

I glanced at our audience and caught movement by the door. RJ. And the grin he flashed before sliding out of sight told me he'd got what we came for. I reached up to scratch my right ear, a signal to Rania to finish this up.

"Let's talk at home, okay? We've bothered these people enough." I turned to Harold. "I'll pay for any damage. Will two hundred cover it?"

The last of my savings. Lloyd Weston had better settle my bill quickly.

Harold opened his mouth, but before he could speak, Lady Fordingham cut in.

"Put any costs on my tab, Harold. This is the most entertaining brunch I've had in years." And to Rania, "Make him grovel, darling."

"I will, don't worry about that."

Still in character, Rania marched off, nose in the air, and I had to tear my eyes away from her arse. In that dress and those heels... I wanted to take her shopping every damn day.

"Thank you," I muttered to the old lady before hurrying off in the footsteps of my wayward fake fiancée.

RJ had already taken off in my car as I opened the door of the Porsche for Rania, itching to smile but playing the apologetic bastard to the end. Only when we'd driven a hundred yards along the road did I allow myself to grin.

"*Darling*, you were perfect." I reached out to squeeze her hand and realised it was shaking. "You okay?"

"Thank goodness that's over," she whispered. "I thought I was going to be sick with everyone staring at me like that. Do you think RJ got the video?"

"I'm more worried about you at the moment. If there had been any other way..."

"I'm fine."

Fine. That damn word again. A small sign pointed out a car park, a rough, gravelled area used by walkers heading for the nearby woods, and I skidded into one of the spaces so I could get a proper look at Rania.

She stared straight ahead.

Oh, hell. I unbuckled both of our seat belts and pulled her into my arms. She went rigid, but she didn't push me away. Good idea or bad idea?

"I'm sorry, Nia." The pet name fell out of my mouth without me even thinking about it. "I'll never put you in that position again. And I won't shag Loretta either."

That at least got me a strangled sob of laughter.

"A man would have to be insane to want anyone but you, and if you'll let me, I'll spend my life proving I'm not that man."

What was I saying? Feelings came pouring out of me uncensored.

"But I might be crazy. You've taken over my mind."

Silence. Too much silence.

"Nia?"

"I'm no good at this people stuff," she mumbled into my shoulder.

"Good thing I like you just as you are, then."

I kissed her hair, and she rewarded me with a quiet sigh. Happy Christmas Eve, Will.

But good things never lasted, and the buzz of RJ's email arriving on my phone made us both sit up.

"Fingers crossed," I said, scrolling down and hitting play on the video attachment.

Helene walked through the doors we'd narrowly avoided being thrown out of, hand in hand with a blond guy. Only one suitcase between them, and he was carrying it, so either she wasn't staying the night or they knew each other well enough to share. From the way she stood on tiptoe to kiss him as they waited to check in, I was betting on the latter.

"I recognise that man," Rania said. "He works for Weston Corp. Aiden? He's in marketing, I think."

"Aiden Rafferty, and he's in sales. I interviewed him on the same day I met you."

Less than three weeks ago, but so much had happened since then, it was an effort to recall the details.

More so because nothing had stuck out about the guy. Sure, he'd bounced one knee under the table as he talked, but most of the people I'd spoken to had been edgy. A couple of the girls had even broken down in tears.

No, neither Aiden's answers nor his demeanour had hinted at more than a business relationship with Helene, but the video didn't lie. Was he a closet sociopath or merely a good actor?

Time to head to work and find out...

CHAPTER 23 - RANIA

"AIDEN'S GONE," WILL said when he arrived to pick me up from Daylesford Hall.

As it was Christmas Eve, Mr. Weston had sent everyone home early, which meant I'd finished cleaning by seven.

"What do you mean, gone? I only saw him yesterday."

He'd been leaving the kitchen on the ground floor. Aiden Rafferty was one of the few people who understood the concept of loading the dishwasher.

"His house is dark, his car's missing from the drive, and the lady next door said he'd asked her to feed his cat for a few days."

"Do you think he's running?"

"I don't know. Lloyd said Aiden's on annual leave until the new year, but he told the girl who sits next to him that he was spending Christmas at home on his own."

"Maybe he took a last-minute trip?" I asked as I climbed into the car. Will had swapped back to his own vehicle now, but the BMW was still a hundred times more luxurious than the bus.

"Maybe." Will didn't sound convinced.

"What else?"

"When I mentioned Aiden's name, Lloyd was more

angry than surprised. Apparently, Aiden had a run-in with Anthony a couple of years back. A proper fist fight. They both accused the other of starting it."

"I'm surprised Aiden kept his job."

"Guess Lloyd understood how tempting it must have been to knock Anthony's front teeth loose. Son or not, the guy's a world-class prick."

Even with the heater on full blast, I still shivered at the memory of Anthony climbing past on the stairs soon after I started work. Although there'd been plenty of space, he'd pressed up against me on more than one occasion. Close enough for me to smell the alcohol on his breath, and close enough for me to feel his arousal. Pervert.

"Even so..."

"Aiden's been their best salesman since he joined. Guess Lloyd couldn't afford to let him go. But my contacts said there was no love lost between the pair of them."

"I guess he wouldn't have been too thrilled to hear that Aiden and Helene were having an affair."

"Especially with Derek lined up as his heir elect."

"So, what do we do now?"

"Enjoy Christmas. Weston Corp's closed until the twenty-seventh, and nobody'll want to answer questions about Aiden while they're opening presents and tucking into turkey."

"What are you doing for Christmas?" He'd mentioned he didn't see his family. "Are you spending it with RJ?"

"RJ gets summoned home every year. Kinda funny —he has to put on a suit and make small talk until his folks keel over from too much sherry."

"So you'll be on your own?"

"It's not that bad. I can get caught up on paperwork. Lloyd Weston wanted this case wrapped up by Christmas, and I'm already behind."

How could I enjoy dinner tomorrow thinking of Will alone at his computer? Especially when our tiny apartment would be full of festive music and too much food because Shannon loved roast potatoes and misjudged the quantities every single time she cooked.

"Why don't you eat with us? Shannon always makes plenty to spare."

Silence.

"I mean, you don't have to come for the whole day if you don't want to. Or we could parcel you up dinner. Does the pizza place even deliver on Christmas Day?"

He paused at a traffic light and turned to face me. Was it my imagination or were his eyes glistening?

"I'd love to spend Christmas Day with you and Shannon. And Aisling. The paperwork can wait until Boxing Day. Uh, I haven't bought any gifts."

"Doesn't matter. We don't go all-out for presents." I shrugged. "Money." Or rather, the lack of it.

Just Will's company would be enough.

***

Dinner with Will and Shannon was beginning to feel like the new normal. Shannon obviously thought so too because she'd even bought an extra chair, a giant wooden monstrosity upholstered in orange velour.

"It's only from the charity shop," she said. "But it's better than the fold-up one."

Her bigger seat meant Will needed to move closer

to me, and our knees kept touching under the tiny table as we ate. Once, the contact would have put me off my food, but between the main course and dessert, I found myself shuffling a little nearer.

"Who's ready for afters?" Shannon asked once we'd cleared the crockery away.

"Afters?" Will asked. "We already had pudding."

She put an arm around his shoulders and steered him towards the sofa. "This is Christmas Eve, and the night is still young. It's time for everybody's favourite movie."

"*Terminator*?"

"*The Sound of Music*, dumbass."

Will glanced towards the door and shuffled a step in that direction. "I've never seen it."

Shannon's jaw dropped. "How can that be? It's a classic."

"Well, I haven't."

She grabbed his arm and tugged him back towards the sofa. "In that case, tonight's your lucky night. And because I'm such a good friend, I'll take the armchair so you can share the couch with Rania."

Only then did Will smile, and I couldn't help returning it. I'd never been a huge fan of that movie either, but watching it with Will? Maybe I'd discover a new-found appreciation.

Or maybe not.

When I woke up, the von Trapp family were walking into Switzerland, and I'd keeled over into Will's lap. Gentle fingers combed through my hair, pausing to brush a few strands out of my face. I stiffened, and Will's hand stilled, but when I forced myself to relax, he ran his thumb over my bottom lip.

"You look so peaceful when you're asleep," he whispered.

For once, he was right. Usually, the nightmares came, but this evening... I'd dreamed of nothing.

"I'm sorry I, uh, fell on you."

"I'm not. But unless you want to end up with a cricked neck by morning, we should probably get you to bed."

Over in the armchair, Shannon hadn't stayed awake either, probably because she knew every word in *The Sound of Music* by heart.

"We should wake Sleeping Beauty too," I said.

"Why ruin the fairy tale?"

Even as the words left Will's lips, hairs on the back of my neck prickled. I'd had the feeling many times before, that light tickle as if a spider were tippy-toeing over my skin. I brushed my hand across, just in case an eight-legged freak had decided to pay me a visit, but instead, I connected with Will's fingers.

"What's up, beautiful? You've gone all tense."

"I'm not sure."

The creepy feeling had come almost every night in Syria, but rarely in England.

"Is it me? Something I've done?"

"No." I sniffed the air. "Can you smell that?"

"What? The incense stuff Shannon lit after dinner?"

The scent of jasmine still lingered, but that wasn't it. I rolled off Will's lap and padded across the room in the comedy socks Shannon bought me for my last birthday—red and blue with the Wonder Woman logo in yellow.

Another inhale, and my throat tightened. I knew that acrid aroma, but it had no business being in our flat. Could I be mistaken?

I made it through the arch into our tiny hallway, and the smell got stronger. A scratching sound came from the front door, and time slowed as my gaze fell to the floor, to the dark puddle spreading out from underneath the welcome mat.

A rattle.

A click.

I leapt back a split second before the petrol ignited, flames tearing across the carpet towards the lounge as the wave of heat washed over me.

"Get out!" I screamed, loud enough to wake Arthur, Helene, and the rest of the dead. "Fire!"

But we couldn't go through the front door, not with the wall of orange rapidly advancing. Will already had a groggy Shannon on her feet, and I shoved both of them backwards into the bedroom she shared with Aisling—it had a window, whereas mine didn't.

"Aisling!"

Shannon snatched up her daughter, who began crying, her wails eclipsing the crackle of fire right outside the door.

"We'll have to go out the window," Will said.

I was already a step ahead of him, stuffing a towel in front of the crack at the bottom of the door and stripping down Shannon's bed. We only had one sheet plus the duvet cover—the other bed linen was in the airing cupboard off the hallway.

Shannon hugged Aisling and backed away. "I can't! We're three storeys up."

I cursed under my breath. "Is now a good time to tell you Shannon's scared of heights?" I asked Will.

He put one arm around her as I tore at the seams of

the duvet, ripping it in half with sheer desperation. Once I'd knotted all three pieces together, the makeshift rope would reach almost to the ground. Pulse racing, I threw the windows open and tied one end of our lifeline around the centre support.

"Shannon, you have to climb down. There's no other way."

She glanced at the door, but even with the towel in the way, wisps of smoke were curling underneath it. Seemed our landlord didn't pay much attention to health and safety—I doubted the ancient carpet or anything else was fire retardant.

"I-I-I can't."

I shoved her towards the window, trying to keep calm as my heart clawed its way up my throat. I'd been here before, with black smoke rolling towards me in a choking cloud, bringing death to all it touched. Back then, the enemy had been shooting too, so at least I had small mercies to be thankful for today.

"Will's right. You'll have to climb."

She froze, arms tightening around her daughter. "What about Aisling?"

Will gave the sheets a tug, testing their strength, then stepped forward. "I'll take her."

The little girl had gone from sobbing to shocked silence, and I had to unpeel her fingers from Shannon's jumper to pass her to Will.

"Hold on tight, sweetie. Can you do that?"

She nodded, her face pressed against Will's chest, and clasped her arms around his neck. I helped to shove him up onto the windowsill.

"Send Shannon down next," he said. "If you go first, she'll never leave."

"I planned to."

Then he was gone, no time to talk further as the smoke grew thicker. The inside of my nose stung, and Shannon began coughing beside me. Will lowered himself down the makeshift rope, hand over hand, muscles bulging. When he reached the end, he still had half a floor to drop, and he fell backwards as he landed in order to cushion Aisling from the frozen ground below. I held my breath, and time stood still as I waited for him to move.

Finally, he rolled sideways and scrambled to his feet.

Thank goodness.

"They made it," Shannon gasped, leaning out the window to get some air.

"Your turn."

"I don't think—"

I grabbed her with strength I hadn't used for years and didn't even know I still had. "Go!" I hauled her up and stuffed her through the window. "Grip the sheets with your hands and feet."

For a second, I thought she wouldn't let go of the windowsill as she gripped the edge, knuckles white. But when the first tendrils of flame showed at the bottom of the bedroom door, she released her grip and lowered herself.

One floor, two floors, three floors. Will caught her at the bottom and Aisling clung to her legs, crying loudly enough for me to hear over the roaring fire.

My turn.

Except a yowl from behind caught my attention, and I turned to see Taffy shoot out from under the bed. He cowered in the corner, quivering.

Aw, hell. I couldn't leave him behind. How could I sleep at night knowing I'd condemned him to burn? I needed a tote, a rucksack, some sort of bag I could stuff him into, but there was nothing, and I worried that if I wrapped him in something small like a cardigan or a T-shirt, he'd fall out. I tried to grab him, but he hissed and lashed out with a paw, leaving claw marks oozing blood on the back of my hand. Shit. He was terrified.

And I only had one option left.

My fingers trembled as I worked at the knot holding the sheets to the window frame, but I finally got it undone. Sweat popped out of every pore, not just from the heat, but from fear, as I threw the shredded bed linen over Taffy and bundled him up as best I could.

"Catch him!" I screamed at Will.

"What the hell are you doing?"

I flung Taffy out the window in his cocoon, and I barely had time to see Will grab him before the bedroom door gave way completely. Oh, hell. Literally. Satan himself would have been quite at home in what was left of our poor flat.

Deep breaths, Rania.

I climbed out the window, gripping the crevice that ran above the frame while I balanced on the tiny ledge. An inch at a time, I shuffled sideways until I could reach out for the window next door. For the first time in my life, I thanked whoever designed the ugly concrete building for making the rooms so tiny. If the window ledges had been farther apart, I'd have been dead.

Another six inches, a foot, a yard. Three more windows, four, five, and I reached the outstretched boughs of the old oak that nobody had bothered to trim in years just as the first sirens sounded in the distance. I tore off a fingernail as I dug into the bark, but I kept hold of the tree limb because my life depended on it. Twigs tore at my hair as I crawled towards the trunk, and I closed my eyes as a branch snapped back and almost blinded me.

Get to the ground. Get to the ground.

I repeated the words over and over, the way I had six years ago on the night I'd come so close to dying in Syria. I'd crossed two continents to get away from violence, but it seemed the Grim Reaper had hitched a ride too.

But I beat that asshole into second place, and the instant my feet touched the dirt, strong arms wrapped around me, holding me up as my knees buckled.

"Shh, it's okay," Will murmured as the first sob tore from my throat.

Okay? How could it be okay?

I stared up at the place I'd once called home, tears pouring down my cheeks as firemen unrolled hoses and set up ladders to tackle the flames now shooting from Shannon's bedroom window.

It hit me like a punch to the stomach.

I'd come to England with nothing, and here I was again.

CHAPTER 24 - WILL

THE ALARM ON my phone went off as the firemen rolled up their hoses. Half past six in the morning, and instead of making myself a coffee and staggering to the shower to jack off over Rania, I was stroking her hair as the crew chief told her and Shannon there was nothing left of their flat. Neither of them even had a pair of shoes, for fuck's sake. At least the other occupants of the building had fared better. Their homes only suffered smoke damage.

A reporter snapped another photo, and I wanted to tear his bloody camera out of his hands and choke him to death with the strap. Damn ghouls. Even in the early hours on Christmas Day, I'd still spotted half a dozen of them. One even asked Rania for an interview, but thankfully Chris Turner wasn't around when I shoved the asshole back against his car.

A policewoman climbed into the ambulance and crouched in front of the girls. At least Aisling had fallen asleep in Shannon's arms, too young to understand everything that had happened tonight.

The WPC's radio crackled, and she silenced it as Rania looked up with glazed eyes.

"Have you got somewhere to stay tonight, love?" The woman glanced out at the sky. "Well, this morning."

"I don't—"

"She's staying with me. All three of them are staying with me."

I'd called RJ a couple of hours ago, and he was on his way back from his family's country pad in rural Somerset. He'd actually sounded relieved to have an excuse to leave.

And Rania didn't say anything, just stared back down at her lap. She was in shock. I tugged the blanket tighter around her shoulders and dropped a kiss on her hair.

"It'll be okay," I whispered. "I'll take care of you. All of you."

Even the bloody cat. Somebody had put it in a kitty carrier, and it hissed and spat every time anyone got within six feet. And it was definitely in my bad books, seeing as it had nearly caused Rania to die. I gave it a dirty look as I left Rania with Shannon and went to find a cop who looked as if they knew what they were doing.

Nobody I recognised was there, but I spotted an inspector talking to a handful of the public at the edge of the cordon.

"Got a few minutes to spare?"

He looked at his watch, out of habit most likely, since he didn't have anyplace else to be.

"Sure."

"Any clue who did this?"

"We'll need to wait for the results of the fire brigade's investigation to prove it was arson."

"Don't bullshit me—I used to be a cop. My...my girlfriend saw petrol coming under the door. Smelled it too."

"Used to be a cop?"

"I'm a private investigator now. Will Lawson."

I held out a hand, and when the inspector didn't crush it or look disgusted, I figured he wasn't buddies with Chris Turner and I'd finally stopped being the subject of idle gossip at the station.

"Interesting," the inspector said. "Any disgruntled clients?"

"One or two. But so far, they've mostly tended to slate me on social media. Cheating spouses, mainly."

"Anything recent?"

"Not for a few months."

"What are you working on at the moment?"

"The murder at Daylesford Hall. Helene Weston."

"Ah, I heard about that one. Any suspects?"

"I've got one lead. How about you?"

"Can't discuss an ongoing investigation. Who's your suspect?"

"Sorry, can't discuss that right now."

I parroted the inspector, which probably didn't endear me, but at seven a.m., I was sick of red tape. I also didn't want to give Aiden's name up, because if the police solved the case before I did, I wouldn't get my closing bonus.

Could Aiden have been involved with the fire? He'd disappeared before his name came up in the investigation, but if he'd been feeling the heat, would he really have hung around to incinerate Rania's flat rather than heading for the nearest non-extradition country? Perhaps Helene could give some insights into his character, but we couldn't talk to her for at least two days, and that was if Rania felt well enough to go back to work.

"You're not giving us much to go on," the inspector

said.

"Sorry," I muttered.

His tone softened. "I understand how difficult this must be. Have you been with your girl for long?"

"No." Was I truly with her now?

"Did anyone know you'd be at the flat tonight?"

"I didn't know myself until this evening. I mean, I've eaten dinner there a few times, but I've never stayed that late."

"Could anybody have followed you there?"

"I didn't notice anyone behind us."

"Us?"

"I picked Rania up from work, then drove her home. She's the cleaner at Daylesford Hall."

In all honesty? I'd let my guard down. Normally, I checked for tails, but lately, I'd been so bloody entranced with Rania that a troupe of monkeys could have followed my car on a carnival float and I probably wouldn't have noticed.

The inspector gave a knowing smile. "Mixing business with pleasure, eh?"

My jaw cracked as I clenched my teeth together. "It happens. I don't follow the same rules as you."

The asshole's gaze lingered on Rania, squashed up beside Shannon. "Can't say I blame you."

Now, I itched to smack that smile off his face. Yeah, I'd gone fucking caveman, okay? My girl almost died tonight. I deserved some damn leeway.

"She's not just a fling."

The cop took a long breath, and I wasn't sure he believed me or not. Neither did I care. My personal life was my own business. He needed to do his damn job and find the sick freak who'd tried to kill four people and a fucking cat last night.

Perhaps it was my black expression, but it seemed he got the message. He took out a notepad and tapped his pen on a blank page.

"So, how about the two women? My sergeant says neither of them have spoken much."

"They're in shock."

"We'll need to interview them both as soon as possible." He sucked his teeth. "Could be a bit awkward over Christmas. We're short-handed as it is. Cutbacks."

"I've only met Shannon a handful of times, but she doesn't seem like the kind of girl to have enemies. Apart from... Yeah, Rania mentioned Shannon had problems with her ex. Some rich asshole."

"Do you have a name?"

"No, but I can get you one tomorrow."

"Any arguments with neighbours? Problems at work?" The inspector grimaced. "Apart from the obvious, I mean."

"Neither of them have mentioned trouble with the neighbours. And work? Shannon does the morning shift in a bread factory, but that's all I know. Rania isn't sociable. She goes to Daylesford Hall, does her job, then goes home again. She's only been in this country for four years, and she doesn't seem to have connected with anyone apart from Shannon."

"And now you."

"And now me."

"Is she a refugee?"

"Does that matter?"

"It might." He paused, chewing the corner of his lip as if he was struggling with a decision. "Look, this doesn't go any further, okay?"

"I know how to keep my mouth shut."

"There've been a number of arson attacks in the area over the past few months. Six in total. We can't be sure of the motive, and we've been keeping this part out of the papers because racial tensions are high enough, but your Rania is the third refugee targeted."

"Who were the other victims?"

"A bunch of suspected prostitutes and a pimp. The pimp was from Eastern Europe, but he was here legally."

"Was?"

"None of the others made it out alive."

"Same MO? Petrol under the door?"

"In the second incident, petrol was poured through the letter box. The first was fireworks, and the others were all Molotov cocktails through the windows. I'm not saying they're definitely connected, but..."

"They could be."

The roar of RJ's Porsche engine made everyone turn their heads, and he looked kind of sheepish as he climbed out. Sheepish and knackered. He hadn't shaved either. I gave him a wave, and he lifted a hand.

"Friend of yours?" the inspector asked.

"Housemate."

"You'll be taking the girls home with you?"

"Yeah. We should probably get going." I patted my pockets—pointless because I already knew my wallet had been incinerated in the flat along with my jacket. At least I'd kept hold of my phone and car keys. "I'll give you my number. Can you keep me updated?"

"I will, and I know how tempting it'll be for you to get involved in this one, but try to let us do our jobs, will you?"

"As long as you find whoever did this."

"We won't let it rest."

"Just get them off the streets. Quickly."

***

The police let RJ through the cordon to help with the girls, and it was a testament to Shannon's mental state that she didn't give him any of the evil glares he claimed he'd been on the receiving end of the other night. Instead, she clutched Aisling against her chest while RJ held the blanket around her shoulders and steered her towards the Porsche. Someone had found her a pair of wellies, bright yellow ones, and they looked far too cheerful against the sombre blacks and greys of the most miserable Christmas Day I'd ever seen. And if you'd met my relatives, you'd understand how significant that statement was.

Rania hadn't been so lucky with footwear, so I picked her up bridal style, her sock-clad feet dangling over my arm.

"Time to go, beautiful."

Nothing.

I shoved the cat carrier into the back of my car, then loaded Rania into the passenger seat, clipping her seat belt on while RJ did the same with Shannon. I wasn't sure anyone had ever ridden in the Porsche's tiny back seat before, seeing as it wasn't designed for people with legs, but it fitted Aisling perfectly.

"See you at home?" I said.

"Yeah. I owe you one."

He'd driven all the way from Somerset in the middle of the night, and *he* owed *me* the favour?

"How so?"

"Aunt Millicent knitted everyone Christmas jumpers, and she was insisting we wear them to dinner."

"Doesn't she do that every year?"

"Her eyesight's going, and she messed up the pattern on mine. I got Santa with a massive fucking erection."

The first laugh I'd had all day, but I covered my mouth so I didn't look like an insensitive prick.

"Hey, dealing with Shannon tomorrow'll seem like a party in comparison."

RJ's eyes flicked towards the car, and his half-smile seemed genuine. Which worried me.

"Looking forward to it."

***

Rania didn't say a word the whole way home, and I didn't know what to say that wouldn't make things worse, so I stayed quiet and held her hand in my lap instead. RJ made it back before us—no surprises there because even making allowances for having Aisling in the car, he still had a heavy right foot—and he'd already parked in front of the garage door by the time we arrived. I pulled in beside him and turned the engine off.

"Wait there. I'll carry you inside," I told Rania.

"I can walk."

Words. At last. "I know you can, Nia, but you're not going to."

She didn't argue or even take her seat belt off, just waited for me to come around and pick her up. Once inside, I kicked the door closed and carried her straight upstairs to my bedroom. We'd sort out sleeping arrangements properly later, but for now, she was going in my bed.

I buried my nose in her hair as I tucked her under the duvet, and my stomach clenched at the smell of smoke.

Shit.

That had been a damn close call, and if I'd lost her...

I pulled the curtains closed then pressed a kiss to her cheek before I could dwell on it. She was here, I was here, and we were all alive. Stuff could be replaced. The only things that mattered, breathed.

Including that fucking cat.

I went to fetch him before he clawed his way out of the carrier. I'd seen what he did to Rania's hands in the flat, and even though the paramedics bandaged them up, I still felt sick thinking of the damage.

"Come on, you asshole," I muttered, hauling the cage out of the car and slamming the door.

What was I supposed to do with him? Leaving him in the tiny box would be cruel, but the house wasn't set up for cats. Didn't they need a litter box or something? After a moment of deliberation, I grabbed a pile of newspaper, spread it out on the floor in the games room, and let him out.

"If you shit on the snooker table, I'm kicking you off the balcony," I told him.

He just stared and hissed some more before slinking off behind RJ's games console.

The man himself was standing in the hallway when I closed the door behind me.

"Rania settled?" he asked.

"Yeah. Think so. Shannon?"

"In my bed with Aisling." He nodded at the duvet and pillow he was holding. "I'll take the sofa tonight. You?"

I hadn't really thought it through. "I'll sleep on the floor in my room."

"That's gonna get old, fast."

"They don't have anywhere else to go."

"I know." He sighed. "I didn't say they couldn't stay. We'll just have to come up with a longer-term solution because my back won't take it otherwise."

"Getting old, mate?"

"Just used to my creature comforts."

So was I. And when I crept into my room, I looked at the floor, then looked at the bed. Rania had either fallen asleep or passed out from exhaustion, her dark hair spread out over my pillow.

I knew how she felt.

And rather than finding a spare blanket and bedding down on the floor, I couldn't resist slipping under the duvet beside her, fully clothed, just so I could stay close.

This woman would be the death of me.

If somebody else didn't get there first.

CHAPTER 25 - RANIA

WHEN I OPENED my eyes, slowly, it took me five seconds to work out I wasn't in my own bed. No, this mattress stretched on for miles, a king size compared to my single, a chocolate-brown duvet rather than my thrift-store floral. Matching furniture—two wardrobes and a chest of drawers in light wood. And a window. A window with a glimmer of moonlight shining through and illuminating the hand splayed across my stomach.

Another five seconds, and I realised who was in bed with me, and by extension, whose bed I must be in. Will's. His musky smell was a dead giveaway, but underneath that was a hint of smoke, and before I could freak out about being wrapped up in a man, the events of last night hit me like a rocket-propelled grenade. A punch to the gut that left me fighting for breath.

"Easy, easy."

Will's whispered words brushed over my ear, a veil of calm. I stopped struggling.

"Nothing happened," he said.

What? No, the acrid aroma clinging to my skin told me the fire was more than a dream.

"Everything happened, Will. Someone burned our home down."

"I meant between us." He lifted the corner of the

duvet. "See? We're both still fully clothed. I know you hate people being close, but I couldn't bear to leave you alone."

Somebody had tried to kill us, and he was worried about sharing a bed? My sludgy brain pondered that for a minute. I suppose after what I'd said to him about hating a man's touch, it was sweet that his first thought should have been for my feelings. But that was Will all over—sweet. And his touch? It felt...comfortable. Like I could get used to waking up with him beside me.

And that thought scared me, not the heaviness of his arm.

I rolled away and sat up, squashing myself against the padded leather headboard, and the movement unleashed a tsunami of questions. Why did someone set fire to our flat? Who? How did I get here? The answers wouldn't come. I drew my legs up to my chest, hugging them close as I sifted through memories.

Will turned on the lamp on his bedside table and rolled over, propping his head up on one elbow.

"I won't ask if you're okay, because that's a dumb question. But what can I do to help?"

I burst into tears.

Will's muttered, "Shit," as he crawled up the bed barely registered, but his arm did as he wrapped it around my shoulders, tentatively, as though he was afraid I'd push him away.

"I don't know what's wrong with me," I whispered.

"What do you mean, what's wrong with you? You escaped from a burning building last night—crying's natural."

"You're not crying. And the last time it happened, I didn't cry."

"Last time? Tell me you haven't been firebombed before."

"In Syria. I climbed out of the building and I didn't shut down like this." Another sob burst out. "I'm sorry."

"Fuck."

One arm turned into two as Will pulled me into his lap and wrapped me up in his strength. And yes, perhaps I should have panicked, but this was Will and I burrowed into his chest as he pressed kisses against my hair.

"You've got nothing to be sorry for, Nia. You didn't start the war."

"But..."

He pressed a finger against my lips. "Shh."

No, I couldn't "shh." I ignored his finger and spoke anyway.

"I don't want to be a burden. It wasn't only me who could have died last night. You and Shannon and Aisling and Taffy..." I sensed his eyes rolling when I mentioned the cat. "Where *is* Taffy?"

"In the games room."

A games room? Bloody hell, Will lived in a whole different world to me.

"Well, they could have died, and it was all my fault."

"How exactly do you work that one out?"

"I overheard the police talking. They said there's an arsonist targeting refugees."

"We don't know that for sure. Hell, I've pissed plenty of people off over the years. Or maybe Shannon upset someone."

I half laughed, half snorted, then cursed because I sounded like a pig in distress. "Shannon's too nice to upset anyone."

"What about her exes? Aisling's father or the asshole before him? And she wasn't too polite to RJ the other night."

"I still don't see it. We've kept out of their way."

"Maybe Taffy shat on something he shouldn't have?"

This time, I laughed properly because that idea was so stupid it was funny.

"That's better," Will said. "A smile."

"I still hate being a burden. I mean, Christmas is ruined for everyone."

Will tilted my chin so I was forced to look at him, and I didn't see anger in his eyes, or sorrow, more of a gleam.

"Ruined? I don't think so. It's Christmas Day, and I've got my girl in my bed. Sure, we're not quite as naked as I'd like, but we've got to start somewhere." He dipped his head closer, an inch from my ear. "Because make no mistake, Nia. You're my girl. I don't care how slow we need to take things, but I'm not letting you go."

A month ago, I'd have been running down the stairs already, but today, the idea of being claimed by Will brought a rush of warmth rather than cold terror. Sure, he could be a persistent asshole at times, but I kind of liked the thought of him being *my* persistent asshole. And from the way my heart thumped against my ribcage, it agreed. There were just a couple of problems.

"Will, I'm not sure..."

"I am."

"You can't ask—"

"I'm not asking. I'm telling you: you're mine. No

other woman makes my heart do this."

He pressed my hand against his chest, and sure enough, it was dancing to the same tune as my own. I reciprocated the gesture, and the dirty git let his fingers stray sideways to my breast.

"Will..."

"Sorry." His lips came closer to my ear, brushing against it. "Okay, I'm not."

"Will, what if the arsonist comes back? What if he finds us here?"

"RJ's got a trickshit security system. If anyone sets foot on the property, it sets off an alarm on his phone." He stopped feeling me up long enough to flex his knuckles. "And I'd quite like it if he did stop by. So would my golf clubs."

Another bubble of laughter escaped. "You play golf? I can't imagine you playing golf."

"Hey, I was posh once. And they're actually RJ's golf clubs. I sold mine on eBay when I got short of cash."

Will nibbled my earlobe, and I stiffened. Not because it felt uncomfortable—far from it, I wanted to relax and enjoy his attention—but because I didn't have the faintest clue what I should do next.

"Will, stop."

He did, in a heartbeat, loosening his grip until his arms fell away completely.

"Sorry, Nia. Too fast, right? You have no idea how much I want you right now."

The duvet had slipped to the side, and Will was wearing a pair of sweatpants that showed everything. Yes, I knew exactly how much he wanted me, and a foreign throb pulsed between my legs as my body began to respond. And it felt...good. No, more than good. Delicious.

"I don't know what I'm doing," I whispered. Obviously, I wasn't a virgin. We'd already had that sickening discussion. But I'd never willingly participated in sex before. "I've never kissed a man properly, and I just used to lie there wishing it was over."

Oh, hell, now the tears were back. My emotions were on a roller coaster today when all I wanted to do was ride the fairground horse.

But rather than run, Will gathered me up again, stroking my hair as he murmured the sweet words that would be my undoing.

"Kissing's like everything else, Nia. It takes practice. And you've got a willing partner right here. I'll put in as much effort as it takes for us to reach the top of the league. We'll win the gold medal. With lips like yours, you'll never be anything but a winner. We'll be the world champions at snogging, you'll see."

My eyes strayed to his crotch again. "And I suppose you've got the equipment for us to win the gold cup at sex too?"

Will's lips quirked into a filthy smirk. "I'm pleased you noticed."

Then before I could think, he rolled me underneath him and lowered his lips to mine. Softly, so softly, the merest touch at first. Our breaths mingled, and I wished I'd brushed my teeth. But Will didn't seem to care. That soft caress became a kiss pressed to each corner of my mouth, then a gentle lick along the seam of my lips. My mouth opened all of its own accord and invited him in, and it turned out that when I gagged my brain and gave in to feelings rather than thoughts, I did know how to kiss. At least, I knew how to kiss Will. And by the time Aisling's wails drifted up the stairs, it was me pulling Will closer rather than the other way around.

But nothing good ever lasted in my life, and he lifted his head as footsteps sounded outside the door.

"Where's Shannon?" I asked.

"RJ put them both in his bed. Without him in it," Will hastened to add. "He values his teeth."

"I should help."

I struggled to get out from under Will, but he held my shoulders down and dipped his head to press one last kiss against my lips.

"No, I'll go mediate. You take a shower. Fresh towels are in the bathroom cupboard, and I'll find you something clean to wear."

"Are you sure?"

"I'm always sure."

Now he got up, offered his hand, and helped me to my feet before pulling open the nearest wardrobe.

"Sweatpants, a T-shirt... Socks are in the top drawer," he muttered. "I don't have any girl underwear."

"I'd be more worried if you did."

That gleam in his eyes came back. "I'd be lying if I said I didn't like the idea of you going commando."

"Go and help RJ."

I closed the door to the en suite, but Will's grin told me he'd caught the smile on my face before I did so. And even when I thought about the hell of the fire last night, that smile wouldn't leave. Because those flames had brought me closer to Will, and if I was his, then that made him mine. My own dirty-talking, boundary-pushing, wandering-handed, ex-posh private investigator.

That man would be the death of me.

If somebody else didn't get there first.

CHAPTER 26 - WILL

"WHAT HAPPENED?"

WHEN I made it to the lounge, Shannon was sitting in the armchair by the window with a crying Aisling in her lap, staring daggers at RJ as he paced the room.

"I only offered to take her shopping," RJ said. "Apparently, that was wrong."

"We don't need your money," Shannon snapped.

"Easy, easy." I held my hands out in what I hoped was a calming gesture. "Look, this has been a tough twenty-four hours for everyone. Shannon, RJ isn't trying to buy you. He's just trying to help."

Her narrowed eyes said she didn't believe me.

"He likes to buy everyone little gifts. I mean, only last week he bought me lingerie and fancy shoes. Isn't that right, honey?"

I batted my eyelashes, and this time Shannon's mouth twitched while RJ gave me an evil glare.

"How about I go shopping with you tomorrow, and RJ can take Rania? Would that be easier?"

I didn't remotely want RJ going shopping with my girl, but neither did I want him to get his nuts ripped off. And Shannon didn't display quite the same antipathy towards me.

Silence.

"Or how about you go with Rania and we'll both

stay at home?"

I could give Rania money. Hey, I still had an overdraft.

Shannon's face crumpled, sending her from stunning to sobbing in two seconds flat. I looked at RJ and he looked at me, hands out, helpless as he gave a panicked shrug.

"Shit," I muttered. "Rania's in the shower."

I crouched in front of Shannon and RJ did the same, but five feet back, out of slapping range.

"Shh, don't get upset. We'll sort everything out."

"You must think I'm such a b-b-bitch."

"It's okay. I'm not your type. I get it," RJ said. "But that doesn't mean we're going to leave you without clothes."

Shannon glanced up from under her eyelashes as RJ stood and took a step towards the door. A long glance. Too long.

And in that moment, I got it too.

RJ was exactly Shannon's type. She just didn't want to admit it.

And now they were stuck in the same house together. A snort of laughter worked its way out of my nose, and I turned it into a cough. I already knew how much Shannon intrigued RJ, but his usual "act smooth and toss cash around" approach wouldn't come close to working with her. He'd have to come up with new tactics, and I bet Shannon wouldn't make it easy for him.

Oh, this promised to be entertaining.

"On second thoughts," I said. "I need to talk a few things over with Rania. Work stuff. We can take care of Aisling while you guys head out tomorrow."

RJ shot me a look that was part thanks, part what-the-fuck-did-you-say-that-for? And when I took Shannon's hand and squeezed it, the look turned into a glare.

"And while you're in town, you can stop off at that homeware place next to the library. RJ was just saying that we need a new set of baking trays."

"I was?"

I rolled my eyes at him.

"Oh, yeah. I was. Baking trays. And those things with the holes for cakes."

Shannon gave one last sniffle and looked up. "You like to cook?"

"I like to eat."

I started to stand, and when I got halfway, I gave Shannon's hand a little tug. Distraction seemed like a good option here. Her emotions had to be all over the place after last night's close call, and while I'd seen her sweet side and her fiery tongue, she didn't have that same core of inner strength that ran through Rania.

Although I hated to think about *why* Rania had that core. Every piece of trouble life threw in her direction had made her both more resilient and more broken at the same time.

I wanted to be the person who put her back together again.

Perhaps that thought should have scared me, but no. The closer I got to her, the more complete I felt myself.

"Why don't we make dinner?" I suggested to Shannon. "None of us have eaten today, and I don't know about you, but I'm starving."

"Do you have turkey?"

"Sorry. There might be something edible in the freezer. We can buy proper food when the shops open tomorrow."

She yielded and let me pull her to her feet, still with Aisling balanced on one hip.

"I'm sure I can put something together."

"We'll help. We'll all help, okay?"

"Okay."

***

Lasagne. We ate lasagne for Christmas dinner. Part of the stash I'd bought last month when the Met Office forecast snow and RJ was panicking that the pizza guy wouldn't be able to reach us.

Shannon used the oven rather than the microwave, dressed the food up with garlic bread and salad, and after we'd managed to eat without RJ and Shannon killing each other, Aisling helped Rania to spoon ice cream into bowls for dessert. Okay, so the kid mostly spooned it over her face and the kitchen counter, but the effort was there.

Speaking of dressing things up, Rania looked unbelievably hot in my clothes. Sure, an oversized sweater and tracksuit bottoms shouldn't have been sexy, but they just were, okay? Call me territorial. I should have given her one of my dress shirts and pretended I didn't have any spare trousers. That smooth, tan skin against crisp white cotton, just begging to be unbuttoned. Shit. I adjusted my cock under the table and focused on the food. Now wasn't the time to be getting a hard-on, not with a child in the room.

And after dessert came the awkward conversation about sleeping arrangements. Although Rania hadn't elbowed me in the balls when she woke up this morning, I didn't want to assume we'd be sharing a bed tonight.

"Tired?" I asked.

She yawned as I closed the dishwasher, and I parked all those filthy thoughts about what I'd like to do with that mouth at the back of my dirty mind.

"Exhausted. I don't know why. We only got up three hours ago."

"The body shuts down after a trauma."

"It never used to. I just got more and more wound up."

"But you were living in a war zone, Rania. You're safe here, and I reckon your body understands that."

A smile flickered at her lips. "Where should I sleep?"

"In my bed?" A guy had to hope.

"It's not fair that you should have to take the sofa in your own house. I'll sleep there."

Well, you win some, you lose some. But I'd never give up. "I meant my bed with me in it."

And no matter what she said, she wasn't going anywhere near the sofa.

I'd seen Rania many things, but until now, flustered wasn't one of them. But a hand came to her lips as she gave an adorable gasp.

"Oh! I didn't know... I hoped, but..."

"Didn't know what?"

"I guess I still don't understand why you're interested in me. Beyond the obvious, of course."

"The obvious?"

"That I can talk to Helene."

Talk to Helene? Good grief. Tell me she didn't think I was using her for work purposes? I took a few steps forward, pinning her against the counter with my hips and preparing to duck if that pissed her off.

"I haven't even thought about Helene for the last twenty-four hours."

She looked down at where we were touching, but she didn't struggle. A good sign?

"But Shannon said you wanted to talk to me about work."

I dipped my head, pressing kisses up her cheek until my lips reached her earlobe. "An excuse to get her and RJ to spend some time together. And so I can spend some time with you."

Rania leaned back an inch, breaking the connection. "Is that a good idea?"

"That I spend the day with you? Absolutely."

"No, Shannon and RJ. She's not his biggest fan."

"Oh, she will be. Trust me. Do you trust me, Rania?"

A million-dollar question, but if there was one thing my asshole of a father taught me, it was go big or go home.

Only my pounding heart broke the painful silence between us. *Thump. Thump. Thump.*

Thump-thump-thump.

A nod. Rania's head barely moved, but it was enough for the balloon of tension that had filled my lungs to burst.

"My bed, then?"

Another nod.

"I won't touch you if you don't want me to. I'll be

the perfect gentleman."

That brought laughter, and I didn't know whether to be happy or insulted. Ah, well. I suppose I *had* earned that reputation.

"I didn't mind you touching me this morning." She burrowed against my chest as she said the words, unable to make eye contact.

Ah, thank fuck. "We'll do whatever you want, Nia. You're the boss."

"You're sweet."

"My cock is in your hands."

"You're also an asshole." Her voice grew sleepier. "My asshole."

CHAPTER 27 - RANIA

YES, I COULD definitely get used to this.

Will said I was the boss, and could I help it if my subconscious decided that the place it wanted to be was curled up against his side with one arm across his stomach? And possibly one leg might have draped over his thigh too. Four nights, and my body knew its place. Was Will awake? I risked a glance upwards and saw him looking back at me. Busted.

Not that I really cared, especially when he pulled me all the way on top of him and gave me a good-morning kiss. A little tongue, a lot of heat, and my body responded in ways I never thought it would. Will chuckled, running his thumbs over traitorous nipples covered only by the thin cotton of the pyjamas I'd bought in town yesterday.

We hadn't got naked with each other yet. Will pushed me every day, but only a gentle nudge each time. On Boxing Day, it was his hand on my bottom. Yesterday, he'd held my hand while we shopped. And today? He swirled his thumbs around the pebbled tips, and a mewl escaped from my lips.

"We need to work on that, Nia. I want you moaning my name."

"Did anyone ever tell you what a big ego you've got, Will Lawson?"

"Nope. But they might have mentioned my big—"

I kissed him before he got the word out. I knew exactly what he'd been going to say, and he wasn't lying. I could feel it hard against my belly. But I wasn't ready for that yet. I knew it, and so did Will. He never pushed me further than I could take. And this time, it was him who broke the kiss.

"Much as I'd love to tease you all day, it's Monday morning and we've got work to do."

Yes, the case. Or cases, now, seeing as we also had the arson at the flat to look into. Will had promised he wouldn't let that drop.

For the last two days, we'd pushed the nightmare of real life away. On Boxing Day, we stayed in the house while RJ and Shannon went into town. Somehow, they managed to buy clothes, food for all of us, and a new cot-bed for Aisling without killing each other, although they were still bickering by the time they got home. And I was happy to see that. With Slick Dick, Shannon had acted meek, compliant, always eager to please. I half suspected Will was right and she did secretly like RJ, but at least she wasn't rolling over and playing the doormat this time. And RJ was still sleeping on the sofa.

Yesterday, it had been my and Will's turn to shop. We didn't buy a lot—neither of us had the money, and until Shannon and I found a new place to live, we didn't need much beyond the basics. Clothes, shoes, and toiletries. I had a secret too. I wanted the insurance company to drag their heels over the flat, because I really, really liked sleeping in Will's bed at night.

Except now I had to get out of it because work was calling.

"What's the plan?"

"I need to speak to the police and find out what's going on with your flat. At least Chris Turner isn't the lead on that case, so I might not feel the urge to punch someone every five minutes."

"And Aiden?"

"Yeah, we need to see if he's home yet. And if you're feeling up to it, head to Daylesford Hall and speak to Helene while you work your shift."

Hurrah. My home was a charred box, somebody wanted me dead, and today I got to go and speak to my favourite ghost. Only Will's hand on my hip stopped me from necking back Night Nurse like water under the desert sun and burrowing back under the duvet.

"Do I have to?" I groaned, already knowing the answer but wishing I could shift to a parallel universe where twenty hours of sleep was the norm and Will's bedroom was the only place that existed.

"We need to solve Helene's murder. It's my only paying case at the moment, and I can't afford to string it out." He brought my hand to his lips and kissed it. "This is the first time in years I've wished I still had my trust fund."

"I'm so sorry I brought all this mess to your door."

"Don't be. I've got you, and as long as we don't starve, we'll be okay."

"I'll need to buy more clothes at some point too."

"Nah, you won't. I quite like the idea of you being naked."

Oh, that dirty git... "Could get kind of chilly while I'm at Daylesford Hall, though."

Will gave me a lopsided grin, as if there wasn't a sex fiend hidden beneath his smooth exterior. "Not only will I let you wear clothes for that, I'll escort you to and from the house of horrors and protect your honour." His smile dropped. "I'm just worried that the two problems are connected."

"You mean the fire and Helene?"

"Or Arthur. We've been poking around into two murders, and Aiden's in the wind. Sure, that visit from your friendly neighbourhood firebug could be a coincidence, but I'm not convinced."

My blood didn't just run cold—spiky ice crystals needled at me from the inside out.

"You really think so?"

"I hope not, but..."

Well, shit. "I'll be more careful. I used to be paranoid, but since I got to England, I've let my guard down."

"Shannon's back to work tomorrow, and RJ's going to take her and pick her up every day. He works flexible hours—one of the perks of owning the company."

"Does she know this?"

"Which part?

"Either of them."

"He hasn't told her yet, so if you hear yelling..."

As if on cue, Shannon's screech of, "No way!" followed by a door slamming made us both chuckle.

Perhaps I should feel bad for her, but no. RJ was a good guy, and if she ever saw past his money, I was pretty sure she'd do more than like him.

***

"Helene, we're not saying Aiden definitely *did* kill you, but the fact is, he's disappeared."

Will tried to be the voice of reason as I put my fingers in my ears and slid my back all the way down the wall until I landed on my bottom. Five minutes of yelling, and we'd got nowhere.

"I take it she's being loud?" Will said.

"I definitely need those earplugs."

The dead might not be able to smell or taste or feel, but there was nothing wrong with their vocal chords. When they passed over, they lost half of their senses but kept every last aspect of their stunning personalities.

And Helene had gone from white-hot angry to sheepish to tearful to peeved in the time it took most people to drink a cup of coffee. Or wine. Make that wine. I wasn't sure whether to nominate her for an Oscar or offer pharmaceutical help.

"Look, Helene, I'm not in the mood for this. Someone tried to kill me on Christmas Eve, I'm now homeless, and there's a possibility that the person who burned my flat down is the same person who murdered you. So if you can't see that we're trying to help you here and give us a little assistance, I'm out."

I glanced over at Will, and now he looked pissed off too. What did I say?

"You're not homeless," he muttered.

Dammit, don't get oversensitive, Will. I laid a hand on his arm in an attempt to placate at least one person.

"I'm more grateful than I can put into words that you're letting me stay with you. I just meant that my flat was gone, and all my belongings too."

Helene gave one more shuddering sniffle. "Did that really happen?" she asked Will. "A fire?"

I blew out a long breath and stared at the ceiling,

the little self-control I had hanging on by a frayed thread.

"I'm not a liar, Helene. And unlike some people, I don't conceal important truths either."

Not the ones I thought people could find out about, anyway.

Her ire toned down a notch, and she clasped her hands in front of her in a gesture that might have been contrite if not for her clenched teeth. People like Helene weren't sorry. They were only sorry that they got called out on their lies or rudeness or stupidity. And right now, she was wondering how to avoid answering Will's questions while at the same time keeping us onside to do her dirty work. I just knew it.

And I'd had enough.

"Ten seconds, Helene." Honestly, this felt like bargaining with a toddler. I'd done the whole countdown thing with Aisling more than once. "Ten seconds, and I'm done. I've got more important things to do with my time than listen to you make excuses for Aiden. Anyone would think you didn't want your killer to get caught."

"How dare you! Of course I want him caught. I want him dead!"

"Ten. Nine. Eight."

"It wasn't Aiden!"

"Seven. Six. Five."

"Fine. Aiden was out scouting for hotels that evening, okay? We needed a new place to meet."

Finally, now we were getting somewhere. I relayed the information to Will.

"Which hotels?" he asked.

"I don't know. He didn't tell me. But it was

someplace farther away than Lanefield Park."

"Why? Did room service burn dinner?"

"We almost got caught. Is that what you wanted to hear?"

I left off the snarky comment when I told Will what she'd said.

"Who by?"

"Marshall Owens, and a woman who wasn't his wife."

"Who?"

"One of the non-executive directors," Will said when I repeated Helene's revelation. "I've only talked to him by phone." Then back to Helene. "Did he see you?"

"I don't think so. Aiden spotted him first, and we hid in the emergency stairwell. Marshall doesn't do stairs, the lazy oaf. He threw a fit last year when he came for a board meeting here and the lift was out of order."

"Did you recognise the woman?"

"No. And neither did Aiden, but we only got a quick glance."

"Can you describe her?"

"Blonde. Thin. Younger than me, if I had to guess. She was carrying a Mulberry Bayswater bag in Oxblood Polished Embossed Croc." Helene shrugged, dismissive. "But I suppose it could have been a fake."

That small gesture told me that Helene wouldn't dream of carrying a knock-off handbag. Good thing she never saw me with the Houis Wuitton clutch Shannon gave me for my birthday last April. One of her colleagues had been selling them, and they were so appallingly awful she'd forked out a fiver so we could both have a good laugh. Now it was ash, and I couldn't get too heartbroken about that.

Will chuckled when I told him what Helene had said, but only for a second. His face quickly grew serious again.

"Did you tell anyone you saw them?"

"Of course not. I'd have been a bit of a hypocrite, wouldn't I? Seeing as Aiden and I were sneaking around too. Although..."

She trailed off, and I bit the inside of my cheek to keep from snapping at her.

"Although what, Helene?"

"Well, maybe... Aiden and I discussed it when we got to our room, and we thought...we thought Marshall might have paid for her company. She had that look about her. Short skirt, kind of trashy."

I started to roll my eyes. Stopped. Then realised Helene couldn't see me and went right ahead.

"Did it not occur to you that if Marshall did see you and realised you saw him, it might have given him the perfect motive for murder?"

"Marshall? No way. He's, like, fifty."

"Good grief, Helene. Fifty's not that old. Believe me, a man that age can still do plenty of damage."

I'd seen that first-hand in Syria. One of the rebel leaders had been closer to sixty, and I saw him hunt down men half his age and kill them with a pocketknife. On one memorable occasion, he'd used his bare hands, choking the man until his eyes bulged so much I thought they'd pop right out. I'd been hiding, so close I could see the dirt ingrained under his fingernails. Three minutes, it took the man to die, and I hadn't breathed that whole time.

"What did she say?" Will asked.

I told him, and his eye roll was accompanied by a muttered, "For fuck's sake."

"Exactly."

Will's hiss of breath was like a gas leak—liable to be explosive. "Next time, Helene, do me a favour, would you? Let us decide what's important."

CHAPTER 28 - RANIA

NOW WE HAD Marshall to question, Aiden to find, Arthur's murder to solve, and the small matter of a lunatic with a fetish for matches on the loose. I was definitely getting used to waking up next to Will, but this morning, I'd only got one quick kiss before he stumbled out of bed and into the shower.

"Are you sure you don't need me?" I called after him. "I don't mind getting up to help."

A muffled *thunk* followed by cursing made me jackknife up off the bed. I'd got one foot out into the early-morning chill when Will poked his head around the door.

"Stubbed my fucking toe."

"Shall I get some ice?"

"Nah." His eyes dropped to the tent in his boxers. "I've got to take a cold shower anyway. And no, you stay here and rest."

He didn't mean to make me feel inadequate, and even if I had been able to stomach the *more* my body wanted but my head didn't, we wouldn't have had time, but still... I felt like half a woman. A child whose innocence had been stolen by circumstances. By bombs and bullets and mortars and *men*.

I burrowed back under the covers as the water shooshed out, doing my best not to think about the fledgling relationship I desperately didn't want to screw up. Despite the circumstances, Will had shovelled a thin layer of hope into the empty chasm of my chest, and I craved being whole again. Or at least, something more than nothing.

Will showered fast, in and out in less than two minutes, and I peeked from under the duvet as he dropped his towel to pull on a pair of boxer shorts. I only caught the rear view, but that was enough to make my mouth go dry in a good way. Could he hear my heart racing?

I watched him surreptitiously until he perched on the edge of the bed and pulled the duvet back. Please, say my cheeks hadn't gone too red.

"Wish I could stay with you all day, but the guy I need to speak to walks his dog at six every morning.

"Who is he?"

"A cop. I've still got a few friends on the force. Albie's two years off retirement, coasting along, but he keeps his ear to the ground and if Marshall's been doing business with ladies of the night, Albie would know about it."

"Be careful."

"Always am." He leaned forward to brush his lips against mine. "I'll be back in time to take you to work."

Another opportunity to converse with Helene. "I can hardly wait."

***

Shannon arrived home grumpy after her shift, her pretty face marred by a scowl as she stomped into the living room where I was watching cartoons with

Aisling.

"What's wrong?" Aside from the obvious problem with the flat. "Did something happen at work?"

"No, after work. I told RJ I'd catch the bus home, but when I got out of work, there was a car waiting for me. Not even a cab. Some fancy Mercedes with blacked-out windows."

"To drive you home? RJ sent it?"

"Apparently. And when I told the man behind the wheel I was taking the bus anyway, he followed me all the way from the factory."

"Why didn't you just take the ride?"

"Because I'm not for sale. Not anymore."

"Maybe RJ was just trying to be nice?"

Shannon folded her arms and dropped onto the sofa. "Nice would have been lending me the money for the bus fare until my new debit card arrives."

"I'm only surprised he didn't pick you up himself."

"He wanted to," she mumbled. "But he had an important meeting, and I wouldn't let him cancel it."

Oh, Shannon. I could tell by that wistful note in her voice that she'd wanted him to come, even if she pretended she didn't.

"If he didn't have money, would you be so cross with him?"

Folded arms turned into hugging herself. "If he didn't have money, he wouldn't have been able to do something so stupidly outrageous, would he?"

"But what if he'd spent his last twenty pounds on a taxi and had it waiting outside?"

Her mouth twisted as she considered my question, and her expression said she didn't like the answer.

"Well, I guess that would have been sweet."

I tried not to sigh, really I did, but sometimes, Shannon was impossible. "So because RJ, who seems like a genuinely nice guy, decided to ensure your safety in a way he could afford, you're pissed off at him?"

"Well, I guess when you put it that way..."

"Just let him help you, Shannon."

She sprang to her feet, and I recognised that look. She didn't want to talk anymore because she knew I was right.

"I need to make dinner."

"But it's two in the afternoon."

"I'm making pizza from scratch. The base, the sauce... It'll take ages."

"Pizza? Because RJ likes it?"

"Shut up."

***

Will dropped me off at work, but a late meeting with a contact who was practically nocturnal meant he left me to deal with Helene and Arthur alone while he dug for more information on Aiden and Marshall. He'd confessed that RJ was spying on Aiden's emails and his credit card too, but so far, there'd been no activity. And according to Lloyd Weston's secretary, Marshall was technologically inept. Every letter had to be couriered because he refused to use the secure network like everybody else.

"I'll be back at nine," Will said. "Earlier if I can get away. I don't like leaving you here alone."

"I'll be okay."

We'd been through the building together, and the only person left was a salesman pacing as he muttered on the phone. According to Will, the guy was married and had a solid alibi for Helene's murder.

"Any problems, call me. I won't be far away."

While I'd never loved my job, before Helene's death, I'd felt secure in the solitude that came with being alone in Daylesford Hall after everybody else left for the day. Not so tonight. After the salesman called out a goodbye and slammed the door behind him, every creak and groan of the building grated on my already frayed nerves.

It was strange—my years in Syria had numbed me to shootings and bombings and screams in the night, or perhaps I'd just been resigned to the fact I was going to die. But in England, the passage of time had let me feel again. A ringing phone made me twitch, the whooshing sound of the dishwasher was far from soothing, and when I caught the vacuum cleaner's power cable around a coat rack and pulled the whole thing over, my heart pounded so hard I thought I was having a coronary.

"Stop being so stupid, Rania," I chided myself.

"Now what have you done?" Helene asked.

She'd been mercifully quiet so far this evening. Sulking again, most likely.

"I haven't *done* anything. It's just not much fun being here on my own at night."

"But you're not on your own. I'm here."

"If whoever killed you comes back, you're not going to be much help."

"Do you really think... Did you hear that?"

Yes, I did. I froze at the sound of a door opening on the ground floor, then quiet footsteps padding across the industrial carpet in the reception area.

"Are you expecting a visitor?" Helene asked.

I shook my head, then realised it was a pointless gesture.

"No," I whispered.

"Then who is it?"

If I knew that, my heart wouldn't be threatening to claw its way out of my chest, would it? I reached into my pocket out of habit, but my trusty knife had burned up in the fire. I had nothing.

Well, nothing but my phone. Could it be Will downstairs? Had Lloyd Weston given him a key card?

I backed away from Helene, all the way to the cleaning cupboard. My strange little sanctuary. Cursing under my breath as my fingers shook, I pulled out my phone and dialled Will.

"Are you downstairs?" I whispered the second he answered.

"At Daylesford Hall? No."

"Shit."

"Why? Is somebody else there?"

"I heard a door. Footsteps."

Background noises blurred as Will hurried through wherever he was. "On my way. Stay hidden, okay?"

"Okay."

That was what I said, but I'd lied. Because my mind fought my insecurities, and a little of the old Rania came back. I didn't cower. I calculated and took the best course of action. Tonight, the last thing I wanted to do was hide and become a sitting duck.

I grabbed a can of spray polish off the shelf next to me. Not a great weapon, but I could use it to blind a man and it was better than a duster. Blood rushed in my ears as I clicked the door open and peered out, listening for the slightest sound.

Nothing. Well, nothing but Helene.

"Rania? Who's there?"

"Shut up," I hissed.

Every limb hummed with tension as I scuttled along the corridor, always ready to duck into a doorway for cover. Which stairs should I take? The middle set was closer, but the staircase at the back of the building lay beside an exit.

Shit! Footsteps were approaching. I ran into the nearest office, then pushed the door almost closed and peered through the crack.

Closer... Closer...

Anthony came into view, wearing jeans and a leather jacket rather than his usual scruffy suit. Light glinted off something in his hands, and I leaned forward for a closer look. Wine? He'd come back to the office late in the evening to drink?

Or rather, drink more. He stumbled against the door I was hiding behind, sending me backwards across the room as I struggled to stay upright.

"Whaaaat the...?" Anthony slurred. He struggled to focus, eyes rolling like errant roulette wheels. "The hell are you doin' here?"

"My job," I snapped. Now I knew who it was, my fear turned to anger. "What are *you* doing here?"

He didn't answer, just slumped to the floor, leaning against the wall with the bottle wedged between his legs.

"Do you want me to call your father?"

"Fuck you. Call my father? 'You're a drunk, Anti... Anthy... Anthony,'" he mimicked. "'You're not welcome in my house until you're sober.' That hypo...

hypotipicral bastard."

Anthony heaved the bottle up and hurled it at the wall. Shards of glass flew everywhere, and a red stain splashed across the white paintwork.

"He never liked me. Always Helene. Little bitch could do no fucking wrong."

I backed away, not wanting to make him any angrier. "Fine. Just sit there, then."

His head lolled to the side, farther, farther, until he keeled over entirely. A soft snore rumbled from his lips, and two seconds later, someone hammered on the door downstairs.

Will! Oh, hell. I'd overreacted, and he must have driven like a maniac to get here so quickly. I sprinted down the stairs, and he was rattling the door as I ran to open it.

"Sorry. I'm so sorry. It was just Anthony."

"Anthony? What's he doing here at this time of night? Not work, surely?"

I stepped back so Will could get past, and my skin tingled from the waves of worry radiating off him.

"No, he's drunk." I peered past into the car park. No cars apart from Will's BMW. "I don't even know how he got here."

"Where is he?"

I led Will up to the meeting room where Anthony was curled up in the foetal position, drool running from one corner of his mouth. Charming.

"What's with the wine?" Will asked, nodding at the mess.

"Anthony threw the bottle. He was kind of angry."

"Angry?"

"Something about his parents hating his drinking.

Helene too."

"He was angry at Helene?"

I saw where he was going with this. "Will, he couldn't have drugged then stabbed Helene in that state. He'd probably have stuck the needle in himself instead."

"Maybe he was in no fit state tonight, but if he was harbouring a grudge..."

"Killing his own sister?"

"It happens. And his alibi wasn't great. He had an argument with his girlfriend at lunch, she stormed out, and he spent the rest of the day watching football apart from a phone conversation with his mother at five."

I glanced over at Anthony's slumbering form again. Some people had all the luck—money, a good job, family—yet they were determined to waste it.

"So what do we do now?"

"Well, we can't leave him here."

***

Forty minutes later, I held the door open as Will helped Lloyd Weston to carry Anthony out to his car.

"I can only apologise for my son scaring you," Lloyd said, grunting under the weight. "He came home drunk, and my wife locked him out of the house, so he must have come here to sleep it off."

"Has this happened before?" Will asked.

"Once or twice, but not for a year or so. Helene's death... It's affecting everybody."

Secretly, I had my doubts that grief was responsible for Anthony's drinking spree, but I kept my mouth shut.

"Perhaps it would help if he talked to somebody?" Will suggested, ever the tactful one.

"I doubt he'd agree to that. Anyway, it's a good thing you happened to forget your jacket."

That was the story we'd both told Lloyd, that Will had left his jacket behind yesterday and he'd stopped by to pick it up because he knew I'd be working late. Neither of us wanted to broadcast our fledgling relationship to our boss.

"Yeah, luck's funny like that."

Back in Will's car, I slumped against the seat. The adrenaline had seeped away, and now I felt exhausted.

"Sorry I messed up your evening."

He reached over to squeeze my hand. "Never be sorry for that. Anthony's a prick."

"Did you get everything done that you needed to?"

"No, but I can talk to the guy tomorrow instead."

I checked my watch—almost nine o'clock. "Unless you could go now?"

"Nah, tomorrow's fine. I hate this damned job. If we didn't need the money, I'd jack it in. Want to run away to a desert island?"

We. He'd said if *we* didn't need the money. Despite the chill in the air, that one word warmed my heart.

"An island sounds good to me."

"It's a date."

CHAPTER 29 - WILL

"YOU'VE GOT TO be kidding."

I'd been on my way out, but the cold squelch as I put my left shoe on stopped me in my tracks.

"What's wrong?" Rania called out from the kitchen.

She'd got up to make Aisling breakfast seeing as Shannon had gone back to work, but Rania should have stayed in bed. Nightmares had left her tossing and turning, and I suspected she'd slept even less than me.

But now I blinked exhaustion away and peered into my leather brogue. The stink made me want to vomit, much as that fucking cat had obviously done earlier.

"Taffy's puked in my shoe."

Footsteps came running, and Rania stooped to look before recoiling in horror.

"I'm so sorry! It must be the new brand of cat food. He's used to eating the cheap stuff, and I guess organic salmon disagrees with him. Uh, I'll buy you a new pair of shoes."

With money she didn't have.

"It's okay. Shit happens." Not that I had the money either.

"Not quite shit. I mean, that would have been worse, wouldn't it?"

We stared at each other for a beat, then doubled up with laughter. Only with Rania could this situation be funny. Her smile made even the worst days bearable. I held the shoe out at arm's length and dipped to kiss her.

"Let's go into town later once Shannon gets back. I need shoes, Taffy needs different food, and you need a Kinder Egg."

As I hoped, that made her smile. The little things always did, and she returned my kiss, softly on the lips.

"Sounds like a plan, Mr. Lawson."

***

Except you know what they say about plans...

We got into town, all right, and we even got the cat food and a pair of decent brogues in a half-price sale. But just a few yards from the car, we passed a pharmacy, and I made a schoolboy error. I asked a simple question with far deeper connotations than I ever imagined.

"Nia, how about we get something to help you sleep?"

She froze. "What do you mean?"

"Night Nurse, or maybe some of that valerian extract?"

Silence.

"You tossed and turned all night."

"Can you unlock the car?"

As I climbed into the driver's seat, I hoped I might have been imagining the stiffness in her tone, but there was no mistaking the tears that rolled down her cheeks.

"What did I say?"

"Doesn't matter."

"Clearly it does."

"Will, I'm never going to stop having nightmares, and I'm sorry if they disturb you. I'll sleep somewhere else."

Oh, Rania. I wanted to give her a hug, but I didn't want to upset her further, so I settled for squeezing her hand instead. Most of the time I felt as if I were walking a tightrope around her, and it was one I never wanted to fall off. As for her idea of sleeping alone? I sucked back the snort that tried to escape.

"I sincerely hope that's tiredness talking and not a serious suggestion."

"I'm sorry, okay?"

"You've got nothing to be sorry for. How many times have I told you that? I just thought an over-the-counter remedy might help. Getting through the day on a couple of hours' sleep can't be easy."

"Nothing helps. *Nothing*. My mother gave me herbs and pills, but they only made the dreams worse, not better, because then I couldn't wake up from them."

"Wait—you got the nightmares before your mum died?"

I thought all the real shit happened to her after that, when she was left to fend for herself in a war zone and travel across Europe. She was saying her problems started as a child? What the hell happened to her back then? The detective in me was dying to know, but the smart man who occasionally made an appearance told me I'd be stupid to ask.

Rania bit her lip and nodded. "Yes, since I was little."

"What are the dreams about?"

Yes, before you ask, I'd put my foot in it once more. Nia turned away, arms folded, and I'd rather have trodden in the cat sick again.

"Death," she whispered.

"Whose death?"

"All the people..." Her voice grew stronger. "Can we just go ho—back to your place?"

"Home," I told her. "It's our home."

***

Rania didn't say a word for the entire journey. The only sound she made was the occasional sniffle, and I vowed never to mention the nightmares again. I'd hold her, I'd comfort her, but I wouldn't talk about them.

What could I do to distract her from her turmoil? We had two hours before she needed to go to work, which had the power to stretch into an eternity if she kept giving me the cold shoulder. A movie? A snooze? Perhaps I could make her a snack?

Except when I opened the front door, the sound of Aisling wailing greeted us. I stuffed my fingers into my ears while Rania dashed into the house.

"What's wrong?" she called.

I expected to hear Shannon, but instead, RJ replied with a note of panic in his voice, rare for him.

"I think she pooped."

Oh, shit. Literally.

I followed Rania into the lounge and found RJ sitting on the sofa with Aisling on his lap, her nose wrinkled as she continued to screech.

"Where's Shannon?" I asked.

"She had to go to the supermarket, so I offered to help with Aisling. I mean, she's two years old. How can it be this difficult?"

Man, RJ had it bad if he'd offer to look after a baby to impress Shannon. I choked out a laugh, then regretted opening my mouth because for such a tiny person, that kid sure could create a stink.

Rania held out her arms. "Give her here."

RJ and I both breathed a sigh of relief, followed by a gulp of fresh air as the two girls headed for the bathroom. I shook my head, trying not to laugh, and RJ glared at me.

"What?"

"You've got your work cut out with those two, mate."

"I'm only trying to be nice."

"Sure. Whatever you say. But since you've been relieved of babysitting duties, could you do me a favour and see if Aiden's materialised anywhere yet?"

***

Time with Aisling mellowed Rania enough that I got a smile as we pulled up outside Daylesford Hall, although that was quickly followed by a yawn. She clapped a hand over her mouth, and I resisted the urge to offer sympathy. No, tonight I'd help Rania to clean, run interference if Helene's bitchy side came out, and get my girl home to bed.

"What shall I do to start? Vacuum? Or empty the dish—?" Dammit. My phone rang with the theme song to *Inspector Gadget*. Rania stumbled out of the car while I answered, and I cursed RJ's timing.

"This had better be good."

"Oh, it is. An hour and a half ago, Aiden's credit card was used at the Odeon in town."

"He's back?" And he'd gone to the fucking cinema?

"Well, I can't say for certain that *he's* back, but his Visa card definitely is. Fifteen quid isn't enough for two tickets, so whoever spent the money's probably alone with only a bucket of popcorn for company."

How long did the movie last? I could get to town in twenty minutes, but would Aiden still be there? I couldn't afford to pass up the opportunity to find out.

"Rania, get back in the car."

"What? No. I have to work."

"RJ's got a lead on Aiden. We need to check it out."

"What sort of lead?" She yawned again.

On second thoughts, if Aiden had killed Helene, did I really want Rania anywhere near him? The chances of him lashing out in public were slim, but desperate men sometimes resorted to desperate measures. "You know what? It's probably a false alarm. I'll check it out and be back in no time."

"Is that safe?"

"I'll be careful."

I expected an argument, but she nodded meekly and walked away instead. Shit. What happened to the smiles I'd got this morning?

Before I left, I made sure Rania got safely through the front door. Daylesford Hall was in darkness, and the red light of the alarm blinked in reception. Everybody else had left for the evening already.

"Lock the door behind you," I told her. "I'll call you to let me in when I get back. Are you sure you don't want to come?"

"I'll be fine. If Anthony turns up, I'll hide and phone you."

"Ring the police too. That asshole deserves to spend

the night in the drunk tank."

CHAPTER 30 - RANIA

I DIDN'T RELISH the idea of spending the evening at Daylesford Hall alone, but after my stupid admission to Will this afternoon, I needed some space to die from embarrassment.

Exhaustion and the agony of carrying my secrets inside had almost led me to confess my secrets. My sins. That I dreamed of the people I'd killed.

Because I hadn't always shied away from my destiny. My training started when I was a little girl, living with a father who saved people and a mother who killed them. Ironic, huh? My father spent his days healing people with good hearts and damaged bodies while my mother dispatched those with damaged souls to free those they left behind.

In the daytime, she'd masqueraded as an artist, filling canvases with such love and light that nobody ever suspected the darkness lurking beneath her flawless skin. But by night, she'd been the Angel of Death– judge, jury, and executioner—and as my curse grew stronger and hers began to fade, she'd passed all her skills and knowledge on to me.

The first man I ever killed was the army captain who shot my father. As a child, I'd been small enough to slip through the tiny window into his room, light enough on my feet to tiptoe across to his bed without waking him, and quick enough to slit his throat before he could struggle. His black soul had floated free from his body and scattered like dust as I watched, and while I'd felt satisfaction, his death didn't bring me any pleasure.

Each person to die by my hand had stained my conscience with more blood, and the day my mother died, from a bullet meant for me, I quit the game I'd never wanted to play in the first place. I hadn't asked to become a member of the Electi, and I didn't want to be in that elite yet deadly club any longer. I'd dispatched her killer then vowed to change my life.

But how could I tell Will that? Bursting into tears before saying, "By the way, honey, I used to be an assassin," was hardly conducive to a happy and lasting relationship, was it?

No, I'd keep my mouth shut, and the next time Will suggested sleeping pills, I'd smile, accept, then flush the damn things down the toilet.

But first, I had to deal with the mass of dirty coffee cups at Daylesford Hall and if I got really lucky, another tantrum from Helene.

"On your own tonight?"

And Arthur. *Don't forget Arthur.* He hovered at the bottom of the stairs, head tilted as usual, eyes gleaming with curiosity.

"Yes, I'm on my own. Will's gone to hunt for Aiden."

"Aiden?"

"The guy we suspect killed Helene."

Either him or Marshall, anyway. Why couldn't Arthur do the honourable thing and just tell us which one? As I watched him closely, puzzlement crossed his face, but only for a split second. Did that mean…?

"Oh, Aiden Rafferty? The salesman who always wears an expensive suit?"

"Uh…" I racked my brains. "Yes."

Whenever I'd seen Aiden, he'd been striding around in French-blue trousers and a crisp white shirt. Not bad if a girl liked the preppy look, but he did nothing for me.

"Well, I suppose I should wish your young man luck."

"Why? Does he need it? Is Aiden dangerous?"

Arthur shrugged, and even though I'd sworn off violence, I wanted to slap him.

"Any man can be dangerous given the right circumstances," he said.

"What about Owens?"

"The director?"

"Yes, him."

"Oh, Marshall's got a temper. I remember the day he drove here in his brand-new Jaguar, racing-green it was, and a delivery driver bumped into it in the car park. Must be fifteen years ago now. Old Marshall gave the man a black eye for his trouble."

Was that a roundabout way of giving me a clue? Arthur hinting that Marshall had a tendency towards violence?

"Can't you just tell me who Helene's killer is and stop all this guesswork?"

"We have a deal. You find out who threw me over the balcony, and I'll give you the answer you're searching for."

Grrr. Bloody men. Why did they have to be so complicated? Will, RJ, Arthur… I didn't understand any of them, and I probably never would. Instead of listening to more of Arthur's complaints, I stomped off towards the cleaning cupboard, my bad mood even worse. Arthur was the most irritating person on the entire planet.

"Has your boyfriend solved the case yet? My father isn't paying him to slack off."

Okay, so Arthur was the second most irritating person on the planet.

"Good evening to you too, Helene."

"You're late. Don't you usually begin work earlier than this? Everyone else went home ages ago. Well, at least half an hour."

"I don't suppose it matters what time I arrive, as long as I remember to empty the rubbish bins."

"Even so—"

"Helene, don't start."

There was only one solution to my current predicament, trapped in a house of horrors with two talkative ghosts. I hurried to the cleaning cupboard and got out the vacuum cleaner.

CHAPTER 31 - WILL

I PUSHED THE accelerator to the floor in the BMW, wishing I'd borrowed RJ's Porsche so I could have shaved two minutes off my journey into town. I hadn't wanted to leave Rania alone at Daylesford Hall, but I couldn't afford to pass up the chance to speak to Aiden. Why had he suddenly reappeared and gone to the cinema? That was hardly the action of a guilty man.

RJ couldn't tell me what film Aiden had gone to see, so I bought a flat white in the coffee shop some enterprising soul had opened in the foyer of the Odeon and found myself a table overlooking the escalator that brought the moviegoers back from the screens. Please, say I hadn't missed the guy.

Ten minutes passed, then twenty, and I was just studying the film listings on my phone to see what was on when I caught sight of Aiden coming towards me from Screen Four, head down and shoulders slumped. He was alone, and he looked thoroughly miserable considering he'd just watched—I quickly checked the schedule—the new James Bond movie.

I fell into step behind him, then accidentally-on-purpose bumped into him as we both went to open the same door.

"Sorry, I— Aiden?"

He gave me that blank look. You know, the one

where you have no idea who a person is, but you desperately don't want to admit that? Then it came to him, and relief washed over his face, quickly followed by the shutters coming down.

"You're that detective."

"Will Lawson. How are things going?"

"Okay," he said, but he sounded far from sure about that.

"Really? I thought you might still be struggling to get over the death of your girlfriend."

He stopped dead in his tracks, exactly as I'd hoped. First, his face paled to a deathly white, then brightened to red, and he glanced around at the thinning crowd in the cinema. No, still too many people. He didn't dare make a scene. So he tried for denial instead.

"I don't know what you're talking about."

"Let me refresh your memory. Wednesday evenings, the Lanefield Park Hotel, Helene, room service, a little—"

"Stop!" Now his eyes glistened as he battled the full spectrum of emotions.

"We need to talk. You've lied to me, you've lied to the police, and I'm betting you're smart enough to understand that's bumped you right to the top of the suspect list."

"I didn't kill Helene!" A couple of people turned to stare, and Aiden lowered his voice. "I loved her."

He tried to push past me, and a woman who reminded me of my high school biology teacher glared as he bumped her arm.

"If you don't talk to me, you'll have to talk to the police, and I doubt they'll be so understanding about your bullshit."

Aiden hesitated.

"And if you tell me the truth, I can help. I want to see Helene's killer caught as much as you do."

He turned back and wiped his face with his sleeve. "Can we talk somewhere else?"

His voice cracked, and I would have felt sorry for him if he hadn't potentially held up the investigation by weeks. After all, he'd lost the girl he cared for, loved even, no matter how underhand their relationship might have been. If I lost Rania, devastated wouldn't even begin to cover it.

"Sure. How about Jeanne's Café?"

Aiden wrinkled his nose in distaste, the asshole. Jeanne's may have been past its best, but back when I'd been a copper, she always welcomed us with open arms and a free cuppa on a cold night. Even now, I still stopped in for a drink or a fry-up to support her, and I knew she'd have a quiet table free at this time of night. Private, but not too private. If Aiden was a killer, I didn't want to invite him back to my place for an intimate tête-à-tête.

"I suppose Jeanne's will do," Aiden said, shrugging.

Too damn right it would.

Five minutes later, we were tucked into a corner after Jeanne had laughed off Aiden's request for an Americano and poured him a strong black coffee from the filter jug.

"Go on." I leaned back in my wobbly chair. "This had better be good."

Aiden picked at the corner of a packet of sugar. At first, I feared he wasn't going to speak, but there was only so long a person could bottle up all the shit inside.

"I started seeing Helene two years ago. Right after

the company Christmas party. We'd both had too much to drink, and when we...when we woke up together, I should have been horrified. But she had this sweet side she kept hidden, and before I knew it, we were sneaking off every moment we could. Except we almost got caught by a friend of Helene's mother, and that was when we started with our evening arrangement."

"How did Derek fit into this? Were you planning to keep screwing after the wedding?"

Aiden cringed then stared into his cup. "Helene didn't love Derek. They got on okay, but she was only marrying him because her father insisted. Derek's father has connections, you see, and Lloyd Weston wanted to use them to expand the company. He threatened to cut Helene out of his will if she didn't help."

Cold, damn cold. "He didn't mention that to me."

Aiden barked out a harsh laugh. "Well, he wouldn't, would he? Lloyd Weston likes everyone to think he's a caring, sharing guy, but he's only out for what he can get. There's no way he'd have let me marry Helene without her having to suffer the consequences."

"What consequences?"

"He'd have fired both of us out of spite, and Helene worked damn hard to build that business. Her good-for-nothing brother would have got the lot, and all the profits would have got pissed up walls."

"So, what was your plan? Long-term, I mean."

"Lloyd wasn't getting any younger, and once Helene got her rightful share of Weston Corp, she was planning to get a divorce."

Arranging the divorce before the wedding? Nice. So far, I'd struggled to see Helene's so-called sweet side.

"And what about Derek? He was just supposed to step aside?"

"I doubt he'd have been that bothered. After all, I saw him and that blonde yoga teacher sneaking out of the disabled toilet at the company's summer barbecue, and he still had his fly undone."

Fucking hell. Was everyone in Weston Corp shagging someone they shouldn't have been? Management's exploits made Martha the receptionist look tame. And worse, if what Aiden said was true and Derek realised Helene and her father were both using him, it gave him a motive for her murder too.

"An interesting tale. But why should I believe it? We've still got the fact that you lied about everything else, and you don't have an alibi for the night of Helene's death."

"Actually, I do. I drove to Nottingham to check out a hotel. I wanted to take Helene somewhere special for her birthday next month."

"You mean to say I've wasted a week trying to track you down, and you could just have eliminated yourself in the first place."

"But I couldn't. When the manager showed me around the Royal Suite, I mentioned Helene's name a time or two, and I couldn't risk that getting back to Weston. Helene may be gone, but I still need my job, and besides, I didn't want to tarnish her memory."

"Give me the details. I'll need to check it out myself."

I pulled out my phone, and Aiden raised an eyebrow. "What, now?"

"No time like the present." I pushed a napkin and pen towards him. "Do me a favour and write everything down. The hotel, the phone number, the name of the person you spoke to."

While Aiden scribbled, I dialled RJ, who sounded thrilled to hear from me at this time of the evening.

"Tell me you're phoning to find out what topping I want on my pizza."

"I don't need to call for that. You have the same every time—pepperoni with mushrooms and peppers."

"So what do you want?"

"Got a minute to check an alibi for me?"

"Only because I want this case to be over just as much as you. Shannon's worried about Rania. But if it takes more than half an hour, I'll have to finish it later, because I've got a conference call with a bunch of Russians to discuss a possible joint venture. These negotiations have been going on for months. Sometimes, I'm tempted to slip them fifty grand through the backchannels and avoid all the bullshit."

"Bribery?"

"Yeah. My competitors still do it, but I always swore Wonderland Enterprises would stay above board. That and I don't fancy going to prison. Go on then, what do you want me to do?"

I read out the details Aiden had given me—the Sherwood Luxe Hotel and Spa—but even as I spoke, my mind was churning. What if we'd been going about this totally wrong? This whole time, we'd been hunting for a thief, but what if the money that went missing from Weston Corp didn't get stolen at all?

"Are you all right?" Aiden asked. "You look kind of spacey."

What if the money had been used as a payoff, and Arthur was murdered so he'd take the truth to the grave?

"How long have you worked at Weston Corp?"

"Thirteen years. I started as a marketing assistant. Why?"

"Twelve years ago, did the company sign any big new contracts?"

"What's that got to do with Helene's death?"

"Maybe nothing. I'm not sure. The contracts?"

Aiden rearranged the ketchup sachets in the basket at the side of the table as he thought, and I wanted to shake the answer out of him.

"We got hired by the Mongolian government around that time, to advise on the construction of a hydropower dam on the Eg River." Aiden shook his head. "I still remember Lloyd Weston making the announcement. Everyone thought he was joking at first, seeing as Weston Corp was the underdog in the tender process."

"How much was the contract worth?"

"Tens of millions. That was the project that turned Weston Corp into a global player."

"Who led the negotiations?"

"Lloyd Weston himself. Back then, he used to work rather than playing golf and taking three-hour lunches every day."

Shit, shit, shit. That had to be the answer! It all fitted. The way Lloyd kept the theft quiet rather than reporting it to the police. His reluctance to discuss the case. And he was a big guy, easily strong enough to have upended Arthur over the balcony. Even now he kept in shape. Which meant... Fuck! Rania was alone at Daylesford Hall.

"I've got to go."

"You've uncovered a clue?"

"Sort of. There was another murder at Daylesford Hall, twelve years ago."

"What murder? I don't remember a murder."

"Arthur Brady."

"The guy who went over the balcony? I thought that was suicide?"

"So did everybody else. But..." Should I trust Aiden? Instinct told me he was being truthful now we'd uncovered his secret, and he spoke of Helene with a fondness I couldn't understand. Not when she'd been so bitchy to Rania. And there was no love lost between him and Weston senior. "I think Lloyd Weston may have helped Arthur to take a nosedive."

"Are you serious?"

"Unfortunately, yes."

Aiden nodded slowly. "I guess I could see that happening. Lloyd may be lazy, but he's got a ruthless streak he tries to hide. When Helene was thirteen, he had one of her teachers fired for— Wait! Where are you going?"

"My girlfriend's on her own at Daylesford Hall."

And I needed to make sure she was safe until this investigation was over. She'd have to take time off work. Call in sick, or just quit. I could borrow money from RJ to tide us over, and...

"I'll come with you."

"I don't need—" On second thoughts, an extra pair of hands could come in useful. "Can you call Lloyd Weston while I drive? I want to know where he is."

I'd parked in a metered bay on the next street, and Aiden jogged behind me as I headed for the car, trying to convince myself that I was overreacting. Rania would be fine. I'd been away from her for less than an hour, and Lloyd Weston was probably relaxing in a high-backed leather armchair, drinking Scotch.

"No answer," Aiden said. "Odd. He always picks up."

Dammit. I ran faster.

CHAPTER 32 - RANIA

BACK IN SYRIA, I'd learned to trust my gut. That instinct had got me out of trouble on more occasions than I could count, and tonight, I chalked up another point to intuition. I felt rather than heard the person behind me rushing forward while I vacuumed.

He grabbed my legs and lifted me effortlessly, and as I flew over the balcony, I saw Arthur's startled face looking up at me from three floors below. But that split second of warning gave me enough time to grab the railing, and rather than falling to my death, I swung myself under the balcony in an arc, landing heavily on the floor below. My ankle buckled on impact, but I gritted my teeth against the pain, and then the adrenaline rush hit. *Run, Rania.* I had to get out of the building. In the dark, I could disappear.

Footsteps thundered down the stairs as I raced for the door at the far end of the corridor, fumbling with my swipe card. My assailant knew his plan had failed, and he wasn't giving up.

"Is something wrong?" Helene asked. "Why are you running?"

The door lock beeped at me, and the light flashed red. Why wouldn't it open? A black-clad figure appeared behind me at the end of the hallway, shadowy and sinister, a man wearing a scarf across his face and a hood that left his eyes in darkness. He advanced slowly, taking his time as if he was enjoying my predicament.

"You can't escape." His voice came as a harsh whisper. "I've revoked your privileges. This new security system's so versatile, don't you think?"

Shit, shit, shit.

Now what?

One of the newly installed panic buttons flashed to my left, and I allowed myself a small flicker of hope as I hit it. Silence. Shouldn't there be an alarm or something?

"I disarmed those too."

Great—a tech-savvy killer. My pulse raced almost out of control as I dashed left into the executive office suite, now shrouded in darkness. For one frozen moment, a millisecond between heartbeats, I thought how strange it was that I should be so scared. I used to face worse on a daily basis, and I'd once been dulled to the fear, but four years of safety had acted like a reset button for my resilience. A decade spent learning to fight and kill had been softened by mornings playing with Aisling and afternoons in front of the TV.

For the first time since I arrived in England, I regretted my transformation, but I didn't have time to lament.

Should I hide? No, he'd find me within minutes, most likely by listening for my pounding heart. I ran past Mr. Weston's office, past Helene's, and into Anthony's in the far corner. *The window. I could go out the window.* I choked back a strangled laugh as I realised I was making a habit of that.

Fumbling for the catch took precious seconds I didn't have, but I finally thumbed it free and gripped the handle. Why wouldn't it open? I tugged harder, but a voice from the doorway interrupted my efforts.

"Having trouble? The decorators painted that one shut years ago, but Anthony didn't care. He likes it stuffy."

The rough voice made me shudder. Why bother disguising it when he planned to kill me? Just an extra precaution? I squinted, but all I could make out was his silhouette backlit by the light from the hallway.

"Why are you doing this?"

"Because your boyfriend just can't stop raking over the past."

The past? So this was Arthur's killer rather than Helene's? Still, I played dumb.

"I don't know what you mean."

"Oh, I believe you do. I tried to refocus his efforts to no avail, then I thought the fire would distract you both from any extraneous activities. But he's dedicated, isn't he? The perfect man to find Helene's murderer if he could only keep his mind on the job. Still, let's see how young Mr. Lawson copes with the death of his girlfriend."

Refocus? Young Mr. Lawson? That meant Arthur's killer was an older man. All these little clues. If only I could stay alive for long enough to pass them on to Will.

"How do you plan on making that happen?"

"I'd hoped to do things the clean way, but I hadn't bargained on you being an acrobat. So, it looks like we'll have to get messy." He shrugged. "Sometimes, these things can't be helped."

Moonlight glinted off the blade in his hand as he switched it to a better position. Oh, hell. I backed away until my ass hit Anthony's desk, and still the Grim Reaper kept coming. Why had I sent Will away? With both of us here, we might have stood a chance.

Tick, tick, tick.

Now we were in a standoff. Who would move first?

The man lunged, and finally, *finally*, the old Rania made a reappearance. Years of my mother's training took over as I did the only thing possible—ducked and grabbed Anthony's vodka bottle, smashed it on the edge of the desk, and rammed the jagged end into my attacker's neck with the full force of my fear and anger behind it.

His howl of anguish suggested I'd hit my target, and warm blood spurted over me as he dropped the knife and clutched at his wound. Acting on instinct once more, I kicked his legs out from underneath him and shoved him to the floor.

"You...you bitch!"

The voice sounded kind of familiar now, but I couldn't quite place it.

"You only got what you deserved."

The metallic tang of blood filled the air, and when I moved my feet, they squelched in the puddle spreading across the floor. Seemed I'd hit an artery. The man's breathing grew laboured, and I knew from experience he didn't have long left.

And neither did Arthur.

I scrambled away from the dying and ran for the dead, almost tripping in my haste to get downstairs. Arthur was already beginning to fade, but his eyes widened as I skidded to a halt in front of him.

"What happened to you?" he asked.

"Did you not see the person throw me over the

damn balcony?"

"Yes, but you didn't go splat. How did you save yourself? Where did all the blood come from?"

"We don't have time for questions. Just know that I've bloody done it. The man who killed you has about thirty seconds left on this earth, and so do you. Which means you owe me a name."

"Who was it? Who was the bastard that killed me?"

"No idea. He was wearing a mask, and I didn't stop to check. Funnily enough, I had another priority."

"But I want to know."

Arthur grew fainter. The stairs behind him showed quite clearly now, but the frustration of dealing with him hadn't lessened at all.

"Arthur, give me the name. You promised!"

His lips pursed into a thin line that blurred as I watched, and I knew the man upstairs only had seconds to live. Was he suffering? I hoped so after what he'd done to Arthur and then tried to do to me.

"I suppose you did keep your end of the bargain, more or less," Arthur conceded.

More or less? I'd fucking freed him.

"Arthur..."

"I don't actually know her name."

Her name? "A woman killed Helene?"

"Blonde, comes every Monday evening with one of those camping mats rolled up under her arm. You know, like they use in tents."

Camping mat... A yoga mat? "Do you mean the yoga teacher?"

"Probably. Always wears tight trousers. Anyhow, after Helene died, she came downstairs covered in blood, even in her hair, and—"

He left.

Arthur disappeared, and I sank to my knees in the spot where he'd rested for the past twelve years, breathing hard. It was over. Arthur was dead, I was alive, and one more black soul had been banished. I should have felt relieved, happy even, but instead I gulped back tears. My life in England was supposed to have been a fresh start, away from blood and death, but war had followed me here to this elegant office building and made me fight again. And I was so, so sick of fighting.

Hammering at the door startled me, and I clutched at my chest as my heart lurched and sputtered.

"Rania! Are you there?"

Will! I used the bannister to pull myself to my feet and staggered towards reception as he yelled again.

"Nia, can you hear me?"

Too late, I remembered my security pass didn't work anymore, and the light beside the front door flashed red. Through the glass, Will's expression turned from fear to relief to horror as he took in the blood dripping down my front.

"Get back," he shouted.

"Why?" I mouthed, but I did as he asked.

Before I could stop him, he'd hurled one of the fancy flower pots that bordered the path through the window, then kicked the last few broken shards out of the frame so he could climb through. And he wasn't alone.

"Aiden?"

Will ran his hands over me, probing for damage, frantic.

"It's not mine," I said. "The blood. It's not mine."

"Whose is it?"

"I don't know, but he tried to kill me and now he's dead. It was the man who killed Arthur."

"Lloyd Weston."

"*What?*"

My hands flew to my mouth, and I stopped them an inch away, bile rising into my throat at the sight of the sticky red stains still covering them.

"I'm ninety percent sure Lloyd Weston killed Arthur. Where is he?"

"In Anthony's office."

Will tucked his arm around my waist without a care about the mess while Aiden took off ahead of us at a jog.

"Why is he here?" I whispered to Will.

"He offered to help. I'm almost certain he didn't kill Helene. RJ's checking his alibi at the moment."

"No, he didn't. That was the yoga teacher. Arthur told me."

Will stopped dead, frozen into a statue. "Geri? Blonde hair, bubbly?"

"Apparently so. Although I've got no idea why. Helene's never mentioned falling out with her, or even knowing her at all."

"Possibly something to do with the fact that Geri was sleeping with Derek."

Holy shit. "Are you sure? How did you find that out?"

"Aiden saw them together."

Why did I get the impression I was missing an awful lot of pieces of this jigsaw? Aiden, Lloyd Weston, Geri... Nobody was who I thought they were.

Will helped me upstairs, and on the landing, my

heels dragged. The last thing I wanted to do was revisit the scene of my desperate battle. But I didn't need to. Aiden popped out of the door to the executive suite before we could get there, face ashen, and I ground to a halt completely.

"You were right," he said to Will. "It *was* Lloyd Weston. The old bastard's finally shuffled off this mortal coil."

Helene's wail almost perforated my eardrums. *Oh, shit.* Aiden looked at me funny as I clapped my hands over my ears and sagged against Will. Now what? With Aiden there, I couldn't even offer words of comfort, and Helene wouldn't stop screaming.

"My father? You killed my father? Was that what you were doing in there?"

I backed away, and my stomach lost the battle with my head as I deposited lunch on the stripy blue carpet. Well, one thing was for sure—I wouldn't be cleaning it up.

I quit.

I bloody quit.

"I'll call the police," Will muttered, gripping me tighter. His glance at Helene's spot said he knew exactly what was happening. "Aiden, can you let them in while I sit Rania down? I think she's going into shock."

"Sure thing, buddy." Aiden backed away, and he didn't look all that comfortable either. "There's a sofa in the meeting room at the top of the stairs."

Once he'd gone, Will gathered me up in his arms. "I'm so sorry I left you here, beautiful. If I'd realised sooner…"

"It's not your fault. None of this is your fault."

Helene's wails turned to sobs, and I stepped forward again. "Helene, I didn't mean to hurt your father. Honestly, I didn't even realise who he was. But he came at me with a knife, and I didn't have any choice but to fight back."

"Why? Why would he try to stab you?"

Will's turn to speak. "Because twelve years ago, he bribed a member of the Mongolian government to get a contract, and he killed a man to hide what he did. Now that his little scheme had begun unravelling, he just kept digging that hole deeper."

Interestingly, she didn't try to deny it. Perhaps she knew what her father was capable of?

"What's Aiden doing here?"

I relayed the question to Will.

"He helped me to put the clues together," he said. "Oh, and we know who killed you too. Did you have any problems with Geri the yoga teacher?"

All I got from Helene was puzzlement. "The yoga teacher? Are you kidding? I stopped taking her classes because I didn't get on with the holistic mumbo jumbo, but Derek said she didn't seem bothered when I stopped turning up. You're serious? That perky little bitch gouged my eyes out?"

"It looks that way."

For a moment, Helene could only sputter. "That... That... What was it? Envy?"

I nodded because I trusted Will's judgement. If he said Geri and Derek had been having an affair, then it was true, no matter what Helene thought. Geri had been jealous over Derek, and no doubt envious of Helene's appearance too.

"We think so."

Helene's face crumpled, and she'd have cried if she'd been able to. "I can't believe this. A month ago, I had a good job, and my family, and Aiden, and now I've got nothing. I'm nothing. And I'm stuck here, aren't I? Stuck here for good."

"I'm sorry."

She turned her back on me, and her shoulders shook as she sniffled. "Just leave me alone."

CHAPTER 33 - WILL

BACK WHEN I was a copper, the brass had always been on our backs about response times. Well, they'd have been proud tonight. Only three minutes and twenty seconds between me calling 999 and the first police car screaming into the car park. Chris Turner took another half hour to arrive, and when he did make an appearance, I made a point of looking at his non-regulation slippers before meeting his eyes.

"Get dressed in a hurry, did we?"

He glanced down and went scarlet. "Why are you here, Lawson?"

"Picking up my girlfriend."

It took him three seconds to put that together. "The cleaner? I knew you were screwing her."

No, Lawson. Punching a police officer is a one-way ticket to jail. Especially if that officer was a prick like Turner.

"At least I'm not sleeping alone. How's the hand? Got RSI yet?"

For one delightful second, I thought Turner would take a swing at me instead, but then he caught himself and backed off.

"If I do, it'll be from writing the report that gets your woman locked up. Heard she killed a man tonight. Let's see how much trouble she's in, shall we?"

"Don't you dare take your problems with me out on her."

"Oh, I'll do things by the book. Always do. It's you who's got the problem with sticking to the rules."

The worst of it was, I could only watch as Rania got bundled into the back of a police car, still covered in Lloyd Weston's blood. I was a witness, to be questioned separately while she got interrogated. Same with Aiden. He sidled up next to me followed by a female constable. Young. Perhaps she hadn't heard about my reputation yet?

"They want us to go in for questioning," Aiden said.

"Give me a moment."

The WPC gave it a try. "Sir? I need you to come with us now."

"Am I under arrest?"

"No."

"Then you can wait for ten minutes."

I knew a lady in the legal aid office—no, not like that, Deborah was old enough to be my mother—and I wanted to find out who the duty solicitor was. Before the police arrived, I'd told Rania not to say anything until she'd got legal advice, but the quality of that advice varied hugely depending on the rota. A quick chat with Deb would tell me whether a big problem was about to get even bigger.

"Please, sir," the constable said. "Detective Turner wants me to bring you straight away."

"You do everything Turner says?"

"Not if I can help it," she muttered.

I flashed her a grin. "It won't hurt him to wait. In fact, he'll be grateful since he'll have more time to fill all his forms in."

She returned my smile. "You know him well, then?"

"Too well."

"I'll tell him we got stuck in traffic."

She'd go far, that one. Constable Joanne O'Dowd, according to her badge. I filed the name away for future reference and pulled out my phone, but RJ got in first and it buzzed in my hand.

"Where are you? Shannon's worried that Rania's not back yet. I tried to tell her you'd only have stopped off for a quickie, but she insisted I call."

"Tell me I'm not on speaker."

"No—hold on." A door slammed. "Okay, what's up?"

Deep breaths. "Rania just killed her boss. Self-defence, but she's been arrested and I need to get to the police station."

RJ sucked in a breath. "Fuck."

"Yeah, that pretty much sums this evening up. Don't tell Shannon, whatever you do."

"She's gonna ask questions. What am I supposed to say?"

"Use your imagination. Just distract her, okay? I need to call in a favour and get Rania a decent solicitor from legal aid."

"Forget that. I'll call mine."

"RJ, we can't afford—"

"Look, if I leave Rania with some schmuck from legal aid and Shannon finds out, she'll cut my knackers off."

I had to laugh. "You really like Shannon, huh?"

"She spends most of her time bitching, and she drives me crazy, but all I want to do is tear her clothes off. Reckon I need counselling."

The policewoman huffed from behind me, and with RJ adding his high-priced lawyer into the mix, there was nothing keeping me from going with her.

"Gotta go. I'll update you when I can. And thanks, mate."

"You owe me a beer."

***

The sky had turned from pitch black to a dusky grey by the time we got Rania out of the police station. Several cops with actual brains turned up, and despite Chris Turner's mutterings about forms and procedures, they'd soon realised that Rania was the victim in all this and let her out on bail. The assholes hadn't even allowed her to take a shower, just confiscated her clothes and given her the same baggy outfit they dished out to prisoners who deserved to be there. She still had bloodstains on her face, for fuck's sake.

"What happens now?" she asked, paler than I'd ever seen her.

"Now I take you home."

While Rania spent hours being questioned, Aiden and I had given our statements then been sent to wait in reception. Despite him being involved with Helene, I couldn't dislike the guy. He'd been caught up in a difficult situation too, even if he did have dubious taste in women. In the end, I'd dropped him back at his car in the town centre so at least one of us could get some sleep, then I'd spent another hour snoozing at the police station while the desk sergeant gave me dirty looks.

"I'm sorry," Rania whispered. She'd barely said a

word after our initial conversation at Daylesford Hall, and I was in two minds whether to take her to the hospital instead because I feared she might be in shock. But the idea of a stranger poking and prodding her made me start the engine and turn the car towards RJ's place instead.

"Never apologise for something that wasn't your fault."

"I didn't want to kill him. Just stop him from hurting me."

"He came at you with a knife, beautiful, and he was too arrogant to realise you might fight back. Lloyd Weston deserved everything he got."

"What about Helene?"

"What *about* Helene?"

"She was so upset."

"Nia, she's dead. There's not much you can do to help her."

I reached out and squeezed Rania's hand, keeping hold of it so it rested on my thigh. I'd have kissed her palm if not for the pink tinge that still lingered on her skin. Nausea churned in my guts just thinking about how close she'd come to being hurt tonight at the hands of a madman. Or worse.

I drove, and she fell silent, looking out the window as the BMW took us farther away from the horrors of the evening. Yes, we'd have to talk more about this, but tonight—or rather, this morning—wasn't the time. We needed a shower then bed, and tomorrow, I'd do everything I could to help Rania start healing.

The light was on in the lounge as I carried Rania up the garden path, and I wondered how late RJ had stayed awake. Fingers crossed he'd managed to keep

Shannon calm. When Rania got upset, she went quiet, but I had a feeling Shannon would be the opposite.

I kept my arm around Rania as I lowered her to her feet so I could get the door open. Part of me wanted to carry her over the threshold, but that could wait for our wedding night.

Our *what*?

Lawson, have you lost your damn mind?

Probably, but if I had to lose it for anybody, Rania was the one.

"Let's get you upstairs," I whispered, happy when I got a nod of agreement.

First, I pushed the lounge door open to turn off the light, which with hindsight was a mistake.

"What the...?"

Clothes lay strewn across the floor, some RJ's, some Shannon's. The two of them were on the sofa, Shannon's fiery hair draped across RJ's naked chest as they both slept. At least he'd covered most of her with a blanket.

Rania's eyes went wide as I put a finger to my lips and backed out of the room.

"Forget we saw that," I muttered.

Would this little stunt result in a happily ever after or RJ losing his wedding tackle? Only time would tell, but I had other priorities at the moment. I picked Rania up again, only letting her go when we got to the shower. Now what? She could barely keep her eyes open, let alone undress herself, but I wasn't letting her go to sleep covered in Weston's blood. She'd hate herself when she woke up.

"Nia, I need to undress you, okay? I promise I won't try anything. I just want to get you clean."

Another nod, and she stood quietly while I threw her clothes into a pile in the corner of the bathroom. Those could go in the bin tomorrow. When the water was hot, I lifted her underneath and climbed in with her, still wearing my boxers. It felt weird washing her, touching her without any ulterior motive, but there was nothing sexy about this shower. The water ran pink, then bubbly, then finally clear as I rinsed the filth of yesterday evening off us.

"Time for bed, beautiful."

I dressed her in one of my old T-shirts and tucked her under the duvet with me. My last thought as I fell asleep?

Fuck, I love this woman.

CHAPTER 34 - RANIA

THE VICIOUS EDGE of the bottle sliced into the Reaper's neck like the teeth of a shark, his skin resisting before it gave way and the glass embedded itself in the carotid artery. Warm blood gushed over my skin, and I twisted to get away. But I couldn't move. Could. Not. Move.

"Shh. It's okay."

I slowly joined the land of the living and realised it wasn't blood covering me but sweat, and I was stuck because Will had his arm wrapped around me, snaking under the shirt I was wearing so it cupped my breast. I stiffened as his thumb brushed across my skin, but while my head told me to run, to get away from this violation, my body relaxed against him while he caressed my nipple. A nipple that hardened under his touch because it knew what it wanted, even if my mind didn't.

"Tell me what happened last night was just a nightmare," I said.

"Don't talk about it. Today, you're going to rest and I'm going to spoil you."

Will shifted his hand to my stomach, holding me tighter as he pressed a soft kiss into the crook of my neck. I wriggled a little, kidding myself I was trying to get comfortable when really I just wanted to be closer to him.

Hang on. Why wasn't I wearing knickers?

More memories came back. The ride home, the shower, Will tucking me into bed and holding me all night long. RJ and Shannon, naked on the sofa downstairs. Shit!

"Did RJ and Shannon...?"

"Sure looked that way. But I haven't heard him scream yet, so I've got to assume she didn't relieve him of his balls when she woke up."

And speaking of balls, I could feel Will's resting against my ass, along with his cock. He didn't move, didn't press into me. They were just there.

Will was just there.

He'd been nothing but kind to me, and I knew at that moment that I'd never want any other man the way I wanted him. Sure, he took liberties—the thumb stroking the underside of my breast was proof of that— but he'd never intentionally hurt me or push me too far.

But I owed it to him to push myself if we were going to have a future together.

"Will?"

"Yes, beautiful?"

I took a deep breath, half-tempted to keep the words inside. "Will you sleep with me?"

"I am sleeping with you, sweetheart. There's nowhere else I'd rather be."

"No, I mean will you *sleep* with me?"

His turn to stiffen, and I didn't mean his cock.

"Nia, you've been through a lot in the past twenty-four hours. Why don't you just rest today?"

He was turning me down?

"Are you seriously trying to talk me out of sex?"

"Reckon I've gone crazy, but yeah. You don't need any more stress right now."

"But what if I want to?" Now I'd had the idea, I was determined to go through with it. "You know, like ripping the Band-Aid off."

"Ouch. You're really expecting it to be that bad?"

"Well...yes."

Sex had never been good before. At best uncomfortable, at worst agonisingly painful. But I knew Will would want it, so getting the first time over with seemed like the best idea.

"Thanks."

Shit. "That's not what I meant." Dammit. *Think before you speak, Rania.* "Please? Can't we at least try?"

Will twisted me around to face him, and I resisted the urge to look away.

"Tell you what. We'll fool around, and if you're enjoying it, I'll make love to you. Deal?"

Bargaining over sex? Well, at least we weren't arguing over the price as I had in a previous life. "Deal."

I thought Will would go straight for the good bits, but instead, he feathered soft kisses across my lips and down my jawline. With each sweet touch, the darkness that had plagued my dreams grew a little lighter.

He lay beside me, using the lightest strokes to keep me prisoner rather than his body weight. A giggle escaped as he ran his fingers down my side.

"That tickles."

He grinned and did it again, but I could only laugh. Then he shifted so his tongue followed his fingers, lower, lower, lower... Oh!

"Will, you can't!"

"Do you want me to stop?"

I wasn't sure. Did I? He blew warm air over my most sensitive spot as I considered my options. Finally, I shook my head.

"Don't stop."

So he didn't. He licked and sucked and kissed and caressed as...as...all that was right with the world gathered in my stomach then exploded outwards like an overstuffed firework, leaving me gasping as I clutched at his hair.

"What happened?"

He looked up, smug. "You've never had an orgasm before?"

"Not if that's what that was."

"Shit, Nia. I'm gonna make you come every night if you smile like that."

Will crawled up the bed and kissed me, and the taste of myself on him didn't gross me out the way I thought it would. Probably because I was still floating on a cloud somewhere near the ceiling. It was only when Will guided my hand downwards and wrapped my fingers around his cock that I drifted back to earth.

With one hand, he smoothed my hair away from my face.

"That's what you do to me, Nia. But if you don't want to go any further today, we won't."

"I do."

"Sure?"

I nodded, even though I wasn't. Nothing could be as bad as the sex I'd had before. Sweaty, flabby bodies that pounded into me for a few euros. This was Will. I loved him.

Wait. I *loved* him?

Yes, I did.

"Yes, I'm sure."

He rolled on a condom, and from the moment he pushed inside me, I knew it would be different. He slid in smoothly, easily, as if he was meant to be there, not like the previous intrusions which had always felt forced. Then he waited until I smiled before he moved again.

My eyes were opened that day, to love and happiness and new possibilities. Will wrapped me tightly in his arms as he came, and it was only when he wiped my tears afterwards that I realised I'd been crying.

"Are you okay? Fuck, tell me you're okay?"

"These are good tears."

He buried his face in my hair and muttered something I didn't quite catch.

"What was that?"

"Maybe I'll make you cry every day too."

I drifted off in Will's embrace, and for once, I didn't dream. Not a snippet. Nothing but smooth, delicious darkness.

Oh, Mr. Lawson, you certainly know how to turn a girl's life upside down.

***

And...back to reality. This afternoon's shower with Will hadn't been nearly so innocent, but now his phone had forty-seven missed calls, the police wanted to ask me yet more questions, and there was still the small matter of Helene's killer walking around free. Plus Shannon. What had happened last night between her and RJ?

The man himself was in the kitchen when we went downstairs for a very late breakfast, engaged in a standoff with Aisling, who absolutely didn't want to eat whatever he was offering her on a fork. Every time he moved it close, she clamped her lips together and turned her head away.

"Is there a secret to this?" he asked.

"Yup. You need to use a pink fork. Aisling thinks she's a princess."

A look of alarm crossed RJ's face. "Pink? We don't have pink cutlery." His head swivelled between Will and me, and he broke into a smile. "Holy shit. About time."

"Huh?"

"You forget how long I've known your boy. That self-satisfied expression means he got action last night."

My cheeks heated, but Will only laughed. "At least we got as far as the bedroom."

Now RJ turned red. "Shit."

"Look on the bright side—you survived the experience."

"Barely. And if she'd chopped my knackers off, it would have been your fault."

"How do you work that one out?"

"You told me to distract her."

"I meant make her a cup of tea or something."

"Well, I panicked."

"And? What did you do?"

"Kissed her."

Will doubled over laughing. "Brave."

"Then she slapped me. Then kissed me back. And I'm not telling you the rest."

"Don't worry, I don't want to know. She's at work?"

"I'm picking her up in half an hour. Fingers crossed she's still speaking to me."

I hoped so too. RJ would be good for Shannon, even if she hated to admit it. And he was trying hard with Aisling, which was more effort than her father had ever made. Yes, RJ was one of the quiet heroes in this world, and he'd helped me too. Will had told me what he'd done.

"Thank you for sending your lawyer last night. I didn't know what to say when the police started with all the questions."

"It was nothing."

No, it was everything. I'd never had friends other than Shannon before. "Still, thank you. Do you want me to help with Aisling?"

"Please."

He held out the fork, but I shook my head and rummaged through the cutlery drawer instead. I was sure I'd seen... Yes! A white plastic spoon. Let's hope it was good enough for Aisling.

"Try this." I crouched to her level as RJ aimed again. "It's an angel spoon, sweetie."

Hallelujah, she opened her mouth, and RJ looked beyond pleased that he'd managed to feed her. Yes, Shannon would be crazy if she let this one go.

"Thank goodness," RJ muttered. "She chewed up my iPad stylus earlier, but she wouldn't eat a banana."

I choked back a laugh, and Will coughed into his sleeve.

"Can you do me a favour once you've finished playing happy families?" he asked.

RJ paused to peer over his glasses at Will. "Pretty

sure you've used all your favours up." But he was smiling, and I knew he and Will would always have each other's backs, just like Shannon and me.

"We think we know who killed Helene Weston, but now I need to prove it."

"Really? Who?"

"Geraldine Canning. She teaches yoga at Daylesford Hall, and she had a fling with Helene's fiancé. I'm betting she got a serious case of the green-eyed monster."

RJ gave a low whistle. "Is everyone at that place shagging a colleague?"

"Seems that way."

"Well, I'll have a dig. You think Mrs. Weston will pay your bill?"

"Doubt that. But I'm not letting a murderer get away with her crime on one of my cases."

"Then let's hope we can put her away."

Will arranged my follow-up police interview for first thing the next morning, citing exhaustion, and while RJ went to collect Shannon, we took Aisling out for a walk. I desperately needed some fresh air after a night in a cramped interview room that smelled of body odour and fear, and Aisling always settled better after she'd felt the sun on her face. Plus I think she had a little crush on Will, much like me, because when he picked her up seeing as we hadn't replaced her stroller yet, she snuggled against him and gave him the smile she usually reserved for chocolate.

"I'd like to take you out for that dinner I keep promising you," Will said to me, "but that'll have to wait until I've landed more work. Someone must have told Mrs. Weston we were together, because she gave me a right earful on my voicemail. Blamed the pair of us for the fact that her husband was a greedy fucker who thought he was above the law."

"Sorr—"

Will pressed a finger against my lips. "Stop apologising."

"I'll get another job. Agency work, maybe. It doesn't pay as well, but for now..."

"And I can hunt for lost dogs again. It pays surprisingly well."

"I can't talk to dog ghosts, just people."

Will chuckled. "Maybe I should specialise in grisly murders?"

"I've had enough of those to last a lifetime, thanks."

He took my hand, still holding Aisling in his other arm. "We'll be fine. We've got each other, so we'll be fine."

We would. If I'd been on my own through the Daylesford Hall fiasco, I'd most likely have been in a jail cell right now, and quite honestly, I'd have been relieved about that. No worries about day-to-day survival, just a plain box to live in and square meals served up morning, noon, and night. But now I had a nice albeit temporary home, Shannon's cooking to look forward to, and a hot, sexy boyfriend.

Who was currently staring in horror at the dark-green Jaguar parked outside the house with its engine running.

"What's wrong?" I asked. "What is it?"

"It's my father."

Chapter 35 - Will

WORSE. IT WASN'T only my father who'd turned up, but my mother too. She unfolded herself from the passenger seat, perfectly poised as always, while my father slammed the driver's door and went to take her arm.

I hadn't seen either of them for...how long? A year, at least. More. Eighteen months, at my niece's christening. My older sister had invited me because she felt she should, I'd gone out of an ingrained sense of obligation, and my parents didn't do more than glance at me as I skulked at the back of the church.

And now they'd turned up here. Were they feeling all right?

I studied my father as he walked. He'd always cut an imposing figure, but today he seemed subdued. Frailer.

"William," my father said.

"What do you want?"

Maybe I should have been more polite, but we'd passed the point of civility when he threw me out of the house eight years ago.

"Your father needs to speak to you. We both do." My mother peered closer at Aisling. "You have a family? Nobody told us."

"She's not mine."

Mother peered down her nose at Rania, reminding me once more why I decided to go it alone. "You're dating a single mother?"

Rania took a step back, and I couldn't blame her. I had no desire to be around my parents either.

"No, Mother, I'm not." Might as well summarise to get this meeting over faster. "Aisling's mother and Rania are staying with me and RJ since their home got burned down. Why are you here?"

"Aren't you going to invite us in?" Mother asked.

I'd rather not have, but the only thing worse was having a conversation with the pair of them in full view of the neighbours. I'd already seen one curtain twitch.

"Sure. Welcome to my humble abode."

Inside, I shoved RJ's duvet off the sofa, and my mother wrinkled her nose again as she perched on the edge of the seat. If she knew what he'd been doing in that spot last night, she'd have bleached it first, and I swallowed a snort at the thought. My father took a pew next to her, looking as though he'd rather be somewhere else. At, say, a dental appointment or a funeral.

"Would you like tea or coffee?" Rania offered.

Escape to the kitchen—good tactic.

"Do you have decaf?" my father asked.

I raised an eyebrow. "Decaf?"

"Your father had a heart scare earlier in the year. He's cut out caffeine, alcohol, and saturated fat."

Boy, dinner at their place must be fun now. Even eight years ago, red wine had been the only thing that got me through three courses.

"Sorry to hear that. Do you want a drink, Mother?"

"Tea would be lovely."

"How do you take it?" Rania asked.

"Darjeeling made with filtered water and a slice of lemon."

For fuck's sake. "You get the choice of black or white, sugar or no sugar."

Mother looked pained, while Rania mouthed a silent, "Thank you."

"Is the milk organic?"

"It's bog-standard stuff from Tesco."

Mother pasted on the half-smile, half-grimace she used at parties when the champagne wasn't up to scratch. "In that case, perhaps I'll just have a glass of iced water."

Rania practically ran out of the room, and I perched on the very edge of an armchair, ready to spring up and show them to the door at a moment's notice.

"Why are you here?" I asked again.

Mother shifted uncomfortably, and Father cleared his throat.

"Might as well cut to the chase, son. We saw you in the newspaper last week."

"What newspaper?"

I avoided them wherever possible, and the TV news. Nothing good ever seemed to happen in the world anymore, and I didn't want to depress myself, or worse, Rania.

"The local one. One of your mother's friends at the country club found the article and passed it around. It's all got very awkward for us."

"Awkward? What are you talking about?"

"You were jumping out of a burning building."

"And not just any building," Mother put in. "It looked like a council flat. People keep asking if we've hit hard times."

"I'm sorry?" Did I just hear that right? "I almost got burned alive, and your biggest concern is that I didn't escape from a mansion?"

"Well, obviously we're glad you're not hurt, but some of our acquaintances think you might actually have been living there."

What was the sentence for matricide? Because right now, I was tempted to drop arsenic in her iced fucking water.

And she wasn't done yet.

"I suppose we shouldn't be surprised that you've taken up with a girl of that sort after everything else you've done. At least she's pretty, even if she doesn't make the effort to put on make-up."

"Don't you care about anything but the superficial?"

My father leaned forward. "You have to be considerate of your mother, son. She's in the running to be ladies' captain at the tennis club, and the vote's taking place next month. We need to limit the damage here."

Damage? How much damage would I do if I rammed his smug attitude up his backside?

"Well, I promise I'll try to avoid the papers." I stood and took a step towards the door. "How about you take Mother for a nice cup of Darjeeling on your way back to the palace?"

"Son, at least listen to our proposal."

Why did he keep calling me son? I hadn't been his damn son since I was eighteen. Was it because he kept forgetting my name?

"Fine. Spit it out."

I dropped back into the chair and kept my fingers

crossed Rania wouldn't come back before they left. This awkwardness would only be amplified if they acted like arseholes in front of her too.

"When we withheld your trust fund, we thought it would only be a matter of time before you came to your senses, but we've given up hope of you taking up a sensible career now. So we need to look to the future. Your mother and I have decided that you can have full access as long as you promise to buy yourself a proper home and not a cheap flat in a bad area. Something with a garden, because you'll need to let your mother have photographs to show her friends."

This was his version of damage control? He wanted to buy me a fucking house so Mother wouldn't get embarrassed at tennis? Part of me wanted to stick to my principles and tell them to get lost, but then I thought of Rania. She deserved better. She deserved everything. And with the money in my trust fund, which was comfortably seven figures if not eight, I could give it to her.

"Fine. We'll buy a damn house. Is that it? A fancy show home and some photos?"

"A Christmas card might be nice."

"One of those personalised ones," Mother added. "And that girl needs to see a proper hairstylist."

"Deal," I said through gritted teeth. "Let me show you to the door."

I'd just slammed it behind them when Rania appeared with a glass of water, puzzled by the empty lounge.

"Did they leave already?"

"My relationship with my parents works best when we see as little of each other as possible."

"Oh."

She stood holding the water, and I unpeeled her fingers and put it on the coffee table. Yes, I should have been working, but one more day of Geri running around wouldn't make much difference seeing as Helene's murder was a crime of passion. Plus I still needed to work out a way to get her onto the police's radar. It wasn't as if I could rock up at the police station and announce a ghost had told me who the culprit was.

The most sensible plan seemed to be to sleep on the problem. And that meant I had the rest of the day to spend with Rania, who bit her lip as she studied my face.

"Forget my parents. They don't matter."

I wanted to keep the news about my trust fund quiet until I saw the money. While my father usually kept his word, I didn't want to get Rania's hopes up until I had the access codes and some smarmy guy from the bank kissing my arse in the hope of earning commission.

"But you look upset. Can I do anything to help?"

"Yeah. You can take me upstairs and distract me."

What would she say to that? Her forehead crinkled as she frowned, but then a secret smile spread across her face. So she *had* enjoyed this morning. Thank goodness. I was sure she must have, but I'd also realised that Rania's mind didn't always work as anticipated.

But now she took my hand. "I'd like that."

"You and me both, beautiful. You and me both."

***

Seven o'clock, and I didn't care about dinner because I was curled around a naked woman and she tasted better than any food. But her silence suggested she was thinking, and thinking could be dangerous when there were two X chromosomes involved.

"Everything okay?"

Rania twisted in my arms so she was lying on her back, hair spread across the pillow as she stared up at the ceiling.

"I've been thinking."

Uh-oh.

"Do I need to apologise for something?"

"Huh? No."

"Then what are you thinking about?"

"The future. Our future."

She turned again, and there was no mistaking the worry in her eyes.

"Good. Our future. I like that."

And she relaxed. Not completely, but enough that the knot of tension in my chest loosened.

"About work. I need a job, and I was wondering if I could help you with your cases? I know what I said last night, but I've had time to consider it properly now. And I can find clues that you can't."

"You mean talking to ghosts? Talking to ghosts to solve murders?"

She nodded, and I ran my thumb along her bottom lip until her teeth released their grip on it. Hmm. Interesting idea. Not one I'd have dared to suggest myself, but if she was offering... Because money or no money, I didn't want to quit my job and become a man of leisure. I'd started solving crimes because I wanted to help people and I believed in justice, and that would never change. But the opportunity to get an edge that nobody else had? I couldn't afford to pass that up.

"If you're sure, I think that's an excellent idea. But I'm not putting you in danger again. We'll work the cases together, and I'll do whatever's necessary to keep you safe."

She burrowed her head into my chest, and I held her tight against me. No, I'd never let this woman go.

"You're too damn sweet, Will Lawson. You turn the bad times good and soften all the pain."

"I'll always be here for you. Always."

That sigh? It made more than my dick twitch. My heart pounded too.

"I love you," Rania whispered.

Holy shit.

"I love you too, beautiful."

Epilogue - Rania

SIX MONTHS. SIX months had passed since I banished my last black soul, and five months since my life changed completely.

Dealing with Geri had been our first task—an interesting challenge since Mrs. Weston had officially fired Will, I was still on bail, and Detective Turner was busy following the misguided theory that Lloyd Weston had murdered his own daughter for reasons unknown.

But everyone chipped in, even Shannon, who went to a yoga class to keep an eye on Geri while RJ stayed at home with Aisling. He'd got better at babysitting now, and he refused to put on yoga pants.

That left me to visit Geri's house with Will in my first role as his sidekick. RJ had offered to go instead, but Will said a couple would arouse less suspicion than two men. If a neighbour saw us, we could always claim to have misread the address when we went to pick up our newly purchased second-hand bookcase.

But nobody noticed us, or at least, nobody living. While Will picked the lock on the back door and snuck off to explore Geri's cottage, I hung around in the kitchen, keeping an eye out for her return and chatting to fifty-seven-year-old Doris, who'd died from a single punch to the jaw when her drunk husband returned from the pub many years ago. He'd long since perished from cirrhosis of the liver, so she said, leaving her to spy on Geri for all eternity.

"She's a strange one," Doris said. "Lives on mushed-up fruit and vitamin pills, but then she smokes those funny cigarettes every evening while she watches crime dramas on the television. So graphic. Back in my day, we had *Dynasty* and *The Golden Girls*."

"Funny cigarettes? You mean hash?"

Back home, so many of the teenagers had smoked it. Hash was the only pleasure they got in our broken city.

"Marijuana, love. She grows it herself. A right little gardener. Sometimes, she watches those DIY shows too, but mostly it's the crime programs. Although that chap on *CSI*'s quite dishy. You know—the one with the brown hair."

"I'm not sure who you mean." I looked around, taking in the back garden, or rather, the patio, seeing as the entire thing was paved with ugly pink-and-yellow stones. A sparkly fairy balanced on an ornamental toadstool, and a small fountain reminded me I really needed to pee. "Where does she grow her marijuana? She doesn't seem to be much of a gardener."

"In the cupboard right behind you. One of those fancy setups with the lights."

"What cupboard?"

"Behind the wall tapestry."

Yup, Doris was right. Behind the ugly orange-and-blue scene of a duck kissing a turtle lurked a full-height door. I covered my hand with my sleeve to avoid fingerprints and pulled it open. Wow. Geri had gone to a real effort. Trays filled with water and some kind of porous stones, bright strip lights, and half a dozen healthy, bushy pot plants filled every bit of space.

Footsteps signalled Will's return. "You'll never guess— Hey, what's this? She likes to smoke roll-ups?"

"Seems that way."

"How on earth did you find that?"

"Doris helped me out."

"Doris?"

"You're treading on her foot."

Will leapt to the side, and Doris laughed. "Your young man's easier on the eye than that TV cop. You should hang on to that one."

"I intend to."

On the way home, Will told me all about Geri's bedroom, complete with its life-size cutout of Derek standing by the window.

"It's freaky as fuck. She's got his face printed on her pillow, and every wall's covered in little Derek-photos. And she's got a bunch of chocolate wrappers pinned in between them with dates written underneath. I'm guessing he ate the contents at some point. There's even a wadded-up tissue and an empty Viagra packet."

"Yuck."

"She's sprung in the head. I didn't find any fentanyl, but I didn't look that hard. Reckon I saw enough."

"But we can't tell the police we broke into her house, can we?"

"No, but thanks to your friend Doris, I do have an idea."

Two days later, Constable Joanne O'Dowd followed a not-so-anonymous tip that a kooky yoga teacher was cultivating cannabis plants with intent to supply. While searching for other hidden cupboards, she may have accidentally stumbled across Geri's shrine to Derek, which might have led to Geri freaking out and confessing her undying love for a man who'd shagged her once while drunk at a party and then getting arrested when she mentioned removing his darling fiancée from the scene. Oops. Better still, Constable O'Dowd got all the accolades while Detective Turner only got pissed off.

That was two weeks after Lloyd Weston's death, and I closed the door on one chapter of my life and turned to the next—titled Loving Lawson. Sharing a bed with Will was where I felt the happiest, and some mornings I never wanted to leave it. But I needed to get a job until Will's business made enough money to support both of us, even if Will didn't seem particularly enthusiastic about the idea.

"There's an office in town looking for a cleaner. Five evenings a week, which would give me the mornings to take care of Aisling and the afternoons to help you."

"Why don't you leave it for a few weeks? Take a rest?"

"Because we can't afford to."

"We'll be okay. Trust me."

I did, even when he led me to the bottom of the garden a fortnight later. What was he planning? A quickie amongst the shrubs?

Not quite.

"Why is there a fence panel missing?" I asked. "Did it blow down?"

He didn't answer, just took my hand and pulled me through the gap.

"Will, we shouldn't be in here."

"It's okay."

"No, it isn't. What if the owner finds out?"

"She already has."

"What do you mean? You know her?"

"Intimately."

Intimately? "Are you having a bloody affair?"

Will burst out laughing while I fought back tears. Why were we here?

"It's your house, beautiful. I bought it for you because I never want you to run again."

"Huh? You're not making any sense."

What did he mean, he'd bought the house for me? Last week, we didn't even have enough money for a takeaway pizza.

"When my parents came over the other day, it was because they'd seen the report about the fire in the paper and thanks to that, they finally decided to give me access to my trust fund. Which means I've got the money to spoil you now, and the first thing I did was buy this place. I figured you'd want to stay near Shannon, and since she seems to have this weird love-hate thing going on with RJ, I reckon she'll be sticking around here for a while."

"Are you crazy? You can't buy me a house."

"Actually, it was easier than I thought. My lawyer's already done the paperwork."

"Tell me you're joking."

"I'm deadly serious. Besides, RJ needs the space. Aisling can have our old room so him and Shannon can get up to some serious filth without an audience."

I began shaking, and Will kept me steady while I tried to process everything he'd said. *He'd bought a flipping house?*

"Do you want to look inside?" he asked.

"Uh, I guess?"

"This is the part where I keep my fingers crossed that there aren't any ghosts. We researched it, and we couldn't find that anyone died here, but..."

Even if there were ghosts, I'd deal with it. Because Will had *bought us a freaking house.* And— *Wait.* My heart stopped mid-beat. "What did you just say?"

"We couldn't find that anyone died here. Apparently, this used to be a forest until the developers flattened it. I know records aren't perfect, but—"

"The 'we' part. Who's we?"

"Uh, me and RJ?"

"You told RJ about the ghosts?"

Silence.

"Will?"

"Just that you can see them. None of the other stuff. He's my best mate, Nia. I couldn't keep him in the dark forever."

"And what did he say?"

"Well, he was kind of sceptical at first, but then Shannon told him it was true. She also told him she'd cut his tongue out while he sleeps if he breathes a word to anyone, so he'll definitely keep his mouth shut." Will laid a hand on my arm, tentative. "Don't be mad, beautiful. RJ knows how to keep a secret. When I was fifteen, I accidentally set the school on fire, and he'll take that to the grave."

"You what?"

"Cross my heart, I only meant to set off the smoke alarm. There was a maths test, and I hadn't revised."

This was what it meant to have friends, wasn't it? That you shared your secrets and they trusted you with theirs. And I'd never find better friends than Will,

Shannon, and RJ. I slipped an arm around Will's waist and pressed a kiss to his cheek to show him I wasn't mad.

"Let's look inside."

The style of the place was totally different to RJ's. White, modern, a single storey wrapping around three sides of a central courtyard. A lump stuck in my throat as I was reminded of my family home back in Syria. Will led me into the kitchen, a large, airy space with a marble-topped island in the centre and a dining table at one end. A door at the far end took us to the lounge, decorated in pale green with floor-to-ceiling windows that opened out onto the courtyard and took up the whole of one wall. And the best part? No spirits lurking in the shadows.

"Nia, say something? Perhaps I should have told you, but I wanted it to be a surprise."

Well, it certainly was that. And it made this day all the more special.

"I love it. I love you. I can't believe this is happening."

Will grinned and waggled his eyebrows. "Want to check out the bedroom?"

"You're such a man."

"Do you have a problem with that?"

"No, not at all."

***

We'd been in the courtyard house for five months now. The back fence was gone completely, and Shannon brought Aisling over in the mornings while she went to work. Which was only three days a week now. She still insisted on keeping her job at the bread factory even though RJ said she didn't have to, but he'd talked her into dropping her hours so she could spend more time with her daughter.

And how were they getting on?

Well, Shannon had started bringing Aisling to our house rather than me picking her up after I accidentally walked in on her and RJ doing the deed in the hallway one morning when I got there a few minutes early. I still reached for the bleach to rinse out my eyes just thinking about it. So, there was that. And Aisling had called RJ "Dada" for the first time last week and he didn't even freak out. He and Shannon bickered constantly, but better to see her like that than the mouse she'd been with Slick Dick, and far from driving them apart, it seemed to bring her and RJ closer together. Fiery. That was the best word for their relationship. It matched Shannon's hair.

Which promised to make our holiday interesting. We were due to leave for the airport in an hour, and according to RJ, she was still packing.

"Will you get a move on?" he shouted up the stairs.

"You'll be the first one to complain if we forget something."

I stifled a giggle and shifted Aisling on my hip. We were going to Portugal, not the Arctic. RJ had wanted golf, Shannon had wanted the sea, I'd wanted sun, and when I'd asked Will, he'd just looked me up and down and said he could get what he wanted anywhere. True. Anyhow, we'd compromised on the Algarve. RJ had booked the flights, and even that caused ructions.

"These are first class," Shannon had said.

"And?"

"I keep telling you, I don't want you to spend so much money on us."

But RJ was learning how to handle Shannon. "Okay, sweetheart. I'll swap yours for economy. But the rest of us are sitting upfront with the fancy food and the big seats." He'd relieved me of Aisling and lifted her onto his lap. "You like the fancy food, don't you, princess?"

"Disney?"

Guess where we'd be going next year?

***

Finally. After two hours in a plane—my first flight ever —an argument between Shannon and RJ when she found out he'd rented a Porsche Cayenne rather than a small family hatchback, and an hour's drive to our beachfront villa, I finally began to relax. Will helped, insisting on rubbing sunblock over every inch of me even though I had the type of skin that rarely burned.

"Well, we finally made it," Will said. "I began to fear we wouldn't when RJ bought Shannon that handbag at the airport."

"I think it helped that she really liked the colour."

"Two weeks to do nothing. At least we got that last case wrapped up before we left."

With money no longer an issue, we both worked for the satisfaction instead. And being able to tell two grieving parents that the neighbour who murdered their ten-year-old daughter had been arrested was worth the heartache of having to talk to that confused and scared little girl. Since Geri got charged, we'd worked three more cases and solved every one, Joanne

O'Dowd had been promoted to detective, and Chris Turner was pissed off with all three of us. That made me smile too.

"What's that look for?" Will asked.

"I just can't believe the way everything turned out. From a disaster to, well, this." I waved a hand at the pool we were lounging beside, set in tropical gardens with the smell of sea air drifting over us. Not quite the island we'd once talked about escaping to, but in many ways, this was so much better.

"Me neither. And to think that when we first met, I had you down as a suspect." Will shook his head. "Lloyd fucking Weston and the yoga bitch. Who'd have thought?"

"I still feel bad about Helene. You know, stuck at Daylesford Hall on her own."

Neither of us had been near the place since that final night. I got the feeling Anthony Weston would finish what his father started if I so much as set foot over the threshold. According to Aiden, most of Weston Corp's customers had jumped ship following Lloyd Weston's death and the bribery allegations, and the company had collapsed. Aiden had gone to work for a smaller firm near Manchester, but he still heard whispers from his ex-colleagues.

"What do you want to do? Stop by for coffee and a chat? I doubt Helene will have anything pleasant to say."

"I know, but she's been through a lot. I just wish there was a way to free her that didn't involve hunting and killing. To free all of them. Sometimes, I wonder if the others might know more than me."

"The other Electi?"

I nodded, running two fingers over the gold necklace I still wore every day. My mother had told me it was important—life or death important—but she'd never elaborated on what it truly meant. I wasn't sure if she'd even known.

"Have you ever tried to find them?"

"I wouldn't know where to start. As I said before, they'll keep their powers well hidden."

"We could both take a look if you want? Maybe there's a clue out there."

"Maybe."

For now, I just wanted to enjoy my first ever holiday. If I focused on the dead, I'd forget to live myself. My nightmares about Lloyd Weston had faded, consigned to the depths of my mind along with memories of Syria, and for a few days at least, I vowed to block out my past and enjoy the present.

"Fancy a swim?" I asked.

Will's answer was to pick me up and jump into the pool. I came to the surface coughing and spluttering as he laughed.

"Need the kiss of life, beautiful?"

"From you? Always."

LEANAN SIDHE

Do you want to know what happened between Shannon and RJ the night Will and Rania found them in the lounge? I've written their side of the story in a little extra book, Leanan Sidhe, available FREE to members of my reader group from the following link:

www.elise-noble.com/51dhe

WHAT'S NEXT?

The Electi series continues in Spooked...

A casual date for wedding planner Kimberly Jennings goes horribly awry when a stranger whispers that her new beau is a killer. Kim's conscience won't let her turn a blind eye, but how does she go about explaining that her informant was the ghost of a previous victim?

Private investigator Reed Cullen needs money to fund the search for his missing sister. What doesn't he need? A neurotic party organiser on a personal crusade for revenge against a slimeball who spiked her drink. Or her secrets, or her pretty little face either. But like it or not, he's stuck with Kim and he's stuck with the case, for better or for worse.

For more details: www.elise-noble.com/spooked

My next Blackwood book will be Platinum, the fifth book in the Blackwood Elements series, releasing in 2018.

After a run-in with her new boss costs junior doctor Roksana Bartosz her job, her friend Sofia has the perfect solution—a short break in Virginia to take her mind off the problem. Little does Roxy know that Sofia and Emmy Black are intent on playing matchmaker in the craziest way possible.

Gideon Renard avoids relationships, especially with girls as fragile as Roxy. Taking a new job in Washington, DC seems like the perfect way to put space between them. But his friends have other ideas, and in between hunting down three missing assassins, resisting the temptation to strangle his ex, and fighting the demons of his past, he has a big decision to make. Can he walk away from Roxy for the second time?

For more details: www.elise-noble.com/platinum

If you enjoyed Cursed, please consider leaving a review.

For an author, every review is incredibly important. Not only do they make us feel warm and fuzzy inside, readers consider them when making their decision whether or not to buy a book. Even a line saying you enjoyed the book or what your favourite part was helps a lot.

WANT TO STALK ME?

For updates on my new releases, giveaways, and other random stuff, you can sign up for my newsletter on my website:
www.elise-noble.com

Facebook:
www.facebook.com/EliseNobleAuthor

Twitter: @EliseANoble

Instagram: @elise_noble

If you're on Facebook, you may also like to join Team Blackwood for exclusive giveaways, sneak previews, and book-related chat. Be the first to find out about new stories, and you might even see your name or one of your ideas make it into print!

And if you'd like to read my books for FREE, you can also find details of how to join my review team.

Would you like to join Team Blackwood?

www.elise-noble.com/team-blackwood

END OF BOOK STUFF

Back in the dim and distant past, I spent a bit of time working in a beautiful old manor house converted into a corporate headquarters, and that was the place that inspired me to start writing in the first place. The story was Pitch Black, and rather than getting dirty in a stables, Ashlyn worked for Luke as a secretary in the old manor. No spirits, just a nervous breakdown and a lot of filth. That part of the story got changed long before publication, but I still wanted to give the building the story it deserved, because it's a truly fascinating place with its isolated location, a layout designed by someone on drugs, and—allegedly—a ghost. So, this is the tale.

I never thought I'd write a paranormal story, but I was a huge X-Files fan as a kid, so I figured I'd give it a go. I quite enjoyed the challenge! Originally, it was just going to be one book, but I had too many unanswered questions about the Electi and why they existed to quit there. And who are the others? The answer is three very different girls, and their stories will be following in the future...

Happy reading!
Elise

OTHER BOOKS BY ELISE NOBLE

The Blackwood Security Series
For the Love of Animals (Nate & Carmen - prequel)
Black is my Heart (prequel)
Pitch Black
Into the Black
Forever Black
Gold Rush
Gray is my Heart
Neon (novella)
Out of the Blue
Ultraviolet
Glitter (novella) (TBA)
Red Alert
White Hot
The Scarlet Affair
Quicksilver
The Girl with the Emerald Ring (TBA)

The Blackwood Elements Series
Oxygen
Lithium
Carbon
Rhodium
Platinum
Lead

Copper (2019)
Bronze (2019)
Nickel (TBA)

The Blackwood UK Series
Joker in the Pack
Cherry on Top (novella)
Roses are Dead
Shallow Graves
Indigo Rain
Pass the Parcel (TBA)

Blackwood Casefiles
Stolen Hearts (2019)

Blackstone House
Hard Lines (TBA)
Hard Tide (TBA)

The Electi Series
Cursed
Spooked
Possessed
Demented (TBA)

The Trouble Series
Trouble in Paradise
Nothing but Trouble
24 Hours of Trouble

Standalone
Life
Twisted (short stories)

A Very Happy Christmas (novella)

Printed in Great Britain
by Amazon